Need You for Keeps

by marina adair

Heroes of St. Helena series

Need You for Keeps

St. Helena Vineyard series

Kissing Under the Mistletoe
Summer in Napa
Autumn in the Vineyard
Be Mine Forever
From the Moment We Met

Need You for Keeps

HEROES OF ST. HELENA SERIES

MARINA ADAIR

Montlake
Romance

Published by Montlake Romance, Seattle

www.apub.com

Amazon, the Amazon logo, and Montlake Romance are trademarks of Amazon.com, Inc., or its affiliates.

ISBN-13: 9781477825587
ISBN-10: 1477825584

Cover design by Shasti O'Leary-Soudant, SOS CREATIVE LLC

Library of Congress Control Number: 2014907538

Printed in the United States of America

To Miss Peepers, Patches, and Princess,
for a childhood full of furry hugs
and unconditional love.

chapter
one

"Someone will come for me," Shay Michaels said, eyeballing her newest client—who looked as convinced by her statement as Shay felt. Maybe it was that she'd said the exact same thing over an hour ago or that she'd been saying the same thing her entire life without any success.

But this time Shay had faith that someone would come. Call it eternal optimism or romantic rebellion, but one of these days karma would stop flipping her the bird and pay it forward.

And that day was today.

Please say that day is today, she thought, looking down at the client in question.

Domino sat stoically, tail wrapped around his massive feet like a statue, gazing up at her with his wet, brown doggie eyes that were so big they could persuade anyone with a heart to do something colossally stupid. Like crawl into a dog kennel that locked from the outside.

Okay, to be fair, when Shay was tired she made questionable decisions. And today she was exhausted.

As the top stylist to the town's most elite and furriest residents, she had been on her feet since the crack of dawn preparing the shop's luxury kennels for the day's long list of canine clients. She was hoping to leave on time to pamper her own four-legged kids.

In addition to her position at the pet spa, Shay was the resident saint at St. Paws Animal Rescue, a foster service she ran out of her home for a variety of animals that needed a little extra help finding their forever families. As much as she wished to keep every animal in need, her home—and the law—prevented her from having more than four animals in her residence at any given time. This weekend she had the chance to show off her foster dogs at the community park, so it was imperative they looked their best—which meant head-to-tail makeovers.

Only Domino had thrown a wrench into her already hectic schedule. So when he started whimpering as she steered him toward the kennel, which meant scooting all two hundred pounds of dog across the floor by his spotted Great Dane tush, she'd decided to climb in and show him that kennels at Paws and Claws weren't scary, they were comfy, more chic than her rental, and almost roomy enough for a human to live in. In fact, with the right kennel mate, they could be fun.

Shay retracted *that* statement the minute the door slammed shut and locked behind her.

"You know, with your height and retrieval skills, you could grab me the keys off the counter over there," she said, pointing to the neon-green lanyard that was a mere two inches out of reach.

Two inches!

"Woof." Tail wagging, tongue lolling, Domino meandered over to the table, right past the keys, and stuck his head in a fifty-pound bag of kibble that sat in the back corner of the shop.

"That's puppy chow. It will make your butt big, and no one wants to adopt a dog with a big butt," Shay warned, then remembered the box of chocolate minidoughnuts she'd inhaled for lunch and made a mental note to run at least five miles tomorrow before work.

Domino, however, seemed unconcerned about his figure and stuck his head in until it disappeared in the bag. At the sound of the crinkling paper, all of the dogs ran to the fronts of their kennels, noses pressed through the bars, straining for a handout. When none came, they started barking—all dozen of them. Which did nothing for Shay's headache.

She was just tired enough that she could sleep in a dog kennel, and since she was the only stylist on the Paws and Claws Day Spa's schedule today, Shay figured this could easily become an all-nighter. Luckily her superpower was the ability to fall asleep anytime, anywhere, no matter what—something she'd learned by her third foster home.

When the dogs' barks reached DEFCON 1, along with her headache, Shay closed her eyes and rested her forehead against her bent knees, needing a moment.

"If you ask me, small butts are overrated," said a masculine voice with a rich grit.

Her eyes opened just as a pair of rugged, manly, steel-toed boots stopped at the edge of the kennel door. Shay lifted her head up, way up, and—*gulp*—found herself staring at the last man on the planet she wanted to see today.

Jonah Baudouin flashed her that department-issued smile and something low in her belly tingled. She would've liked to blame it on a natural reaction to the weapon holstered at his hip or quite possibly the badge he carried, but she had a sinking feeling it had more to do with the way he filled out that uniform.

Six feet two of hard muscle on a body that was built to protect and serve, he was the perfect catch if one was into brooding hero types. But Shay didn't do brooding or heroes, and she most certainly did not do cops.

Ones who made her tingle or otherwise.

Not that it mattered, because the only reactions she seemed to inspire within him were irritation or amusement. Today he was packing both. He was also sipping on a giant-sized coffee cup that made her mouth water.

"Sheriff," she said casually through the bars. This wasn't her first time in the pokey.

"Deputy," he corrected. "Still got a few months before the election."

"If you're here soliciting support, I have to be honest and say that I'm voting for the other guy." It was a lie and they both knew it. Deputy "Do-Nothing" Warren could bring a snow machine into hell and still not win. He was lazy, shady, and only had a badge because his dad was mayor. "But since you're here, could you hand me the keys off the grooming station behind you?"

"I'm investigating a stolen property claim," he said, not even pretending to get the keys. "Mr. Barnwell reported his Dalmatian missing about three hours ago." He was cool and casual, not a feather ruffled in his perfectly pressed uniform. A bad sign.

"How awful." Shay placed a horrified hand to her chest.

"Yeah, awful," he agreed mildly. "Have you seen him today?"

"Mr. Barnwell's *Dalmatian*?" She shook her head, hoping she looked more baffled than guilty. "Nope."

"You wouldn't lie to an officer of the law, would you?"

"Not today."

"Huh." He took a leisurely sip of his coffee, which she'd bet the keys to the kennel was a plain old-fashioned drip—no frills. "That's odd, because a Caucasian female, wavy light brown hair, about five four and a buck twenty was seen shoving Domino into the back of a late-nineties Honda Civic."

Domino, the *Great Dane*, emerged from the bag of kibble and, expression dialed to *woof?* cocked his head at the sound of his name. He eyed Jonah's crotch eagerly and Shay could almost see the dog vibrating with indecision.

Kibble or doggie high five to the crotch? So many choices.

Thank God the kibble won out.

"Lots of people drive Civics," Shay challenged, tucking a light brown wave of hair behind her ear.

"Yeah, well, only one five-foot-four Civic owner is on record claiming Mr. Barnwell to be"—eyes locked on hers, he set the coffee right next to the keys and pulled a little official-looking notepad from his front shirt pocket, flipping to the middle—"cruel, criminal, and a bad neighbor with questionable hygiene."

She'd called him a lot more in private. "He really should brush his teeth twice a day if he intends on making a habit out of yelling at me."

"The getaway car had a St. Paws Animal Rescue sticker on the door—"

"*Getaway car*? Is that official cop jargon?"

"—and the shover in question was reported to be wearing a pair of faded jeans and an orange T-shirt that reads I BRAKE FOR SQUIRRELS."

He lifted his gaze and zeroed in on the squirrel on her orange shirt.

Shay crossed her arms over the cute critter and shrugged. "Sorry, Deputy, can't help you."

"Jesus, Shay," he said, sounding all put out, like he was the one behind bars. "I'm trying to help you here. My bet is that dog is worth a few grand, which means if you have him in your possession, it's a felony. So just hand Domino over and we can call it a day."

Either Domino had finished all fifty pounds of kibble in record time or hearing his name again was too tempting, but he lifted his head and barked. Twice. Really loud. Then bounded across the floor at NASCAR speed, skidding to a stop at Jonah's feet, his nose going straight to the crotch for a big welcoming sniff.

"You want to change your statement?" he asked, deflecting Domino with a few complex swishes of the hand. "Or do I need to get out the cuffs and haul you in?"

Maybe she was more exhausted than she thought. Or maybe she'd just been too long without a bedmate who didn't shed, but her entire body perked up at the thought of Deputy Serious and his seriously hot cuffs. Which was annoying because uptight, by-the-book men were not her type.

Then again, it had been so long she wasn't sure she even had a type.

An awkward silence hung in the air while they glared at each other and Domino stared between them, panting.

Breaking eye contact, because he was better at it than she was, damn it, Shay bent over to pet Domino's head through the bars.

He stopped, dropped, and rolled to assume the belly rub position. She obliged the best she could, her heart going heavy when his tail slapped the floor with excitement and he looked up at her adoringly.

Domino was a lover. He needed attention, affection, unconditional love—a family who wanted him, not one who felt obligated to feed and house him.

There was the perfect family out there—she just needed to find it.

Determined, Shay stood to face down one very pissed deputy, the top of her head grazing the kennel's roof. Apparently hauling her butt in was not how he envisioned his afternoon going. Or more likely, it was all of the paperwork she'd just added to his plate.

"For the record, I didn't lie. Domino is a Great Dane, not a Dalmatian. A Great Dane, Jonah, who weighs two hundred pounds." She grabbed the bars and pressed her forehead against the cool metal. "Have you seen the size of Mr. Barnwell's crate? It's built for a Chihuahua. He can't even stand up and he is locked in there all day long. Can you even imagine?"

"Shay," he sighed, looking up at the ceiling as though seeking divine intervention.

"It's cruel and it's mean and no one will help me," she whispered.

Jonah stepped forward until she could smell the summer heat on his skin, and that normal cool and distant expression he wore like Kevlar softened.

"Hard to do when you go breaking in to other people's property, steal their pets, and start trouble."

"I don't start trouble." He raised a disbelieving brow. "I don't. And I called your office three times last week, when the temperatures hit surface-of-the-sun levels and I had to give him water through the bars." She didn't mention she'd spent most of yesterday sitting by his crate, rubbing his head, and giving him an ice pop and that she'd only decided to take him when Mr. Barnwell threw out the pamphlet she'd put on his doorstep about crate cruelty.

But a felony? This situation was so beyond what she could handle. Mr. Barnwell wasn't mean, at least she didn't think so. He was just misinformed—and stubborn.

She looked up at one of St. Helena's finest and admitted—silently, to herself—that she needed help. She needed his help.

And didn't that just piss her off.

"If you promise to do something so he isn't locked back in that crate ever again, then I promise to give him back."

"You're making a list of demands?" He laughed, and even though it was aimed at her, she had to admit he had a great laugh. "I have a gun and cuffs and you're locked in a cage."

And why did that image have her hormones short-circuiting? No wonder all the women in town pawed over him. The uniform and high-octane testosterone radiating from his every pore were a lethal combination.

"But do you have enough manpower to watch him twenty-four/seven? To make sure he doesn't 'run away' again?"

Jonah braced his hands overhead on the top of the kennel's door, his mighty fine arms bulging tight against the fabric of his shirt as his frame towered over her. He looked at her long and hard, then at the dog, who was staring up at him like he was a god. Which just meant that he thought Jonah had a stash of doggie treats stuffed in his pocket.

She knew the moment he gave in—his shoulders relaxed and those intense blue eyes narrowed.

"Fine," he sighed. "I'll talk to Mr. Barnwell, but I can't promise you anything."

"Thank you, thank you, thank you." With a smile, Shay stuck her arm through the bars to shake. "You can take Domino then."

When Jonah's big, rough hand engulfed hers, a zing of something hot raced up her arms and spread out to every happy spot she owned and a few she'd thought she'd lost. And Shay had no business getting zings or tingles for any man, let alone this one.

Nope, Jonah Baudouin was stable, a straight shooter, and sexy or not, the soon-to-be sheriff of a place she'd started to think of as more than a temporary stopover.

This wasn't their first tangle over the law, and she was pretty sure based on her history that it wouldn't be their last. So finding out if he used those cuffs for business or pleasure wasn't in her best interest.

She shook once and waited for him to release her hand. When he just stared at her, she snatched it back. "And I'll try to stay out of your hair, but I can't promise anything."

His mouth twitched. "You do that." He clipped a leash on Domino and tipped his hat. "Have a good day, Shay." They started for the door.

"Wow, thanks for all that protecting and serving," she said, sure he was just yanking her chain.

"Anytime," he threw over his shoulder.

"Wait," she hollered after him. "What about letting me out?"

"Call the other guy. You know, the one you're voting for. Make him earn that support you're so eager to throw his way."

"Thank you for your support," Shay said, handing a discreet paper bag to the next customer and putting the money in her cash box.

"I can't believe how many people showed up," her friend Harper Owens said, taking in the line of women stretching across the grass field. A line that made it impossible for Shay not to smile.

"Me either. Although I think it's Emerson's bottomless Salty Chihuahuas that have people roughing the heat."

Emerson stepped out from behind her food cart with a cold pitcher of said Salty Chihuahuas and snorted. She wore her hair short, an even shorter black skirt that was covered in a million zippers, and a tank top that said PITA PEDDLER STREATERY across the chest. Her red Converse hi-tops, matching lipstick, and bite-me attitude made Emerson appear every bit the tough troublemaker of their trio.

Shay had met them at the farmers' market a few months ago. She had been doing five-dollar pet-icures, Harper was working a kids' art table, and Emerson was passing out baklava samples. The triple-digit day had scared off the crowd and had them bemoaning their poor sales under Emerson's food cart umbrella. Two hours and three batches of the gooey Greek dessert later, the trio was cemented.

"I think it's the half-naked men," Emerson said, gesturing to the tray she balanced on her hand. Behind the two full pitchers of her trademark tequila-infused cocktail sat a stack of cups that read BOTTOMS UP right above a picture of a magnificent butt in nothing but a pair of red boxer briefs.

"Good point."

Naked hotties and free booze were just smart business tactics in a town where a good portion of the female population carried a senior discount card. But today's turnout was more than Shay could have hoped for, especially since summer was showing her nasty teeth. It was late morning and already the heat hung thick on the valley floor, bringing with it the sweetness from nearby vineyards. Not that a little heat could stop today from being a success.

A solar storm couldn't have stopped today. Because just like the sun would rise each morning and set each evening, the women of St. Helena would do anything to get their hands on St. Paws' extended edition Cuties with Booties calendar. And Shay was the town's only supplier.

Last year, kitten and puppy season had been brutal, so Shay, wanting to raise awareness of the staggering number of homeless pets, started Cuties with Booties, a pet-adoption blog. Each week she paired one of St. Helena's sexiest working men with a pet in need. Contractors, vintners, service men, even a forest ranger—all barefoot while their partners-in-crime wore their work boots.

Cuties with Booties had gone viral in a matter of days, helping Shay place nine pets with their forever families and raising enough donations to help offset spaying and neutering costs for another dozen. It also made local stars out of the men brave enough to pose and the animals who'd captured the town's hearts. The women of St. Helena had even started up a fan club, Booty Patrol, printing off the photos of the pets—and men—and asking for their paw prints.

This year Shay had bigger dreams, and with the blog's success putting her on the map as the patron saint of St. Helena's strays, she regularly received calls from people needing help finding an animal a good home or from the local shelter when its facility was maxed out.

But it seemed that for every one she placed, another two would appear on her doorstep, and her heart had already outgrown her house. Not to mention her checkbook.

Every life counts, she reminded herself, which was why turning away a stray broke her heart, so she was determined to find a way to place more pets. Her current goal was twelve animals over the next twelve months. With Bark in the Park right around the corner, Shay was certain she'd place the four foster dogs currently residing in her home by the end of the summer. The seasonal doggie roundup acted as a place where locals could socialize their four-legged kids and would allow Shay to introduce potential families to her dogs. Dogs that, when adopted, would provide her the extra space she needed to foster more pets. Only more fosters meant more vet bills, more food, and more money.

Money Shay didn't have access to.

But she did have access to the most adorable *and* adoptable pets on the planet. And together with some of St. Helena's finest first responders, wearing not much more than their work pants and a smile, she'd hoped that the Eighteen Months of Cuties with Booties calendar would raise enough to cover the costs of twelve animals.

Shay turned to her friends. "Peggy is being super supportive." Peggy wasn't just her landlord, she was also the owner of Paws and Claws Day Spa, which made her Shay's boss. "She even offered to let me have a few calendar signings at her shop, including one with Warren and then a big meet-and-greet with the cuties the weekend after Bark in the Park. A 'men behind the dogs' kind of signing, where we sell all kinds of autographed calendars and swag. I already have several of the guys from the calendar lined up to do signings with their featured pet."

Shay smiled at the long line of women that wound through the park to the steps of town hall, all waiting to get their hands on the anticipated calendar.

Cuties with Booties was going to make her dream a reality. She just knew it. Helping those otherwise overlooked souls was something Shay not only understood, it was what drove her. Everyone loved kittens and puppies. Who wouldn't? Not many looked twice at a sweet older dog with bad vision and gas problems. Once they reached a certain age, their likelihood for placement dropped dramatically, and during puppy and kitten season the chances of placement were slim at best.

"With that many hot dawgs in one place, every lady in town will show up with their pens. And checkbooks," Harper said, handing a calendar to the next customer—followed closely by a Salty Chihuahua. "I bet your applications will go through the roof."

That was the plan. "Then I just have to come up with the money to cover the cost of the new fosters."

"The number of people willing to stand in the heat and plunk down a cool twenty for a calendar tells me that St. Paws will have enough to take care of as many fosters as you can handle."

Emerson was right. With this kind of crowd, she would be able to afford more fosters than she'd originally thought.

"Who's next?" Shay ushered the next customer forward.

To her surprise the next customer was neither a soccer mom nor an old biddy. A three-foot-tall girl with freckles and a mess of wild blonde curls flying every which way peeked over the edge of the table. She was maybe six, beanpole thin, wearing a faded sundress that was on the wrong side of vintage, and holding a beach bag that was twice her size.

"Well, hello," Shay said when the girl just looked her at her with serious, assessing brown eyes. Shay glanced around to see who she was with, because surely the girl was too young to be there alone. But no one seemed to step up to the table to join her.

Shay shot Harper a questioning look. Harper managed the Fashion Flower, the only kids' clothing boutique in town, which meant she knew just about every munchkin between two and twelve. Harper just shrugged.

Hoping a parent was nearby, Shay leaned forward, getting to eye level. "Are you here to pick up a calendar for someone?"

Goldilocks shook her head, her gaze dropping to the dog at Shay's feet. She reached out a tentative hand, pausing briefly. "Is it all right if I pet your dog?"

"He's not mine." *Not anymore*, she thought, ignoring the ping of sadness that always surfaced when one of her lost ones found their forever home.

Just that morning, before the signing started, a young family had come specifically to meet Tripod and fallen in love. The feeling was mutual. They lived in a one-story home, which was a must with only three legs, and had an autistic daughter who would benefit from Tripod's calm and loving demeanor. It was the perfect match for everyone involved.

"Tripod goes to his new family next week, but he's friendly and loves belly rubs."

On cue, Tripod, the star of today and an attention-lover, rolled over to expose his soft underbelly.

The girl had great animal etiquette. Kneeling next to Tripod in the grass, she stroked him gently, careful not to go near his face.

"Do you have a dog?"

She shook her head. "Grandma's allergic."

Too bad, Shay thought, taking in the way the girl seemed to relax while petting the dog. It was the same thing that happened whenever Shay was around animals. There was something so healing about unconditional love.

"Is it a nice family? Tripod's new one?" Goldilocks asked quietly, giving Tripod a belly rub that had his tongue lolling to the side in ecstasy and all three legs sticking up in the air like roadkill.

Tripod was a two-year-old shepherd mix who'd lost his front leg in a car accident when he'd been dumped on the side of the highway, then bravely bared it all for the cover of the calendar with a local deputy.

Just not the deputy Shay had wanted.

Then again, Shay had learned early on that the things she wanted either gave her a big butt or a broken heart, because the ones she really wanted never seemed to want her back. Or at least not for long. But Tripod had a chance at a lifetime of happiness. Shay had made sure of it.

"The nicest," Shay assured her, but Goldilocks didn't look convinced and Shay couldn't blame her. People could suck, something Shay knew firsthand, which was why she screened all of her applicants thoroughly before approving any adoption.

"It's a rule." Shay handed Goldilocks a St. Paws flyer and pointed to the tagline at the bottom. "See, right here. Only nice families need apply."

Goldilocks gave Tripod one last pat, then stood to study the flyer. She looked at every condition Shay listed, then read the most important part: "St. Paws pets are the 'for keeps' kind."

"Yup." That was the best part of what Shay did. She wasn't interested in finding her animals another temporary stopover, so she took the time and care to ensure that each match ended in a lifetime of love and companionship.

"We only place pets with people who have big hearts," Shay explained.

After a long moment the girl gave a small nod and extended the flyer. "Can I have it signed?"

Shay smiled. "Sure." She reached across the table to grab the organic inkpad she'd brought for Tripod, but the girl shook her head.

"I want you to sign it." She handed Shay a pen from her Mary Poppins–sized bag. "Right there."

Shay took the pen and signed her name right where the dirty finger pointed. The girl looked at the signature, then at Shay and smiled.

Big and bright, exposing a gap where she'd lost a tooth. "Someday I want to be a saint too."

And didn't that just make her week.

Shay swallowed hard as Goldilocks gave Tripod one last pet to the head and, tucking the signed flyer in her pocket, walked toward town hall. Shay was still collecting herself when two bony hands snatched a calendar off of the table.

Estella Pricket, the current president of the Companion Brigade, the local pet owners' society, sucked on her teeth as she looked it over carefully. Estella was about four hundred years old, favored penciled eyebrows over real ones, and had jaws like a pit bull when it came to getting her way. That she was Shay's neighbor only made it that much worse. "How did you pick the models?"

Shay looked at the back of the calendar, over all of the drool-worthy men, and waggled a brow. "I asked them if they wanted to take it off for a good cause and they said yes."

"And all these years I've been suffering through coffee dates," Emerson said, grabbing the calendar.

"At least you get coffee," Harper argued. "I had every one of those cuties and their half-naked booties in a dark room and the closest I got to a date was one of them asking when the calendar would be released."

Harper had donated her set design and photography skills to the cause in hopes of meeting a dark and dangerous bad boy wanting to give her an adventure she'd never forget. Too bad for Harper, the men of St. Helena had a hard time picturing the town's good girl getting down and dirty.

"Maybe you should lose the cardigan and tights," Emerson said before picking up her tray to make her rounds.

Shay laughed. Estella only scowled, which made her forehead fold over on itself and her lips purse out like she needed an EpiPen. It was enough to scare a ghost. The last time the woman had scowled like that in public was when Sheila Stanton mistakenly announced Estella's prized Pomeranian as a papillon at last year's Bark in the Park crowning ceremony.

Sheila was sentenced to doodie duty at all Companion events—for the rest of her life.

"Not the men," Estella said impatiently, narrowing her beady eyes on the calendar. "The dogs."

"Oh." That was an easy answer. "I didn't, they picked me." Which they had. Shay truly believed that each and every stray she rescued picked her—and in return she promised to find a family to love them.

"Then that's false advertising," Estella said, pointing to the tagline at the bottom of the cover, which read WINE COUNTRY'S FINEST TAIL.

"It's just a marketing tool, Mrs. Pricket," Harper said sweetly, scooting a little closer to Shay, which, for a girl who would rather leave the state than face a confrontation, was a big deal.

"No, it's a lie! Because Foxy Cleopatra is the best tail in town," the older woman snapped, and the tiny Pomeranian that sat at her owner's feet started shaking.

Harper laughed.

Shay didn't. She wanted to pick up the poor dog and cuddle her close. It was obvious that Foxy was terrified being in a sea of legs, and Estella's tone was only amplifying the dog's insecurities. But their conversation had caught the attention of Nora Kincaid, who slid closer. Nora was the kind of woman who made a business out of knowing everyone's business, then posting it on her Facebook page—which had over ten thousand likes and was growing daily. And informing Estella of her lacking parenting skills with the town's own paparazzo nearby wouldn't help matters.

"Foxy Cleopatra came from two champion lines . . ." Estella paused to watch Nora pull her phone out of her purse, then turned so that Nora could catch her good side, should the Voice of St. Helena decide to start snapping and uploading pics. "And is, herself, a blue ribbon holder, and you didn't once come to ask me if she'd like to be in the calendar."

"And she is a wonderful dog." A painfully shy and insecure dog who needed gentle reassurance, not a stroll through a forest of drunken legs. "But this calendar is for adoptable dogs."

"Which explains why you only went as far as to search through that ark of misfits you have in your house." An ark of misfits that had been a point of contention since the day Shay moved in. "You should clarify that for buyers."

Then to ensure that everyone in line could hear, Estella raised her voice, which had Foxy cowering and Nora's trigger finger bursting into action. "Because you can't imply that you have the finest tail in all of wine country if you didn't inspect all the tail wine country has to offer." Estella turned back to look—right over Shay's shoulder. "Isn't that true, Deputy?"

Oh boy. Shay didn't have to turn to see which deputy was standing behind her—her nipples already knew. Jonah oozed enough testosterone and confidence that all he had to do was stand downwind and Shay's hormones short-circuited.

"Yes, ma'am," Jonah said without a hint of humor in his voice, but she knew he was laughing. "And I have it on good authority that a thorough search of the best tail in wine country has not been completed by Shay here."

At that she turned to face him, completely ignoring how well he filled out his uniform. Or that his cuffs and more-than-impressive equipment were at eye level. Even his gun had swagger. She looked up and found those laser-sharp pools of blue aimed right at her.

So she aimed back. "I've inspected enough tail to know right away what a cause worth pursuing is and, more importantly, what is not."

Estella, thinking Shay's comment was directed at her dog, snatched up poor Foxy and stormed off, mumbling, "Wouldn't know good tail if it bit you in the ass."

Which was probably true, but Shay kept silent.

Jonah, however, let his gaze fall to Shay's tail, which was sporting her best pair of shorts, and smiled. An arrogant smile that promised to deliver everything Shay could ever want, and more.

Only Shay had seen that smile enough to know that it lied.

People either wanted to control Shay or change her, and she had a feeling that the sweet sheriff fell into the former category. Sure, their chemistry was off the charts, and sleeping with Jonah Baudouin would most likely be a religious experience, but beneath all the swagger and upstanding small-town charm was a man who controlled his world. And Shay was done with being controlled.

"I stand by my earlier statement," she said.

"Following your gut is important." Jonah took in the hordes of women flapping their money in the air, pushing their way forward—and the pitchers of alcohol. "Like when it's nagging you that the hostess probably doesn't have a permit to sell wares in a public park or serve open containers."

"I'm handing out calendars. For charity," she argued, purposefully leaving out the alcohol part.

"Which requires a permit." He leaned in close. "You got a permit, Shay?"

Yeah, that would be a big, fat, apparently illegal no. The way his hands went to his cuffs told her he'd figured it out. The way her body responded said she was crazy, which was the only explanation she could come up with for why she stood and held out her wrists in surrender. "You going to cuff me, Sheriff?"

"Deputy," he corrected, looking as though he was contemplating it, and a whole lot more.

"Deputy," she said with a smile. When he didn't move to whip out the cuffs, she decided to change the topic. "And how is our favorite Great Dane?"

He remained locked and loaded, but his swagger faltered slightly. "Working on it, Trouble."

"That wasn't our deal," she reminded him, ignoring the thrill of him giving her a nickname. "You said you'd handle it and I believed you." Something Shay didn't do lightly.

Trust was a hard concept for her. But for some reason with Jonah she'd been willing to give him a chance. She just hoped he didn't turn out like all the other men in her life—a gigantic disappointment.

"Give me a few more days," he said quietly.

Shay looked at the stack of calendars, each one getting her closer and closer to her dream, then back to his gun. "Only if you give me a few more hours here."

"You're serving alcohol without a permit," he explained, but she could hear the hesitation waver in his voice.

"It's grapefruit juice," Shay said, and Jonah raised a brow.

She sat silent, letting that lie grow and grow until she felt the urge to reach up and touch her nose. "And other stuff," she mumbled.

"It's the other stuff that concerns me." The cuffs clanked against his hip and Shay considered offering him some of that "other stuff."

Personally, she thought Jonah could use a little loosening up— good cop with a touch of wild side was way more appealing than an uptight sheriff.

"If you arrest her, then you've got to take all of us in," Clovis Owens, a portly woman in a Booty Patrol T-shirt, shouted.

"Grandma," Harper warned, and when Clovis crossed her arms in outright defiance, she added, "Last time they took you in, I had to post five hundred bucks in bail."

"A man should know better than to touch a lady's cane without permission," the older woman defended, then looked back at Jonah. "And you should know better than to think we are going anywhere without our man candy."

That elicited a few supportive amens and a damn straight, and soon fifty wrinkled hands were fist pumping bills in the air in protest, all hollering, "We want"—double fist pump—"man candy."

Jonah merely looked at the sky and let out a sigh. Shay noticed the lines of exhaustion bracketing his mouth and felt herself soften. Being a superhero was hard work, and Jonah worked harder than anyone she knew for his town.

"I'll go without a fight as long as you promise me a hot cup of coffee. A latte, something decadent and sweet, not that crap you carry around," she added, and that got a little smile out of him.

"As much as that would make my day, I'll have to take a rain check." She considered asking him if he'd ever call to collect, then thought better of it. With her bold life choices, not to mention her colorful past, the last person she should be spending time with was a no-frills-drip guy who carried a badge.

As though reading her mind, Jonah chuckled, then held a couple of bills of his own over his head, waving it at the crowd and silencing them. "My aunt is recovering from surgery as you all know."

"Lucinda had those bunions removed," Nora added, and the crowd bobbed their heads. "Nasty things."

Jonah grimaced as though he'd gotten an up-close-and-personal look at those bunions and agreed. "The only way to keep her off her feet was if I promised to get her a calendar."

"Such a nice man you've grown into, Jonah," June Whitney, the town's crocheting queen, said, fanning herself at the sight of Jonah flapping bills like he was about to take it all off for charity.

Nora moved even closer.

"So if you all won't mind my snagging one," he said to the crowd, then pinned Shay with his sharp gaze, "I'll be on my way."

"As long as you leave some for us and don't arrest the girl," June agreed.

He flashed that practiced smile that would secure him the race for sheriff, then handed Shay a couple of tens. "Deal."

An excited hum vibrated through the crowd and Harper wisely started handing out calendars before the sheriff changed his mind.

"Thank you," Shay said, picking up a calendar and, forgoing the discreet bag, handing it to him. "It almost makes up for locking me in a cage for days on end."

"You locked yourself in that cage," he corrected quietly, looking down at the cover—and a half-naked Deputy Warren—and shook his head. "And I'm sure you were released within fifteen minutes of my leaving."

Ten. But he didn't need to know that. "You didn't even come back to check on me, so how would you know?"

"Because when I left I called Peggy and told her you were locked in." Which explained why her boss had shown up on her day off. "Then I paid her twenty bucks to take her time getting there."

"Well, you blew good money, Sheriff, because she let me right out." She'd also brought Shay dinner and helped her spruce up Tripod for today, since he was the man of the hour.

That grin went full and he snatched back his twenty. "Good, then we're even." Without another word, Jonah collected every last drop of alcohol and headed back toward the sheriff's department.

"That was interesting," Harper said, adjusting her glasses to get a twenty-twenty on the sheriff's retreating backside.

"Interesting?" Emerson said, coming up behind them. "Hell, that was verbal foreplay."

"*That* was police harassment," Shay corrected.

"If that was harassment, then Deputy Hot Ass can harass me anytime he wants." Emerson laughed.

"Deputy Tight Ass." There was a difference, one Shay needed to remember. "And he just likes to annoy me."

Truth be told, she liked when he chose to annoy her. It felt like flirting without all the pressure.

"So are you going to ask him to take it all off for charity?" Harper asked.

She already had. He'd turned her down. In retrospect it was a good thing, she thought, shuddering at the memory of the last guy she had gotten naked with.

There had been sex, which led to more sex, which led to feelings, and finally Lance moving in. Shay had thought it was a forever kind of situation. Turned out, Lance didn't believe in forever all that much, although he did believe that half of everything Shay owned was his when he left.

"He's not my type."

"If you say so," Harper said.

"I do," Shay clarified.

"Then why are you still staring at his ass?" Emerson asked.

"Doing my due diligence and inspecting his tail."

"Does it pass inspection?"

Shay looked at her friends and smiled. "Oh yeah."

It was by far the finest tail Shay had ever seen.

ch🐾pter
two

A week later, Jonah responded to a call at Valley Vintage, a senior community on the west side of St. Helena, and parked his cruiser behind the fire engine. It was nearly dusk, but he could still make out the perfect cut of steak and chilled six-pack sitting in the backseat. With one last look, he stepped out into the hot July air.

He made his way around the engine blocking the entrance to the complex, and when he saw his brother talking to a group of old ladies who weren't even bothering to hide their ogling, he pulled a box of orange Tic Tacs from his pocket and popped one in his mouth. He had a feeling it was as close to dinner as he was going to get.

"Took you long enough," Adam said, strolling over. He was three years younger, two inches taller, and one of the best smoke jumpers on the West Coast. Today, based on his dark blue work pants and a matching SHFD T-shirt, he was being an average fireman, rescuing cats from trees or some other BS, and had decided to rope Jonah in.

"That's what happens when you call a man in on his day off," Jonah said, thinking again about the steak he'd just picked up for dinner.

"You're just pissy because you got suckered into spending it digging a trench for Mr. Barnwell."

Actually, he was building a fence so Mr. Barnwell would retire the dog crate. And he was pissy because he was doing it to keep Shay Michaels out of trouble. The less chance for trouble, the less chance their paths would cross. A good thing considering every time he was around the woman she seemed to push every single button he owned—including the good ones.

"This had better not be another false alarm, Mr. July," he said.

Ever since Adam landed the centerfold for the Cuties with Booties calendar, the number of female callers had tripled on the days that his brother worked. The weathered faces with bifocals dotting every window, looking their fill of St. Helena's very own Mr. Smoking Hot only deepened Jonah's suspicions.

"Don't hate because you didn't make the cut."

Oh, Jonah had made the cut, and was even offered the cover, but posing in nothing but underwear with the department's K-9 didn't scream *respectable sheriff.* So he'd passed—and Shay had given the spot to Warren. Not that it had mattered, since Nora posted a photo of Jonah shaking his bills like a freaking stripper on her Facebook page last week.

"And I called because Giles is MIA," Adam explained while sending a little wave to a group of senior ladies who were standing patiently with Sharpies in hand, calendars conveniently flipped to the center.

Jonah thought about the steak waiting in his car, begging to be grilled and paired with a baked potato and cold beer, and he sighed. Giles Rousseau was Valley Vintage's most notorious escapee—he was also Jonah and Adam's great-uncle on their mother's side. On Tuesday nights he snuck out to watch the WWE Diva SmackDown on the jumbo screen at the local pub, on Friday it was to play a high-stakes game of Put Up or Shut Up in the basement of the hardware store, and any other time it was to cause trouble with his buddies. "Call Warren, he's the deputy on duty."

"Already did."

"Then why am I here?"

"Because when the nurse reported Giles missing, Deputy Dickwad told her he'd look into it. That was right after lunchtime."

"And?" Giles always made it home by dinner.

"*And* we already checked the Spigot, the bocce ball court at the park, and the hardware store, thinking he might be playing a few hands of cards." Adam shrugged. "No luck."

"This nurse," Jonah asked, taking in the leggy blonde sitting on the end of the fire engine looking their way with Adam's jacket wrapped around her shoulders. "What does she have to do with it?"

"Nurse Nikki?" Adam asked, flashing her that smile that got him laid on a regular basis. "She placed the call. First day on the job and the poor thing lost a patient."

"Yeah, poor thing," Jonah deadpanned, knowing exactly where this was going.

"Seems she needs some consoling," Adam said, and the damn guy had the nerve to grin. "Said if I found Giles before her shift ends at seven then she'd be forever indebted to me." Adam looked back over at Nurse Nikki and her double Ds, and let loose a low whistle. "Do you have any idea how much consoling Nurse Nikki and I could do with forever?"

"You'd be bored by Friday."

Adam shrugged. "Friday, forever. Same thing."

"Not when you're the one getting laid."

"That's why you're pissy," Adam laughed. "You're not getting any."

No, he was not. In fact, Jonah hadn't gotten laid in way too long. And maybe that was the problem. Ever since he'd pulled Shay over a few months back for driving with loose animals in the vehicle—a flock of goddamned geese—he couldn't seem to stop thinking about her. He'd given her a ticket, she'd shown him the bird, and they'd been circling each other ever since.

Which was ridiculous.

Jonah preferred his women sweet, easy-natured, and straight-forward. Nothing about Shay was easy. Oh, she was all woman, with the sweetest ass he'd ever seen, but she was also the most complicated and irritating do-gooder on the planet. Her go-green world was like a nonstop Category 5—spinning out of control and leaving behind a trail of destruction that he usually had to clean up.

Good intentions or not, the woman was a magnet for trouble—something he'd long ago given up chasing.

"Even after you let the cute neighbor off with a warning, she still wouldn't go out with you."

Jonah didn't think Shay would go out with anyone, let alone him. She was beautiful, sexy, and had a distinct fuck-off attitude that sent most men scurrying. Too bad he wasn't most men—it would have made things so much easier.

"You want to talk about it? Maybe I can give you some pointers."

"Call Warren." Jonah smacked his brother on the shoulder and headed back to his steak.

"Hold up," Adam said, catching up to him, his normal humor fading. His brother might play it fast and loose in his personal life, but he was dead serious when it came to his job. "Nikki found Giles's meds on his nightstand."

"Ah, hell," Jonah said, staring at the fading sun. Four hours was a long time for a man with a walker to be out alone. Especially one with a breathing condition.

For once Jonah wished that Warren would man up and do his job. Following up on a known wanderer who didn't want to be found could be boring as shit, but it fell to the sheriff's department to protect and serve all of the residents of Napa County, not just the ones Warren thought could help his career.

Which was why Jonah had decided to run for sheriff. It wasn't that he wanted, or needed, any more responsibility—keeping his adrenaline-junkie siblings out of trouble and making sure his step-mom didn't donate herself right into bankruptcy was a full-time job—but when Warren stepped up unopposed, Jonah knew he had to do something.

He loved this town, loved the people. They'd rallied around his family when his dad died, so to repay the favor he was going to have their backs—and that meant making sure Warren stayed a deputy.

Kissing a night of manning the grill and sipping cold beer good-bye, he popped another Tic Tac in his mouth and said, "Let me radio dispatch and call out Search and Rescue."

An hour later, Jonah stood on the steps to the senior center, patiently waiting for Adam to finish his quick medical eval of their missing Houdini so he could ask his uncle what the hell he'd been think-ing. Although, looking at the window full of ladies in flower-covered swim caps, Jonah already had a pretty good idea.

He had been about to lead his team of volunteers on a canvass of the Vine Street neighborhood when a call came in from dispatch. A suspicious-looking gray-haired man was cornered by the entire water aerobics class for snooping around the pool with a camera in hand. Jonah had arrived right as the first water noodle went airborne. It had taken three firefighters, a handful of Search and Rescue volun-teers, and Adam's promise to stay after for autographs, to get Giles away from the angry mob of biddies.

"You're all good," Adam said, closing up his first aid kit. "But next time you might want to rethink peeping on a bunch of ladies with weapons. Or at least bring your walker so you have a fighting chance."

"That Clovis has some bony feet, got me in the shin real good," Giles said, rubbing the red area on his leg and frowning as though he were the victim. "And I wasn't peeping. I get enough of the saggy breasts back at the home."

"Then what is this?" Jonah held up Giles's camera and scrolled to a photo of enough wrinkled cleavage to make Adam look away in horror.

"That," Giles said, flipping to the next picture of a very beautiful, very stacked blonde in a bikini leading the class, "is a gift from God."

"Those aren't from God," Adam, the resident boob expert, said after a long and thorough investigation of St. Helena's newest swimming teacher. "Those, my friend, can be purchased for about ten grand."

"Too old to know the difference or to care," Giles said, taking his camera back and zooming in on the screen. "Wanted to snap a picture to show the guys back at the home, give them some motivation. Celeste does private in-house lessons. Says so on her website. So we're pooling our social security checks to bring her out, and I needed my investors to see what they'd be getting."

"I saw you swim the length of Lake Donner," Jonah said, remembering the summer after his mother's death, when Jonah had turned seven and his dad had been too overcome with grief to function, let alone celebrate life, and Uncle Giles had taken Jonah and his brothers camping. It had been one of the few bright spots in that period of his life, between losing one mother and gaining another in his stepmom, Phoebe, and his half sister Frankie being born.

"I could forget how to swim for a day or two if it meant seeing Celeste up close in the thing you kids are calling swimming suits."

Jonah couldn't blame the guy. Just last week he'd chosen, for the first time since leaving San Francisco PD, to forget about the law for just a moment and look the other way.

He knew better. Knew all too well just how dangerous relaxing on the job could be. But he'd done it anyway and that didn't sit well. Hell, nothing about Shay sat well. She made him want to strangle her and rescue her at the same time—a bad combo for a guy who liked things cut-and-dried.

Blue lights flashed as Deputy Warren's cruiser pulled into the lot. He approached the group, his eyes narrowing when he spotted Jonah. "What are you doing here?"

"Following up on that missing persons report," Jonah said, returning the look evenly. "The missing senior Valley Vintage called in earlier today that you promised you'd look into."

"I did look into it," Warren defended in a tone that implied none of this mess was his doing. "I opened his file, saw that he goes missing at least once a month, and figured it was a waste of city funds to send out a search party when the guy obviously needs some space."

"Protocol says we respond to every reasonable call, not just the ones we feel like responding to," Jonah countered.

Warren put his hands up. "The missing person was found. All is good."

"You had a senior with a breathing condition who was reported as missing without his proper meds," Adam cut in. "Which means this all could have ended a whole hell of a lot differently."

"But it didn't," Warren said.

Adam sent Jonah a *can you believe this a-hole?* look. And sadly Jonah could believe it. This was typical Warren—lazy, entitled, and always thinking his shit didn't stink.

It was no secret that Warren, wanting to follow in his father's footsteps, had his sights set on mayor. The title of sheriff was the next logical step in his quest to climb the public service ladder. Problem was, St. Helena deserved a sheriff who was in it for the right reasons.

"You're right." Jonah stepped between the two because Adam looked ready to punch Warren in the throat. "We got lucky. This time."

"You're right. My bad," Warren said, not looking sorry at all. It was as though the entire situation were completely out of his grasp. "Won't happen again."

"Then let's clean this up. Because I'd really rather not explain to the sheriff how our missing-person issue turned into a handful of irate grannies threatening to press loitering charges." One of whom had her camera poised in their direction.

"Agreed," Warren said, because the kid might be lazy but he wasn't stupid. And getting caught having a pissing contest over who was in charge in front of Nora Kincaid would look bad for the entire department. Especially since she'd have it all over Facebook in a matter of seconds.

"How about I finish up with the statements and you handle Giles?"

Warren looked at the swim-cap mob, still steaming mad, and back to Jonah. "You sure?"

"Yup." He wanted to get this done right. He could just see Warren somehow managing to rile up the grannies, Giles winding up behind bars for loitering and invasion of privacy, and Jonah spending his morning explaining to Sheriff Bryant how this whole fucked-up situation started to begin with.

"Let me know when you're done and I'll give Giles a ride back to the home," Adam said as if his offer had nothing to do with Nurse Nikki.

"Why not." Jonah rolled his eyes and headed toward the flock of flowered caps. "Wouldn't want my investigation to get in the way of you getting laid."

A few days later, Jonah stood at the edge of the community park with two coffee cups in hand, telling himself to get back in his car and head out. Due to the triple-digit heat, the park was empty.

Except for Shay.

He didn't know what to make of the fact that she was still there. She had been sitting under a tree on a park bench for the better part of the morning. He'd first seen her when he'd stopped by the hardware store earlier that morning, only she'd been sitting with her three-legged mutt—waiting. For what he didn't know, but she had looked eagerly expectant.

It was now lunchtime and she was still there in the same denim skirt and summery top that tied around her neck and floated around her curves, but the smile was gone—so was the dog.

In its place was a half-eaten bag of minidoughnuts.

"I know it's not raining," Jonah said, extending her a paper cup, "but I believe I owe you one of these."

Shay looked up at the cup and eyed it skeptically, then eyed him skeptically, as if waiting to see what the catch was. Oddly enough, today Jonah didn't have any ulterior motives. He'd seen her sitting alone, remembered that he'd promised her coffee, and acted. Not his usual MO.

The suspicious way she was glaring only had him rethinking things more.

"Mind if I have a seat or do I need to stand to enjoy my cup?"

"By all means." Shay picked up what was left of her bag of doughnuts, dusted a few crumbs off the wood, and patted the bench in welcome. "But I'm not sharing my doughnuts, Sheriff."

"Never expected you to, Trouble," he said, not bothering to correct her that he wasn't sheriff yet, then sat before she changed her mind, and placed her cup between them.

She picked it up and took a tentative sniff, watching him over the rim of the cup the entire time. "Salted caramel?"

"As promised."

Her expression went from surprise to sheer bafflement, but for a brief moment he'd caught a flash of something that was raw and vulnerable and—

Oh, crap. Say it wasn't so.

Beneath the bite-me attitude, those big brown eyes of hers were red-rimmed and vulnerable and a little too misty for his liking.

"I can always go back and trade in that cavity-inducing syrup concoction you seem to be so fond for drip crap if it would make you feel better," he said, going for light.

She didn't even crack a smile, instead looking more confused and, *okay*, back to being suspicious again.

"It's just a cup of coffee, Shay," he said because the way she was acting, one would think he'd just offered her an active grenade.

"I know." But her gaze went from the cup to him, carefully assessing—and not in an appreciative way. Not that he blamed her. Jonah was sweaty, covered in sawdust, and in desperate need of a shower. "More home improvements?"

He didn't want her to know that it wasn't his home he was improving. If she heard he was building a dog fence for Domino, she might ask why. A question he wasn't sure how to answer anymore, especially after Adam had ripped him a new one over it the other night.

It also wasn't something he wanted to examine too closely, so he said, "Something like that."

His answer triggered her BS meter, he could tell, but she forced a small smile to her lips. "Thank you. I needed this."

"Rough day?"

"Tripod went to his family this morning, which is awesome," she said in a tone that didn't sound like it had been all that awesome for her.

She took a sip of her latte and went back to staring out at the park. She didn't elaborate, didn't ask him to leave, didn't offer him a doughnut, but after a few minutes quietly admitted, "It sucked."

A strange tenderness washed through Jonah at her honesty. Usually she worked hard at keeping things surface level with him, so the admission was surprising and endearing.

Two of the worst reactions he could have to a woman he wasn't interested in.

"It's obvious you want them as your pets, so why don't you keep them?"

"They're not mine to keep," she said as though completely confused by his question. "I am lucky enough to be a part of their journey, and to help them find their families."

All the struggle and hard work to make families complete yet she goes home alone. Not unlike his own situation. "And that's enough for you?"

Her face softened with resignation and pride. "For now it is."

"How long have you been doing this?"

"Since I was twelve." She picked a doughnut out of her bag and popped it into her mouth. A clear sign that the conversation was over.

Jonah didn't want it to be over, he wanted to know more, so he sat patiently waiting for her to continue. When she plucked out another doughnut, he leaned back, put his arms across the top of the park bench, and stretched out. The *I've got all day* was implied.

With a sigh, she continued. "The summer after my mom passed I found a cat that had been hit by a car. He was still alive and a bit scuffed. I wasn't allowed to have a cat in the house, so I hid him in the garage."

"Your dad wouldn't let you have a cat?" Jonah didn't know the first thing about raising kids, but for a girl who had just lost her mom, giving her something to care for and connect with seemed like a no-brainer.

"Not my dad, my foster parents," she said as if it was no biggie, but Jonah bet that at the time it was the biggest thing in her little world. "I was placed with a couple who wanted a baby, so they didn't feel comfortable letting me keep a pet when they knew I'd be moved. But my teacher had just lost her cat, so I got Commissioner Gordon—"

"Commissioner Gordon?"

"What? I was twelve and a big Batman fan. Do you want to hear the rest of the story, or would you like to keep smirking at me?"

"Sorry." He ran a hand over his mouth. "There, smirk gone. But at some point we are going to talk about how you named a cat after a police commissioner."

She rolled her eyes. "Anyway, I got him healthy and then snuck him to school in my backpack. Mrs. Halliday took one look at Commissioner Gordon and I knew." She lifted one shoulder slightly. "That was my first adoption."

"How many homes were you in?"

"A few," she said, and at his silence admitted, "Okay, a lot."

He'd bet she'd been terrified and scared, because no matter how hard she wished, her world would never be the same.

He had lost his mom at a young age too, then his dad in high school, but Jonah had always had family around, and friends and a town to lean on.

Shay had no one. He got the feeling that over the years that hadn't changed much.

"That's a hard pill to swallow gracefully at any age, let alone twelve," he said.

"I believe the words you're searching for are *temperamental* and *difficult*," she said in a voice mimicking someone who he assumed was a foster parent or social worker.

"And I bet the word *temperamental* didn't help in your file."

She shrugged it off, but he could tell the words still hurt.

"It was true then and sometimes still is now," she admitted without apology, which intrigued him.

Shay was a caretaker, that was obvious, yet she lived her life loud and made no apology for it. Jonah was starting to understand that there was so much more to her that she kept hidden.

And if there was one thing that got Jonah going, it was a good mystery.

chapter
three

Shay arrived for her shift at the Paws and Claws Day Spa a few minutes early. She had to put out the water dishes, make sure she had enough peanut butter pupcakes on hand, and still have time to post her flyers announcing the upcoming signings in the window before the customers started pouring in.

Even though it had been raining when she'd left the house, a freak midsummer storm, Shay had walked to work because her oldest rescue, Jabba, needed to burn off the economy-sized box of pudding cups he'd found in the pantry. Today was his day to find a home, Shay just knew it, and since Jabba was a dump truck of a dog who waddled when he walked and made more gastrointestinal noises than a tent full of Boy Scouts, she was determined not to let a little gas ruin his chances.

What better place to meet his future family than at a crowded pet day spa full of dog lovers?

Okay, so she'd also risked frizzy hair because Wednesday was her neighbor's day off. Not Estella. Her other neighbor. The one with the amazing tail who kept threatening to cuff her. Only to turn around and bring her a coffee.

Last spring, Jonah had purchased the run-down Craftsman across the street and liked to spend his day off doing manly improvements outside, like digging fence posts, lifting heavy things, and working on the roof. And if Shay timed her departure right, which she always did, she'd catch him just as he was starting to get a little hot and a whole lot sweaty.

She'd smile and say good morning, he'd tip his hat begrudgingly, then pretend he wasn't checking out her butt when she walked to work, and she'd pretend she always had that swish to her stride. It was their thing. And she looked forward to it.

Only this morning he'd been a no-show, and for some reason that bothered her. Especially after last week in the park. She'd wanted to tell him how sweet it was that he had remembered how she took her coffee—how she hadn't felt so alone after losing Tripod, but she hadn't seen Jonah since.

It's just a cup of coffee, Shay. And she'd do best to remember that.

Shay dropped her bag in her styling chair, unleashed Jabba, who collapsed on the floor panting as if he'd just hiked the north face of Mount Eiger, and was pulling out her new adoption flyers when Peggy appeared from the back room.

"How many more of those dogs did you adopt out last week?"

"Just Tripod," Shay said but gave a secret smile because she was pretty sure she'd found the perfect family for her nine-year-old beagle, Yodel. The applicant, Ms. Abernathy, was a widow, lived in a house with an enclosed yard, and didn't like to use her hearing aids—a bonus since Yodel more than lived up to his name.

Peggy didn't smile back. Eyes serious and lips grim, she reached under the counter and came up with a cardboard box, which she gingerly set right between a display of cheddar dog biscuits and hanging gem-encrusted cat collars.

"I don't even know why I'm showing you this—you need another charity case like you need a hole in your head—but this was sitting by the back door and it had your name on it, so, here you go."

Shay walked over to the box, her resolve already melting at the little mewing sounds emanating from the cardboard. She knew what was inside—the holes punched in the top told her it was bundles of love just waiting for someone to recognize what they had to offer. She reached for the lid.

"Before you open that," Peggy jumped in, "and your save-the-world attitude takes over, remember that you have four dogs who are already counting on you to save their world. And with Bark in the Park coming up, my kennels are booked with clients."

"I know." And she did. Her house was already at capacity, which meant she had no business opening that box, because if Peggy was giving her a warning, there was another option.

"Booked, dear. As in, no matter what is in there, I can't help because there will be no additional space." Peggy tried to sound stern but failed miserably. It was then that Shay knew Peggy had already peeked inside the box, and what she'd seen was too cute to say no to.

"I wouldn't expect you to give up kennel space, Peg. Plus, I think Yodel found his new family. All that's left is the surprise house inspection." Something that Shay did for all of her pets before she agreed to the adoption. Doing a walk-through when the applicants expected it gave them time to put on their best faces. Shay wanted to see them when they didn't think anyone was watching.

"Which leaves you with only one space," Peggy warned, and Shay's smile went full-blown. For more than one critter to be in a box that size meant—

"Kitties," she cooed as she opened the lid and found a plethora of whiskers and wet pink noses, and five sets of the bluest eyes staring up at her.

They were some munchkin–Scottish fold mix, four of them peaches and cream and the smallest one, a male, charcoal gray with a white dot on his muzzle. She picked up Dot—*look at that, he already has a name*—and cuddled him to her chest, gently inspecting his little body. He was tiny and shivering from the rain, his stomach was so sunken she could see his little ribs poking out, and he was covered in enough filth and neglect that it broke Shay's heart.

"Oh, Peggy, who would do this?"

"I don't know, honey, but it sure makes you rethink public shaming, doesn't it? Time to bring back the stocks."

It made Shay rethink a lot of things, namely how saving just a few here and there wasn't enough anymore. There were so many animals that needed a champion in their corner—like Dot with his sad eyes and gentle spirit—and Shay wanted to be that champion. She just didn't have the space.

"I called the county shelter," Peggy said quietly. "They can take the kittens this afternoon."

Shay was already shaking her head. "It is the height of kitten season. We'll be lucky if any of these guys will find a home, let alone *all* of them." Which meant they would never get the chance to know what it felt like to be loved and cherished. "Call them back and tell them you found another shelter."

Peggy dug her hands into her hips, everything in between giving a jiggle. "You aren't a shelter, missy, you are a foster mom—who is already at her limit for fosters."

"Kitten season, Peggy." Shay narrowed one eye and her boss narrowed back. "Plus with the calendar out, Bark in the Park in a few weeks, and the signings, all that exposure is pretty much a guarantee that Jabba and the others will find their homes by the end of the month. You want me to tell these kittens they don't get a home because of thirty silly days?"

"Fine, you can keep Mr. Whiskers and his siblings here until the end of the day," Peggy said, picking up the biggest one. "But they better be gone come dinnertime."

"Mr. Whiskers?"

"They came with names." Peggy held up a piece of binder paper that had Shay's name scribbled in purple marker and enough fold marks to pass for origami. "And instructions."

Shay cuddled Dot close to her chest and gave him a little scratch under the chin, while Peggy unfolded the letter. It didn't take much before a little rumble of contentment escaped from the kitten, although his eyes remained guarded and glued on Shay.

"Dear Saint," Peggy read, then with a sigh, handed Shay the letter. "Just *Saint*, isn't that sweet?"

Sweet and telling. She stared at the rudimentary letters, and the heart over the *i* in *saint* gave her a pretty good idea of who had dropped off that box. It looked as though Goldilocks was taking her journey into sainthood seriously.

DEAR SAINT,

I KNOW YOU'RE REALLY BUSY FINDING FAMILIES FOR YOUR DOGS, BUT KITTENS GOTS PAWS TOO. THESE ONES ARE NICE AND NEED A NICE FAMILY WHO GIVES THEM TOYS. THEY ALSO NEEDS A BATH BUT I WASN'T ALLOWED TO BRINGS THEM INSIDE. THEY LIKE CHICKEN TENDERS, PURR A LOT, AND MR. WHISKERS IS GOOD AT CHASING MICE.

There wasn't a signature at the bottom, but a list of names with coordinating drawings. Not that they helped distinguish one from the other. Besides Kitty Fantastic, a solid gray one with curled ears, and Dot, whose given name was Patches, they were all orange and white.

"Mr. Whiskers, Princess, MiMi, Lovekinz, Kitty Fantastic, and Patches," Shay read aloud while trying, without much luck, to match the drawing to the kittens.

"I got as far as Mr. Whiskers being the biggest and Patches with his spot, but then I was stumped."

Shay looked from the list to the box, counting three times to make sure she wasn't mistaken. "Where's the sixth kitten? There are six names but only five here."

"I know, I counted several times," Peggy said gently, giving Mr. Whiskers a kiss on the head. "The closest I could come up with is that Kitty Fantastic didn't make it."

Shay gave a single nod and pulled Dot close. "I'd better call Dr. Huntington and see if he has time to check these guys out," she said, referring to the town's vet, whose heart was as big as his belly and who always gave discounts for Shay's fosters. "Do you mind if I get them cleaned up and settled in one of the smaller kennels?"

"Make it fast. We've got a full schedule today."

"If Dr. Huntington clears them, I'll take them home on my lunch break. These guys have had a rough start. The least I can do is get them cozy and settled while I find their families."

"I imagine with all that cuteness, it won't take long."

It was more a sad statement than a question, so Shay stopped fussing with the kittens to look up at her boss doting on Mr. Whiskers. "They will go fast. So if you want to keep Mr. Whiskers—"

"Nope." Peggy didn't sound all that confident, but she put Mr. Whiskers back in the box all the same. "When Chaplin passed, I promised myself no more pets. It hurts too much when they go."

According to Peggy's friends, Chaplin's passing came on the heels of losing her husband, so instead of investing her heart into a new companion, she threw herself into turning her small pet food store into a full-functioning pet spa. Not that Shay blamed her.

Sometimes it was better to just live without than to risk the heartache that accompanied loss.

"If you're sure?"

"I'm sure." Peggy took one last, long look, then closed the lid and handed Shay the box. "Where do you think they came from?"

"I don't know." Goldilocks might have dropped off these cats, but Shay knew the kittens weren't hers. She would never neglect animals this way. "Wherever it was, they wouldn't survive going back."

Twenty minutes later, Shay had the little guys bathed, fed, and sleeping in one of the kennels. Dr. Huntington had agreed to drop by on his lunch break, and Shay was cleaning up the kitty tub when a commotion came from the front of the store.

She dried off her hands on her apron and walked out to find her first customer of the morning looking irritated, drip-dried, and spitting mad.

Ida Beamon, owner of Cork'd N Dipped—a wine and chocolate bar—and founding member of the Booty Patrol, was a shotgun of a woman who favored coral lipstick, dime-store jewelry, and offensive sweatshirts. Today's said QUACK OFF and had a picture of her Norton.

Norton, a tropical whistling duck, had a black belly, brown body, and a bright orange beak. He also walked on a leash, liked playing catch, and believed himself to be a dog. He had been one of Shay's first fosters when she moved to town.

"You see this?" Ida asked, waving the day's issue of the *St. Helena Sentinel* at Shay while Norton gave Jabba a good butt sniff. "First that woman bans Norton and me from the Companion Brigade, claiming he isn't a companion. And now this." Ida pressed her thin lips into an angry line while her gray, spiky hair moved with each flip of the hand.

"Norton is a duck," Shay reminded her, sending a gentle smile at Norton, who had waddled over to say good morning. Normally that consisted of a few beak nuzzles to the thigh and flopping on his back for a belly rub. But midnuzzle he heard the offensive term *duck*, and, preferring to be addressed as a companion like his doggie friends, looked up and—

Quark!

Quark! Quark! Quark!

—abandoned his greeting to instead waddle over and poop in Shay's station.

"A duck who has spent more time socializing with dogs than Estella's snooty Foxy Cleopatra." Ida unfolded the paper and jabbed a bony finger at the front page. "Read."

Shay looked down at the full-page article: MANHUNT TO MAN CANDY: HOW OUR SHERIFF HOPEFULS HANDLE THE CROWD. It had a photo of each candidate posted side by side. Deputy Warren had his arm around the once lost but thankfully found Giles Rousseau and looked as though he were heading up a joint task force with the fire department and Search and Rescue team. Whereas Jonah stood in front of a Cuties with Booties banner, surrounded by a sea of waving twenties, looking for the world as though he were about to rip off his uniform and shake his tail feathers for charity.

The article went on to praise the department in its rescue of Valley Vintage's lost resident, at the same time promoting Shay's calendar, which had Deputy Warren featured. It even went as far as to quote Shay about the success of the day.

"Deputy Jonah handled the crowd like a pro," she read aloud and cringed. Yeah, unfortunately, she'd said that. Not that Nora had told her what the article was for when she'd called—or how bad it would make Jonah look.

No wonder he'd been absent this morning. He was probably handling the fallout of the article, explaining to his boss how he'd ended up in the center of a mob of drunken seniors cheering for their man candy. He didn't seem to be the kind of guy to get angry over a silly photo. But it couldn't be good for his campaign.

Jonah was obviously working hard to cement that upstanding superhero persona he had going on. And Superman did not strip for charity. A shame, since Jonah on her cover would have doubled her profits.

"I should go apologize," Shay said, surprised at the unexpected need to see if he was all right. To make sure he didn't blame her.

"Apologize?" Ida laughed. "For what?"

QuarkQuarkQuark. This from Norton, who was sitting on Jabba's back as though trying to hatch him.

"I agree, dear," Peggy said. "Best press that man's gotten all year. He's actually smiling. See."

She saw all right. A double dose of dimples with a set of lips so kissable that Shay's body zinged. Silly, since she'd long ago stopped believing in zing. Only there was a definite zinging going on in her belly—and lower.

"Damn."

Quark!

"Watch your mouth. Norton's been repeating what he hears and the grandkids are repeating him," Ida explained, then pointed her bony finger at the bottom of the page with so much force she nearly punched a hole right through it. "But I was talking about this."

At the bottom of the page was a color ad for Bark in the Park.

"They moved it to the last weekend in August," Peggy said quietly from over Shay's shoulder.

"What?" Shay looked at the date and felt her stomach hollow out. "But Bark in the Park is always the third weekend. Always."

"Now it's the same day as the big signing here," Peggy said, resting a hand on Shay's shoulder. "I'm so sorry, dear. I know how much you were looking forward to this event."

An event that, if this ad was accurate, was now irrelevant. Because, if Shay was honest with herself, and she always was, she knew that given the choice between attending a fifty-year tradition held by one of the town's oldest families or a cookie and soda mixer with the town's newest tumbleweed-transplant, Shay and her dogs would come in a cool second.

"I guess I'm going to have to change it," Shay said as though it wasn't a huge deal. As though she hadn't already sent out a few hundred flyers. As though it wasn't mentioned in the article above. Changing it now would be a major undertaking and Estella knew that. "She did it on purpose, to get me back for the calendar."

"Oh boy," Peggy said, her face going soft in that grandmotherly way that always had Shay sweating. Having people care about how she felt was unfamiliar and a little scary, because she was afraid that once she got used to it, the caring would go away. "Keep reading."

Shay did, skipping past the list of vendors, the photo of Foxy dressed like Cleopatra and Estella like the Sphinx, reading the fine print under the last line.

"No peddling of pets allowed." Shay looked up, a bad feeling settling in her chest. "What does that even mean?"

"It means that Estella bullied the Companion Brigade to change their policy on allowing breeders and rescues into the event," Ida said. "She says it is about honoring companions, not selling them."

"I'm not selling them." On average, she lost a few hundred dollars with each adoption, which was why she'd come up with the calendars to begin with. Every calendar sold helped to pay for vet bills and keep her fosters fed and housed until they went to their families. "And she can't do that, not so close to the event," Shay said, rereading the ad but knowing there was nothing she could do to change it.

Bark in the Park was run by the Companion Brigade, and Estella was their long-standing and much-respected president. If she said no peddling, then Shay was out of luck.

"Bark in the Park is my biggest adoption event of the year." Shay felt her throat begin to close.

"That's why she did it," Peggy said, laying a hand on Shay's.

"It doesn't make any sense. Cutting out breeders and rescues cuts into the event's profits." Unlike pet owners, who could participate for free, people like Shay had to pay to play—a hundred dollars a pop. "She'd have to refund everyone's money."

"She already cut the reimbursement checks. Justified it by saying distinguished organizations deserve distinguished members," Ida said, and that got a big quack out of Norton.

"She's punishing all those pets because I didn't put Foxy in the calendar."

"She's doing this because she thinks the dogs in your calendar have an advantage to be named this year's Blue Ribbon Barker and will upstage her Foxy Cleopatra," Peggy explained.

Shay snorted. "I wish, but every year a purebred wins." Usually it was Estella's. "There is no way one of my mutts would take the crown."

"Every woman in this town has a calendar hanging on their wall, telling them just who the finest tail is in wine country," Peggy said.

"She's right," Ida agreed. "Not even Estella's reputation and pull can compete with mutts with trading cards and coordinating man candy."

"Yeah, well trading cards and man candy will only find the calendar dogs homes. I was hoping to capitalize on the draw of the calendar to place other animals."

"You still have the big signing," Peggy offered.

She closed her eyes, because no, she realized painfully, she didn't. "My guys aren't available the weekend before." They'd all made it clear that they needed advance notice to make sure they could get the time off work. "Some guys had to take personal days to be there. So if I change the date, a bunch of them won't be able to come, and if I keep the date I am competing with Bark in the Park. It's like this whole calendar thing was for nothing."

"It's not nothing, dear," Peggy said, placing an arm around Shay's shoulders. "You have the money to help dozens of animals get their shots." But if she couldn't find her animals homes, then the money was worthless. "And don't forget those cute kittens back there. You'll find them a good home."

It wasn't the kittens or the pinup pets Shay was worried about. It was the older pets, the awkward ones with special needs who were hard to place. Those were the ones who needed Bark in the Park. Needed a little extra exposure to show how wonderful and loving they could be.

Those were the ones who people like Estella Pricket always overlooked.

Jonah was done.

Done with this shift. Done with the weather. He was done with the whole damn day.

That it should have been his day off only made it worse, but with the department desperately understaffed, three rookies on the schedule, and Mother Nature flipping them the bird by dumping three inches of rain before lunch, Jonah had been called in.

He'd spent the morning doing traffic control and dealing with tourists going faster than the weather permitted, and the afternoon fielding a bunch of BS calls. It turned out the *St. Helena Sentinel* had sold a record number of copies, even doing a rush second print after lunch. Which meant that three out of every four calls he'd responded to after that had been female—single ones, married ones, widowed ones, ones with walkers—all wanting to know if the deputy made house calls and if his gun was really as big as it looked.

Soaked through to the bone and wanting nothing more than to get out of his wet clothes, Jonah dropped his hat on the back of his chair and made his way to the locker room, surprised to find half the squad standing around as though the rest of the team weren't out in the storm, busting their asses trying to keep up with the high call volume.

It was weird. They were all geared up and ready to head out, only they weren't moving, just standing there shooting the shit. And, in a stellar example of what *not* to do on the job, Warren sat on the bench, clicking away on his phone.

Telling himself that it wasn't his business how Warren handled his shift, Jonah opened his locker, took one look at the pair of pink fuzzy cuffs dangling from the hook, and that twitch—the one that had started behind his right eye the second he'd seen the morning paper—gained ground until his whole head throbbed.

Warren was looking for a fight, and after Jonah's day he wanted to give him one. Only he wasn't that guy anymore, couldn't afford to be, so he plastered on a laid-back grin that he sure as hell didn't feel. "I think your girlfriend left these in my locker."

He tossed the cuffs to Warren, who caught them midair, and with a grin that was more shit-eating than good-natured, the prick pulled out a twenty and waved it. "For the record, how much will this get me?"

"Fuck you," Jonah said, turning back to his locker. The faster he got out of uniform, the faster this day would be over. And the less likely it would end with Jonah having to explain to IA how Warren's teeth had ended up down his throat.

"You're not my type," Warren said, sounding highly amused. "But, wow, can't believe a twenty gets me all that."

"Instead of spending all your brain power figuring out how to get in my pants, why don't you put the phone away and try doing your job?"

"Somebody's hormonal," Warren said, but nobody laughed. They were all too busy staring at Sheriff Bryant, who was standing in the doorway. The guy might be old as dirt and three months from retiring, but even Warren knew to watch his step around the sheriff. He was respected, tough as nails, and the one person who could sink what little chance Warren had of winning the election.

"If you ladies are done wasting county money, we've got a four-car pileup on Silverado Trail blocking traffic in both directions," Sheriff Bryant said. "So quit playing grab ass and head out."

"Yes, sir," Warren said, securing his utility belt and shoulder-checking Jonah before he headed out to start his shift.

Sheriff Bryant crossed his arms over his generous spare tire and waited until the room cleared out. "You going to let him be a problem?"

Jonah looked over his shoulder. "No, sir."

"Good to hear." The sheriff took in Jonah's disheveled condition, the pink cuffs on the bench, and chuckled. "We need to talk about it?"

"Christ no."

He nodded, looking relieved. "I took you off the schedule tomorrow."

"What? Why?"

"Because you've worked too many overtime hours this month and I don't need billing on my ass." His smile faded. "If you're going to last as sheriff, son, then you need to find some kind of balance. As tired as you look, I'd bet you haven't had more than fifteen hours of sleep this week."

It was probably less. Sleep and Jonah didn't mix anymore. He just lay there staring at the ceiling, thinking about all the things he wished he could do over. Which was why he needed that overtime.

"That's what I thought." Bryant lowered his voice. "Son, in your condition, you're more of a harm than a help. So do me a favor and go home and spend your TO in bed resting, instead of building a fence to impress some girl."

ch🐾pter
four

Shay looked at the bag in her hand that was getting wetter with every drop of rain, then back to Jonah's front door, but no matter how much she willed her feet to take that last step to his porch, she couldn't seem to make any progress.

It wasn't the idea of apologizing that got her. Shay had made her way through life using the trial and error method, and as such was a firm believer in owning your mistakes. It was apologizing when she wasn't sure how it would be received that was hard for her. And after her earlier attempt with another neighbor, it was no wonder why she was waffling.

Moments ago, Shay had swallowed her pride and gone to Estella to find common ground and maybe end this ridiculous feud by offering to put Foxy Cleopatra's photo on her blog. Hell, she would have offered to make Foxy the Cuties with Booties' official mascot if it meant getting her fosters inside Bark in the Park and finding a few of them families—but Estella had slammed the door in Shay's face.

It seemed no matter how hard she tried, the woman had it out for her, as though she could tell Shay didn't belong, and that hurt.

The truth always hurts, she thought, because she knew that Estella wasn't the problem. Shay was. She had a hard time fitting in. Always had, because every time she started to fit, the space changed, the family changed—and with that expectations.

The last time she'd thought she finally found her place, she'd been sorely mistaken. It had taken her two painful years to overcome that heartache, and ever since she'd been more gun-shy than ever.

But here, in St. Helena, she wanted to do more than fit. She wanted to belong to something bigger than herself. Be a part of this town in the same way as Emerson and Harper. She just wasn't sure she knew how.

She looked down at the bag and took in a humbling breath.

"The last person who threw a flaming poop bomb at a deputy's house wound up with two hundred hours of community service and a permanent record," an amused and incredibly sexy voice said from behind her.

"I've already got a record." To prove that point, Shay slowly raised both hands over her head, the suspicious bag clearly visible, dangling from her fingers. "And this isn't a poop bomb, it's an olive branch."

"Trouble, it sounds like you and I need to have a serious conversation about what *olive branch* means."

At his casual demeanor, Shay turned around and dropped her hands to her sides. "Seriously?" She waved her free hand to encompass the general vicinity of where his holster usually hung. "You aren't even armed."

Jonah leaned against his cruiser parked on the street in front of his house. He was in a pair of worn button-flies and a soft-looking T-shirt, his forearm leisurely resting on the window frame, a ball cap pulled low on his head, looking so solid and together it was annoying.

He looked down to where she was pointing and grinned. "That could be argued."

My oh my, was the straitlaced sheriff flirting? Part of her brain was saying yes, he was. The other part was screaming at her to abort mission. He might not be armed, but when he looked at her like that, she knew he was dangerous—to her mental well-being.

And just maybe her heart.

Jonah pushed off the car, taking his sweet-ass time to stroll up the walkway, not stopping until she could see the rain on his lashes. Eyes on hers, he reached out, and for a second she thought he was going to kiss her. His hands were headed for her hips, and when his lips parted slightly, her knees wobbled and her pulse raced and she made the split decision, right there on Jonah's lawn, that she'd kiss him back.

His gaze slowly dropped to her mouth—then lower.

To the bag—saving them both from making a huge freaking mistake when he took it to test its weight and size. After a thorough investigation, which must have passed inspection, he stepped back and grinned.

"Too heavy to be dog shit," he said as though he were uncovering evidence to prove the identity of JFK's assassin. He shook it and it rattled. His brows went up. "Last I checked, branches don't clink, so you want to talk about why you're trespassing on private property in the middle of the night?"

"It's barely eight and you're not even on duty."

She reached for the bag and he held it over her head. "I'm always on duty."

Didn't she know it.

Admitting she wasn't tall enough to snatch it back, Shay gave up. Then went for honest. "I came to say thanks and to apologize."

"Apologize?" Jonah raised a single brow, then cautiously peeked inside and smiled at her over the rim of the bag.

"You brought me beer." His expression softened, bringing forth that annoying zing. Only this time it wasn't so annoying. It felt—nice. "My favorite brand."

"I know," she said, and damn if her face didn't heat.

He seemed surprised by her statement, but it was true. She'd done a little investigation of her own and discovered everyone's favorite deputy was a beer connoisseur. She'd watched him on occasion, sipping a bottle on his front porch, but until today she hadn't known that it was his thing.

Even though they had never spent any significant length of time together, she knew he took pride in his ability to protect and serve. He showed it every day in the way he cared for his family, his house, his town, and its people—even when it came to pain-in-his-ass neighbors carrying suspicious brown paper bags. And the other day he had cared enough about Shay and her dogs to look the other way when she'd messed up, then he sat with her while she mourned the loss of one of her babies, as though he understood her struggle in saying good-bye.

She wanted to acknowledge that and say thanks.

"You didn't have to do that," he said quietly.

"I wanted to. I mean, it isn't a big deal. It's . . ."

Shay didn't know how to finish that statement. In fact, it was becoming increasingly difficult to speak, period. Jonah had focused all his attention on her, patiently waiting for her to continue. Being on the receiving end of that kind of intensity, and what she thought looked a lot like caring, made her heart do crazy things. Then he took a step forward and her breath caught.

"It's sweet," he said softly, his smile faltering as the last word played off his tongue.

Hers disappeared altogether. Not because she was shocked that he found her sweet, but because she was suddenly aware of just how close they stood, and how badly she wanted him to lean down and kiss her. How badly she wanted him to think she was sweet.

Shay knew she was a lot of things, but sweet wasn't one of them. Yet something about the way he said it, the way he was looking at her, made her want to be just that. At least for tonight.

"Hang on," he said, looking in the bag. "What happened to the rest of the six-pack?"

"Nothing. It is the perfect amount," she said, taking the bag and pulling out the first one. She handed it to him. "This one is to say thank you for not ticketing me for giving away alcohol without a permit."

He laughed—and it was a great laugh. "Your thanks for over-looking your illegal possession of alcohol is to give me alcohol?"

"Legal alcohol," she corrected. "I learn from my mistakes. Now take the beer and say, 'Thank you, Trouble.'"

He did as told, making a big show of popping the top and taking a big swig. He wiped the back of his hand over his mouth. "Thank you, Trouble." Only he wasn't being a smart-ass, he was being serious.

She pulled out the next bottle. Same brand, different brew. "This one is for buying a calendar. Your being supportive meant a lot."

"To be clear, no money actually exchanged hands, and the calendar was for my Aunt Lucinda. If my brothers hear any differently, we are going to have problems." He eyed the next beer in her hand. "Let me guess, that one is for not busting you for selling calendars without a retail license?"

"No it's for . . ." *Shit!* "I have to have a license to sell my calendars?"

"Forget I said anything." He took another long pull.

"Already forgotten," she said and handed him the third one. "This one is to say thanks for bringing me coffee and listening to me whine over Tripod."

"I didn't think you were whining," he whispered. "I thought you handled it with an amazing amount of strength and grace."

Grace.

That word, with regard to her, was a compliment in itself. Coming from Jonah? It made all of her insides turn to mush.

Afraid she might kiss him after all, she quickly pulled out the last bottle. "This one is to apologize for the quote in the paper. I had no idea what the article was about or how it would make you look." She took a deep breath and looked into his deep blue eyes until she wanted to fall in. "I didn't think that—"

Not wanting to cheapen this experience, she stopped before she made up some lame excuse. He deserved more and so did this moment.

"I didn't think. Period. I was so focused on selling my calendars and I didn't think of how it would affect you or anybody else. And I am sorry."

He was silent, just staring at her. She confused him, which was fine by her since she got flustered every time he looked her way.

"So you stood out here in the pouring rain to apologize? To me?"

Unable to hold his gaze any longer, she leaned her head back to look at the rain, which was coming down pretty hard, and put her hands out to the side. "I like the rain."

"Me too."

Shay's body gave a little shiver—but not because of the rain. The heat between them was so tangible it made it difficult to catch her breath. He didn't help the situation, letting his gaze purposefully fall to her shirt—her pastel blue, incredibly wet shirt that was as practical as tissue paper in the rain—taking that shiver to a full-blown zing of anticipation. And when she realized he wasn't trying to hide his interest, she knew she was in trouble.

"Are you flirting with me, Sheriff?"

"Jonah," he corrected and Shay swallowed. Not *Deputy* but *Jonah*. It felt intimate, personal, like he was giving her something in return. It was silly, but with him dressed like a regular guy telling her his name, it made him seem more approachable. It was as if he was sharing part of himself with her, the real part of Jonah who sipped microbrews on the porch, and that Jonah she found incredibly appealing. "And I'm not sure what I'm doing."

"Me either," she said and rolled up on her tiptoes, promising herself that she was just going to give a peck on the cheek, a sincere token of thanks between two friends. Only her lips touched his skin and the last thing she felt was friendly.

His skin was rough with stubble and tasted like a summer rain and sexy man. And okay, her lips may have lingered a little longer than necessary, making her heart feel like it was going to pound right out of her chest, which was the only excuse she had for doing something epically stupid.

Like moving her mouth just enough to brush his.

In her defense, he did groan what sounded a lot like her name. Then again the blood was pounding so hard in her ears it could have just been a groan. Whatever it was sounded needy and hot and like he wanted more. So she did it again, and suddenly she felt air whoosh from her lungs as the cold bottles trailed from her hips around to her lower back as he pulled her to him, taking her mouth in what had to be the most thorough kiss in the history of kisses.

Jonah was slow and languid, taking her mouth again and again, as though he was gearing up for an all-night-long slow kiss.

Never one to be rushed, he took his sweet time to explore every inch of her, gently taking what she offered and nothing more. He wasn't demanding or controlling, which surprised her. He seemed content to let her set the limits. Problem with that was Shay didn't do limits all that well.

In her mind, they were nothing more than recommended guidelines set for the sole purpose of being tested and crossed. And she had a feeling that crossing this particular line with this particular man was either the best idea she'd ever had or the worst mistake she'd ever make. And that was saying a lot.

Thankfully her cell vibrated—the buzzing a reminder to feed the kittens.

"What's that?" he asked against her lips, then tilted his head to look at her butt, which was vibrating and blinking a rainbow of colors.

Not wanting to explain that she had added five more pets to her now over-the-county-limit household—which would undoubtedly lead to her being fined—Shay turned off the alarm and repocketed the phone. "Nothing."

His gaze rose to her lips and he said, "That was a lot of bells and whistles for nothing."

"Yeah?" she whispered, knowing they were no longer talking about her phone.

"Yeah," he said as their gazes met. His was heated and guarded and she knew what he was thinking. This kind of chemistry could only end in disaster. A hot, steamy, life-altering disaster. But a disaster all the same.

She touched her fingers to her lips and shook her head. "I don't know what happened. I just wanted to give you a little kiss on the cheek."

That earned her a smile. "You missed."

"I got distracted by your mouth." Just saying the word had her gaze zeroing in on his lips again, had her breath sticking in her chest, and that zing picking up power and moving south—way south.

His finger, chilled from the beer, traced along her jaw to her lower lip, making every nerve ending inside of her light up. "I know the feeling."

She looked up into his eyes, surprised at the hunger she found there. She placed a hand over his, bringing it to her mouth to deliver a gentle kiss. "This won't work."

"I know that too." Unfortunately their bodies didn't, because even as they dropped their hands, the rest of them swayed closer.

"Then I'll just say my thanks so we can pretend the rest of this didn't happen."

He laughed low and husky. "If you say so, Trouble."

Nope, but she was going to give it her best. "And I wanted to say thank you for fencing in Domino's yard." But giving him a beer for this one just didn't seem right. Didn't seem enough.

It was the deputy's turn to blush, which meant that he'd had zero intention of telling her what a wonderful, sweet thing he'd done for her. Well, for Domino, but it felt good all the same. "It was no big deal."

"To me it was. You promised you'd fix it and you did."

He took a step back and looked at her as though she'd somehow offended his entire sex. "I gave you my word."

He had given her so much more.

Few people in Shay's life had come through for her, which was why she didn't want to mess this up, or complicate things.

"Most people would have looked into it and maybe followed up, but you went to Mr. Barnwell's on your day off, helped him build the fence, even bought some of the supplies."

He shrugged off her words, and for the first time Shay saw a different side of the confident and together deputy. She saw that he didn't do well with praise, and she wondered why.

"You're a good man, Jonah," she whispered, then walked away without another word. Across the street, up her front steps to the porch, and only when she was inside with the door securely closed did she allow herself to breathe. Because that kiss wasn't a kiss. It was the start of something.

"Should I go with the crotchless or red lace?"

Under different circumstances, with a different woman, Jonah would have asked if she had a pair of crotchless red lace. But since he was on the job responding to a call, and Ms. Clovis Owens was the woman asking, he waved vaguely at the red pair. "I'd go with those." He had tried several times in vain to direct Clovis to the point of her call, but she somehow kept distracting him.

"Hmmm," Clovis chuckled, her stare unyielding. "I would have taken you for a crotchless kind of guy."

Clovis dropped the red lace and picked up the crotchless, then relying heavily on her cane, waddled over to slip them on the half-dressed mannequin in the front window display.

With a round face, an even rounder body, and enough aged cleavage to have Jonah shuddering, Clovis looked more like a madam than a shop owner. Granted, she ran the Boulder Holder, a lingerie store on Main Street that specialized in the curvier woman. And this curvy woman, who'd been rumored to have roamed the earth with the dinosaurs, loved to flaunt her wares, which today included a teal-and-black corset—whose seams looked one chuckle away from snapping due to the extraordinary amount of weight—and a button that said LET'S GET INTIMATE.

"I'm spicing up the shop, trying to give customers a reason to wander this far down Main Street," she explained. "Ever since I moved locations, I've had a hard time moving merchandise. I still have my regulars, but the lack of walk-ins is hurting business."

Two years ago, Clovis had purchased one of the five renovated Victorian storefronts on the far end of Main Street with the hope that the luxury live-work-play community breaking ground across the street would bring in high-end customers and raise the price of real estate. The project was nixed by the planning commission before they even broke ground, and the store owners had been floundering ever since.

Satisfied with her display, Clovis walked back through the store, stopping midway to look at her hands, as though just realizing she no longer held her cane.

"Sorry to hear that." Jonah walked over to the window and, eyes averted, carefully extracted it from underneath the mannequin and handed it to her.

"Aren't you a gentleman," she said, and when Clovis sat back behind her counter and thumbed through a box of glow-in-the-dark G-strings as though they were quilting squares, Jonah busied himself retrieving his notebook. "My granddaughter warned me against moving. Said I was counting my bills before they were in the strap."

On that note, Jonah cleared his throat. "You called about a discrimination claim."

That phrasing finally got her attention. "It isn't a claim," she said, her voice firm. "It was an act of discrimination pure and simple, and I want the culprit arrested."

"Why don't you explain what happened."

"I was on that Pinterest, pinning me some pictures of those Cuties with Booties, when I saw that Giles Rousseau had opened him an account." The older woman looked horrified. "The man makes me mail him a paper catalogue every season because he refuses to sign up for my e-mail mailing list, but he's got a Pinterest account! And he pinned pictures from our swim class at the senior center on his Sexy and Single in St. Helena board."

Ah, Christ. Jonah knew where this was going. Warren was supposed to handle Giles, get him to hand over the photos, or at least scare him into not making them public.

"I'm sorry about this, Ms. Owens. I will stop by his place on the way back and have him take your photos down immediately." Then he was going to rip Warren a new one. Competitor or not, Jonah was tired of cleaning up his messes.

"I'm not in the photos," Clovis whispered on a sniffle, and Jonah wanted to head for the door. "That's the problem, don't you see?"

No, he did not see. In fact this entire conversation was starting to make him sweat. Or maybe it was the banana hammock display to his right. Either way he wanted to take the report and get the hell out of there.

"They're all of the new swim teacher, Celeste, and her inflated floaters." The woman looked so distraught Jonah did something he rarely did—he placed his hand on her meaty shoulder and gave her a few awkward pats.

"If you're not in the photos, then why did you call the sheriff's department?" Jonah asked, his patting keeping pace with her sniffles, leaving him feeling completely at a loss as to how to handle this situation.

Not a new feeling. He'd felt displaced and disconnected ever since he'd left San Francisco. Staying there hadn't been an option. Dealing with kids killing each other over the wrong ball cap had slowly taken its toll, until Jonah had started making shit decisions. Decisions that made dealing with, well, pretty much anything impossible. So he'd quit, come home hoping to find a sense of peace. Instead being surrounded by his family and the town he loved only left him feeling more isolated. Lost, even.

The truth was Jonah had felt lost ever since his dad had passed, leaving behind boots Jonah just couldn't fill. Wasn't sure he wanted to. David Baudouin was a complicated man who'd loved his family, yet often confused control with love.

"He cut me out of them. Me!" She placed her hand on her chest with such force it caused a rippling effect that had Jonah looking elsewhere. Only elsewhere was worse, because his gaze fell on a basket of colored coins by the register and, *aw hell*, the woman who used to hand out popcorn balls at Halloween now handed out tropical-flavored condoms. "Clovis Owens, owner of the sexiest shop in town, isn't sexy enough to be pinned on his Sexy and Single board. And that, young man, is discrimination, and I intend on pressing charges!"

And so went his day.

Giles refused to either take down his board or add Clovis to it, claiming his First Amendment rights. And Clovis, heartbroken over not being considered sexy and single, hired a lawyer. Later, Jonah caught a couple of teens stealing spare tires from Stan's Soup and Service Station, ticketed a tourist who'd mistaken Main Street for a raceway, and spotted Shay parading a litter of dogs in nothing more than a pair of shorts and a yellow tank top that said WOOF ME across the chest, the WO and ME straining to be seen around her curves.

He couldn't tear his eyes off her as she ran past, the little necklace she always wore bouncing up and down. It was more the ring that hung on the chain that caught Jonah's attention. Or maybe it was the other bouncing that had him missing his green light.

When Jonah got back to the station he found Warren, who was supposed to be working the front desk, out front signing calendars for a group of ladies in Booty Patrol T-shirts. Which meant that Jonah spent the last hour of his shift fielding calls while trying to get caught up on the mountain of paperwork he'd been putting off all week.

Not that he got all that far, since all he could think about was Shay and how much he wanted her. It took him over an hour to write up one report because he was replaying that kiss over and over in his head until somehow the kiss led to Shay in his bed wearing nothing but panties—red ones.

The sheriff walked over to Jonah's desk, taking a seat across from Jonah. He leaned back, making himself at home, then smiled.

"Got a call from the judge a few minutes ago. Seems his wife's all riled up over something about her neighbor."

"What's Estella claiming now?" Jonah asked, going back to his report and promising himself he was asking because he liked to be informed, not because he was going to get involved.

"Says the neighbor is running a puppy mill. Says there is barking all hours of the night."

"I live across the street from her," Jonah explained. "Sure, there is barking at times, but not any more than coming from Estella's place."

"Estella has one dog. She's claiming the neighbor has more than four. Wants us to arrest her for animal cruelty."

Jonah looked up at his boss. "Shay would rather become homeless than harm an animal."

"Good to hear. Let me know how it goes." The sheriff stood to leave and Jonah felt his palms start to sweat.

He was attracted to her, no question. Hell, with that body and mouth, what man wouldn't be? Smart and sassy with a side of sweet. A tempting combination.

Thankfully, he and Shay were too different, and Jonah knew just how destructive the "opposites attract" situation could be. His dad and stepmom were proof of that. So it was imperative to keep his distance.

"I can't go." Not to mention, putting himself between the judge's wife and the woman he couldn't stop picturing in her intimates, with the election a few short weeks off, was not a smart move. And Jonah was a smart guy. "I've got a pile of paperwork to get through, plus, animal control handles those kinds of calls."

"That's what I told Pricket. He told me that if he couldn't get his wife calmed down, then he'd have to cancel on our fishing trip."

Jonah was hosed. The sheriff had been talking about this fishing trip for months, even dropped a few grand on a new rod and special hook for the occasion.

Jonah blew out a breath. "I can drop by after I finish up here."

The sheriff's phone lit up. He glanced at the screen and held it up so Jonah could get a good look at the caller. It was Judge Pricket's personal number. "Not sure that's soon enough."

"I'll take it," Warren cut in, surprising both Jonah and the sheriff.

Then again, face time with a man as influential as the judge would only help Warren in the race. But the sheriff knew what Jonah knew, that with Warren on the job, this disgruntled neighbor call had a 50 percent chance of escalating into bloodshed. "You two figure it out, but make it go away."

"Yes, sir. I got this, sir," the prick said, all smiles as the sheriff headed back to his office.

Jonah barely resisted telling Warren it would be less obvious if he kissed the boss's ass directly. Instead he thought about the reports needing his attention, Warren's willingness to do his job, and gave in. "You sure?"

"Yeah, man. Wouldn't want the town to think we only handle the calls we want," Warren said, popping in a breath mint and heading to the door. "Plus, have you seen the dog walker's ass?"

Jonah had. Just like he'd seen that smug look on Warren's face before. Which was why the paperwork would have to wait.

ch🐾pter
five

It was way past feeding time for the kittens, so Shay picked up the pace, much to Jabba's irritation. Her oldest foster liked to smell the roses—and pee on each and every one of them. Which made for uncomfortable conversations with her neighbors.

At seeing Mrs. Pricket's prized rose garden ahead, lining the sidewalk like a giant invitation, Shay pulled a treat from her pocket and wafted it in front of the dog's nose while tugging the leash toward the other side of the street. "Come on, you know you want it."

Jabba did want it, by the way his eyes became saucers and his nose went into overdrive, snorting and nudging at Shay's hand to get to the bacon treat hiding inside. He also wanted the roses, and even though he was short, he was built like a tank, which meant she had to really sell that treat—or deal with her neighbor. And since they'd already shared words earlier that morning over Jabba raiding her garbage can, Shay upped the ante, doubling the treats.

It worked.

They had made it to the middle of the street when Jabba stopped. Ears up, tail slowly raising like a periscope, the dog took one last step, then dug his paws in, eyes riveted by the sight of a couple of police cruisers down the street. In front of her house.

Shay's heart did a little digging in of its own, because there, past the rose garden and two driveways down, walking the perimeter of her house in a pair of black combat boots, department-issued pants, and a gun belt that said *your friendly neighborhood badass*, was just the man she'd never want scoping out her house.

She considered dragging Jabba back the way they'd come, or demanding to see Jonah's warrant, but then, with the brute strength that came from being a beat cop for years, Jonah pulled himself up on her fence, balancing on the lip while he proceeded to lean over— way over—so he could peek through her side window and check out, most likely, the source of the barking.

Knowing that there was nothing to see—through *that* window at least—Shay did some checking of her own, taking her time to fully inspect the best ass wine country had to offer, which, in her defense, was practically begging her to look her fill.

And then it happened: Jonah hopped off the fence and his baton caught on a loose board, flipping up and out of his utility belt and landing on the grass. Jabba, taking this as a clear sign that a game of fetch was being called, gave an enthusiastic bark and lumbered down the street, not stopping until he had the baton in his mouth.

The dog made three complete circles of the yard before returning to drop it at Jonah's feet, where he sat patiently, waiting for him to pick up the stick and give it a good throw.

Jonah did pick it up, carefully, with the tips of two fingers, and even from a distance Shay could see the slobber dripping off. She was about to apologize when Jonah dropped down to his knee and gave Jabba a hearty rub behind the ears.

"Hey, Sheriff," she said when she reached her yard. "Sorry about that."

"It's Deputy." Jonah straightened to his full height, tipped his hat back, and quietly studied Shay. His gaze went from her tennies to her lips, and all the good spots in between, only he didn't smile, didn't return the greeting. In fact, he seemed irritated and a little pissed—at her, which wasn't unusual given their past. But given their immediate past, it rubbed her the wrong way.

"And can you clarify what you're apologizing for?" Jonah asked, deflecting Jabba's face, which was heading straight for his goods this time, only to make a hard left for his pocket.

"That's right, you're not sheriff yet, which I bet is why you're here, snooping in my yard." She took in his shirt, damp with the heat from the day, his pants riddled with foxtails and dandelion seeds, and smiled. "If you want to put a VOTE BAUDOUIN FOR SHERIFF sign in my yard, I need to hear your stance on implementing a mandatory spay and neuter law first."

"I'm more interested in your stance on occupancy laws," he said, triggering a spark of something unnerving in Shay.

There was no way he could be referring to the kittens. She'd been so careful to keep them hidden, keeping them sequestered in the spare bedroom with the curtains drawn, and stealthily inquiring about people looking for a kitten.

"Is that your way of asking me to do a sleepover?" she said.

Deputy Warren appeared from Estella's yard and came up beside them, flashing Shay a smile that was too sweet to be trusted. "I'm willing to give you my stance on all things legal and illegal, over a nice dinner of course, if you let me stick *my* sign in your yard."

Shay laughed. Jonah did not. He sent Warren a look that would have had most men taking a gigantic step back. Only Warren was either too stupid to pick up on the alpha male fumes rolling off Jonah, or he didn't care.

"I bet you used that same line on every house on the block," Shay joked.

Warren made a big deal about looking up and down the street, which was devoid of any declaration of support for either candidate, then flashed a practiced smile her way. "I came to your house first."

"You came here because she's running an illegal puppy mill out of her home. I've counted four or five just this week," Estella corrected, marching across Shay's lawn. "Look. She's got another one."

Jabba growled.

"Jabba is not a puppy. He is a mature dog who has been with me for a while, as you well know. And I'm not running a puppy mill, I run a foster-to-home rescue, licensed by the county," Shay explained, sliding Jonah a confident smile. Only something in his expression had her internal alarm going on alert.

Then he took off his hat and—*oh boy*—he knew about the kittens. Knew she had more pets than allowed. And because Estella was pushing her weight around, there was no way this would end with him looking the other way.

"Mrs. Pricket claims you have too many dogs on the premises," Warren said, and Shay could have sworn the man puffed out his chest the second Estella looked his way.

"Can one really have too many dogs?"

"According to the county, yes," Warren said.

"Come on, Deputy. They're cute little fuzzy animals," Shay said casually. "Not worthy of a multiple-officers callout." And when Jonah still looked constipated, she asked, "Tell me, did you run the sirens?"

"Shay," Jonah said in warning, but it was already too late, she had riled the beast.

"This isn't a joke," Estella snapped, wagging a condemning finger in Shay's direction. "You run a kennel in a residential area. They have rules. And you, Miss Michaels, are a rule breaker!"

"I run a foster-to-home rescue," Shay repeated because kennels provided a temporary home, and Shay provided a temporary family. And she didn't comment on the rule breaker part because it was totally true.

"You collect pets no one else wants and then when you get sick of them you pawn them off on people who are too nice to say no."

Shay opened her mouth to speak, but nothing came out. Was that how Estella saw her? How people in this town saw her?

Shay didn't keep the animals she fostered because they didn't belong to her. She knew that going in. She wasn't sure how to be a part of a family, but after years of watching other families interact, she knew how to spot a good one. It was her superpower. What she was good at. And if she kept one of her babies, she'd have to keep them all, and then what would happen to the other animals she would have fostered?

"I foster them," Shay defended quietly, surprised at how close to tears she sounded. "I get them ready for their forever family. And you, Mrs. Pricket, are rude and mean and a terrible dog owner."

Estella's hand flew to her chest, her facing creasing in horror. "And to think, I almost listened to Ida's suggestion and reconsidered allowing you to come to Bark in the Park."

Damn it!

"Okay," Jonah said, inserting himself in the middle. "Let's take a walk."

Without waiting for Shay to answer, he took her by the arm to lead her away from the fuming judge's wife. Only Shay refused to budge. She was afraid that if she walked away, Estella would show Warren her animals and he'd confiscate them.

He gave another little tug on her arm. Shay tugged back until Jonah let out a sigh.

"Are you arresting me?" she asked, because that was the only way she was going to leave her pets.

"Do I need to?"

Shay looked at Warren, who was getting an earful from Estella about obtaining a search warrant, even going as far as to offer to have her husband draft one up immediately. Then Shay glanced at her bedroom window, where she knew her kittens were waiting for her to come home and make their day right. Even thinking about losing her pets made her sick.

Jonah must have sensed her hesitance because he lowered his voice and said, "Nothing is going to happen today, Shay. So walk with me."

She paused to look him over, gauge if he was telling the truth, which revealed nothing since the man was a ninja master at covering up his emotions. But he was reading her loud and clear. His expression softened and he gifted her a warm, reassuring smile that had her resolve melting, and added, "Just to the curb."

"Fine. But I charge ten dollars an hour for my walking services."

"And I carry a gun and cuffs," he said in that authoritative voice that reminded her she was a woman. And she'd been far too long without a man.

"So you keep saying."

When Jonah was confident they were out of eavesdropping range, he sat on the curb and waited for Shay to take a seat next to him. Partly because he was afraid she'd make a break for it. He knew damn well she was over the legal limit for pet occupancy. He just wasn't sure by how many. And she might be tiny, but he knew that those little legs could cover ground fast, and he wasn't in the mood for a foot chase today.

But mainly he chose to sit because Estella's last comment had seemed to knock the floor out from under Shay.

"You know that the county only allows four pets per household," Jonah said, sending his best hard-cop look her way, not that it mattered since she was looking everywhere but at him.

"It's a stupid rule," she mumbled to her shoes.

"Then you also know that if you have any over that amount I have to fine you."

"Okay." She finally glanced his direction and, man, was she gorgeous. She was tough and independent and passionate and a woman who would stop at nothing to protect what was hers. But the look she was giving him right there, in that second, was one he hadn't seen before now. It was one that told him she was also breakable. "Just promise that you aren't going to take them."

He wanted to say yes he promised, so that she'd start looking at him like he was a good guy, the guy everyone had made him out to be. Only he wasn't that guy anymore, hadn't been for a while, and Shay knew that. Knew that he was broken too. She didn't look at him like the others in town, she looked at him as if she understood his struggle. As if she'd seen through the badge and persona to the dark, ugly truth he kept hidden. And that scared him as much as it got to him.

"I spotted one older dog through the side window, another two napping in the backyard, a kitten climbing the curtain in your bedroom, and this one, for a total of five animals. Did I miss any?"

She shook her head and he would have believed her, was ready to stand up and call this day over, but then her shoulders sank and—*shit*—she gave a little nod, sending her dark hair spilling over her shoulder. "How many?"

"Four adult dogs, and a litter of kittens."

"Define litter."

"Five kittens," she said quietly. "There were six originally, but one must have escaped."

"Jesus, Shay." He ran a hand down the back of his neck, cupping it at the base and trying to squeeze out the weight of the town that had settled there. One pet over he could work out—more than that and there was no way he could get Estella to stand down while Shay handled her business. "What do you want me to do?"

"Give me time to find them families," she pleaded. "Yodel is going to his home this weekend, and the kittens, as soon as they are old enough to be fixed, they will go fast. And then I won't go over the legal limit again, I promise."

Jonah leveled her with a look.

"Okay, I won't go over the limit unless it is an emergency." Which could be as simple as her coming across a dog with a cold.

"Do you have any friends who could foster them?" The look on her face said no. Great.

"Shay, you need to call the owner and explain that you have to return the kittens."

"I can't." Shay's face went pale. "The, um, owner, couldn't provide a safe place for them so I promised to find them a nice family."

He was about to ask who the owner was so he could give them a call when Warren stepped off the curb and right into Jonah's space.

"As much as we'd love to help out, Miss Michaels, the law is there for a reason," Warren said, rocking back on his heels. "And like I was just explaining to Mrs. Pricket, we can't pick and choose which ones we follow or the whole system suffers. Right, *Deputy?*"

Warren's tone said *game fucking on.* His cocky stance said he was stepping up that game and was now in this race to win sheriff. And the son of a bitch had used the last person Jonah wanted to disappoint to make his statement clear.

"What's he talking about?" Shay asked, unaware of the tension that was arcing between the two men.

"You have been fined in the past for violating the county's animal-harboring laws," Jonah explained.

"Once," Shay argued, looking from Estella to Warren and back to Jonah, and the desperation he saw there killed him. "Once and that was when I was shooting the calendar, which by the way is done and I have found almost all of them homes already."

Something everybody there knew, but it didn't make a difference. "It still makes you a repeat offender and means there are limits to how we can handle this," Jonah said gently, hating what he was about to say next, hating even more how it would impact Shay. "By law, we have to give you thirty days to find them a new home."

"Thirty days? That's impossible. My kittens won't be old enough to place for another six weeks, I've been banned from Bark in the Park, and it's the middle of kitten and puppy season, which means finding families for my older dogs will be more difficult." Shay hugged her arms around her stomach and Estella had the decency to look ashamed. "I need more time."

"I wish I could give it to you," Jonah said, but once he wrote up the report it would be out of his hands—and it was his job to write that report. Not to mention if he didn't, Warren undoubtedly would—and Warren wouldn't give Shay any time at all if it meant securing Estella's vote. "After thirty days this case transfers to animal control and any pet they find over the four allotted will be removed."

ch🐾pter
six

I'm never going to make it in time."

Shay cracked the oven door to peek at the carrot scones, which were still a few minutes shy of golden. Her cheddar biscuits, on the other hand, were seconds from bursting into flames.

"Crap." She pulled out the charred biscuits and placed them on the stove top, then opened the window, hoping it would combat the smoke.

It didn't help.

Jabba lifted his head to sniff the air, then the floor around the entire room until his nose led him back to the stove, where he sat and looked up adoringly at Shay, giving her a few big doggie eye bats.

"They're burnt," she explained, but Jabba only snorted as though he thought they were at the perfect state of cookedness, and that he was more than willing to take one for the team and be the official taste tester. "Sorry, buddy, but you already ate an entire plate of cream cheese and cucumber finger sandwiches when I wasn't looking." Which were far from dog friendly. "The last thing you need is to add a lump of coal to the mix."

Jabba gave it one more hopeful minute, wishing beyond wishes that Shay would reconsider, then waddled over to the doggie bed in the corner of the spa's lunchroom and lay all the way down with a huff, his bow tie shifting in the process.

Shay knew how he felt. Today was the monthly Paws and Claws High Tea at the spa—and she couldn't afford any mistakes. News that she was running a puppy mill had gone viral, racking up two hundred comments on Nora's Facebook page alone. Peggy, concerned about Shay making her thirty-day time line, had offered to let Shay bring all of her adult fosters to the event.

"What better place to find them a family than around a bunch of dog lovers who know other dog lovers?" Peggy had said. Only her boss forgot to mention that this month's tea had been sold out for weeks, leaving Shay with twenty-five animal attendees—and only food and seating for twenty.

And with Foxy Cleopatra taking the number one spot on the VIP list, today had to go perfectly.

Shay had spent the past two days molding her dogs into well-behaved and respectful hosts, hoping that seeing a new-and-improved side to them might be enough to persuade Estella to reconsider her stance. Not on the citation, that was out of her hands the second Jonah filed the report, but the pet-peddling ban. Shay thought that if Estella saw the best in her fosters, then maybe she'd have a change of heart. She'd almost changed it once—then Shay's thoughtless statement had ruined it.

Today was her chance to fix her mistakes, mend fences so to speak, and get her dogs re-invited to Bark in the Park. She wasn't going to let her impulsive nature, or severe lack of cooking skills, screw up this opportunity. Which was why when she looked up from her mutt-loaf squares to find three smiling Booty Patrol members dressed like they were going to the Kentucky Derby in flowered bonnets and pearl catch gloves, carrying foil-covered plates, Shay nearly cried.

"Thank God you're here," Shay said as Clovis, Ida, and Peggy set their plates of finger sandwiches and dog bones on the prep table, then walked around to get a better look at Shay's contribution.

Clovis leaned way in, gave the black pucks a few pokes, and grimaced, her cane clicking against the cabinet.

Jabba zeroed in on the wooden stick, tail twitching, breathing nonexistent, while he patiently waited for her to drop the stick in the horizontal "game on" position. Shay shot him a single look and, when that didn't deter him, tapped her foot.

Jabba reluctantly disengaged with the stick and called off the attack, but he wasn't happy about it.

"How did you know I'd need help?" she asked, peeking inside of one of the plates to find peanut butter-dipped bones.

"Smelled the first batch you put in." Ida poked at one of the biscuits. It gave a little sizzle, then burst, sending bits of burnt dough onto the floor—and Jabba skidding across the tile to do his part of the cleanup.

"At the second smoke signal we packed up and headed out," Clovis said, pulling an apron from her bag and tying it around her waist. She tossed one to each of the other ladies, and Shay's chest warmed when she saw the St. Paws logo on the pocket.

"Where did you get those?" she asked, running a finger over the pink paw print.

"Ordered them from my guy yesterday," Clovis said. "Told him we needed a rush order and he dropped these off this morning."

Shay didn't know why Clovis had a guy or what her guy did exactly, but she did know that this was one of the sweetest things someone had done for her in a long time. It was just the thing she needed to get her back on track after the standoff with Estella and her hit squad—a heartfelt reminder that not all people sucked.

"Figured if you were going to show that Estella and her yap dog a good time, then you needed backup," Ida said. "Banning you from her event is one thing, but calling the fuzz? Now that is about as un-neighborly as one can get."

"And here in St. Helena we pride ourselves on being good neighbors," Peggy added.

Deeply moved in so many ways, Shay found it hard to speak but managed a shaky, "Thank you."

"Don't thank us yet, this act of neighborliness comes with strings," Ida said, and there went all of Shay's warm fuzzies.

"I'm not big on strings," Shay admitted.

In her experience, strings were a lot like expectations, tying people together, and when not reached the connection was forever severed, sometimes even destroying lives. Something Shay had experienced firsthand at the unexpected death of her mother and then again when her father was a big fat no-show. And from what life had shown her so far, Shay understood that connections came at too high a price for her heart to handle.

The grannies didn't seem to feel the same, since they smiled and scooted a little closer, slipping an apron over Shay's head. It had a picture of a giant umbrella sheltering dozens of pets.

"You need a place where your entire menagerie can have a safe place to live until they go to their forever homes," Ida said, fastening the back of Shay's apron. "And we think you should open up a real rescue."

"I already run a real rescue." Every bit of the love and heartache was real to her. Real to the animals who passed through her life. And real to the families who were lucky enough to find their perfect pals.

"No, dear," Clovis clarified, her voice soft with apology. "What Ida meant to say was we think you should lease a shop in town so folks like Estella can't call the sheriff every time they get their bloomers in a snit."

"A shop? Here in St. Helena?" As in permanently?

"Why not?" Peggy said, obviously surprised at how horrified Shay seemed at the suggestion. "You've got to make a home someplace. Why not here?"

Because even though St. Helena had begun to feel like more than a brief stopover in Shay's ever-changing life, she wasn't sure if it had "home" potential. Sure, she'd made friends, and loved her house and her job, but she'd also made a few enemies and a million mistakes—not that *that* part was new. Only this time her mistake had put her at odds with one of the most powerful women in town.

Then there was Jonah—and that smoking-hot kiss, followed by an official citation and the silent treatment. Well, that might be a bit harsh. Hard to give her the silent treatment when he'd spent the past two days avoiding Shay completely. Yet she couldn't help thinking maybe it was for the best. If he'd reacted that way over a few extra kittens, what would he do when he found out about her past?

Shay sucked in a calming breath, hating how her stomach pinched with nerves. A brick-and-mortar St. Paws was something she had spent a lifetime dreaming about. It would allow her to board up to forty pets, provide a central location that would put her fosters in daily contact with people, and help her save lives without bending laws.

To her, leasing a storefront sounded a lot like forever, and forever was a serious step. She knew this, not having taken it herself, but by the bonds she helped form with the animals and their forever families.

"Even if I could find a place"—storefronts in town were hard to come by—"where would I find that kind of money?" And the support? And the courage to take that step? Because a storefront meant Shay and her pets wouldn't sleep under the same roof.

"The calendars," Peggy said, clasping her hands in front of her face. "You can use the money from the sales to help lease the space."

"Mr. Russell has a vacant sign hanging in the old barbershop next to my place," Clovis said, her giddy smile taking a decade off her face.

"That sign has been there since I moved to town," Shay explained, surprised to realize that it was nearly eighteen months ago that she'd packed up her car and headed north to start her new job at the Paws and Claws. She hadn't even unpacked her car and she'd already fallen in love with the place. It wasn't just the quaint downtown, picturesque mountains, or miles of grapevines that had drawn her in. It was how happy everyone was. How they always seemed to have a ready smile to share, and a friendly word for their neighbors—her current standoff with Estella excluded.

"Yup, but the old coot has a huge balloon payment coming due at the end of next year. We all do," Ida explained. "At this point, some money is better than no money, which tells me I could persuade him to cut you some kind of deal."

Shay wasn't so sure. Mr. Russell was a class-A tightwad who would rather be right than profitable. He'd bought two of the historic Victorian storefronts on the north end of Main Street a few years back for twice what they were worth, and rather than lease them out for the going rate, he'd priced the spaces based on his elevated mortgage. Which was why they were still vacant.

"It would have to be a good deal." She'd made good money on her calendar fund-raiser, but nowhere near what Mr. Russell was asking. It also would have to be the perfect environment, otherwise Shay wouldn't be able to leave her pets alone at night.

Actually, Shay would never want to leave her pets alone at night. Or maybe it was that Shay didn't want to be alone at night.

"He'll see reason," Ida said.

"All we have to do is tell Mr. Russell you're bringing your cuties and he'll see that in a few months he'd be able to lease out his other space for what he's asking," Clovis said, breathless with excitement. "Nothing attracts customers like hot men."

"Hot men?" What kind of shelter did they think she wanted to open? Then all three women nodded in earnest, gray crops bouncing as they pulled out their Cuties with Booties calendars, and Shay got it.

"If we help you get the place, then you have to promise us you'll host a signing every week with one of your cuties from the calendar." Ida's birdlike hands fluttered like hummingbird wings. "My favorite is Mr. July."

Although Adam was lovely to look at in nothing but his fire pants and hat, he didn't hold a candle to Shay's favorite. Not that her favorite was in there. Nope, the uptight deputy didn't think it was fitting to pose for a good cause—at least not her good cause. Then again, her favorite was the same guy who was evicting her dogs.

A part of her knew that Jonah was just doing his job, doing his best to uphold the law. But there was another part, the scared girl who had been disappointed too many times to believe in heroes, who wondered if he would have been as eager if the caller had been an average resident rather than the judge's wife.

Her head said he would have. Her heart wasn't so sure.

Shay looked over at her brood, who were all looking back with their big, trusting eyes, counting on her to make their world right, and suddenly leasing a shop didn't sound half as terrifying as letting them down. Even if it meant that Shay would have a quiet house.

"I know it's a lot to think about." Peggy placed a hand on Shay's. "Just promise me you won't discount it before giving it a chance."

"Fair enough," Shay said, because damn it, Peggy had given Shay a chance, even though she hadn't had a single letter of recommendation.

"Oh, honey," Clovis said, clapping her hands. "Those hot buns will bring more foot traffic my way than last year's *Fifty Shades* display Harper did for my store window. Nothing moves panties like hot men."

"And nothing says sexy better than wine and chocolate," Ida pointed out, handing Shay a list, highlighting her extensive supply of aphrodisiac chocolates and spirits as though Shay had already signed on the dotted line. "In fact, Cork'd N Dipped would like to be St. Paws' first official sponsor and donate one of those pet-friendly crates Peg has at her shop."

Ida flipped over the pamphlet and there was a picture of the exact kind of kennel Shay had dreamed of getting. They kept the animals confined without making them feel caged. And they cost upward of a grand apiece. "I don't understand. Why?"

Ida took Shay's hands in what had to be the first sign of affection Shay had ever seen the woman give another human. "Think of it as an investment, in my shop *and* in you. I was so lost after my Randal passed, then you brought me Norton. He is the best part of my day and I want to help you help other people like myself." Ida cleared her throat and Shay felt hers going thick. "Plus, once you get the ladies of St. Helena dreaming about being corked, the first place they'll come is next door to get dipped."

"And then they can come over to my place and buy crotchless panties."

Mad at herself for putting her animals and job in serious jeopardy, Shay grabbed her running shoes. She pounded down her street toward town, vowing not to stop until she was too tired to be angry—or reached the sheriff's department, whichever came first. Not that either would be far, since the sheriff's department was at the opposite end of Main Street and Shay hated running.

Almost as much as she hated failing. And today had been an epic failure.

Peggy hadn't even waited for the tea time to begin before closing shop because the Companion Brigade finally took an official stance on the pet-peddling ban, one that placed them firmly behind their president. The timing made Shay suspect a conspiracy, then their statement was released following a Facebook post displaying a photo of Friday's "confidential" police report, and Shay knew she'd been set up.

Estella had had several opportunities over the past year to report Shay to the authorities and hadn't called them once. And now Estella was using her judge-y connections and her power with the Companion Brigade to teach Shay a lesson—effectively ruining any hope Shay had of fixing this mess.

If anything, her mistakes were expanding to affect the people she cared about, like Peggy, who had never been anything but wonderful and supportive. It was also ruining Shay's chances of finding her dogs a home. And with the clock now ticking, she was feeling a little desperate. And scared.

The upset stomach and chest pains, Shay convinced herself, were the running's fault.

Any evidence of last week's storm was gone, replaced by an intense heat that seemed to press in on her lungs as she turned onto Main Street. Heading north, she admitted that maybe some of the panting was caused by the bag of minidoughnuts she'd inhaled last night, and not for the first time, she considered giving up the addiction.

Not this week, of course, since even thinking about how guests had been nonexistent at the tea—besides Norton, who had looked dashing in a bow tie and top hat—made her tummy feel hollow. Thinking about Yodel's new mom made her chest follow suit.

Concerned by the news, Ms. Abernathy had called to ask if she could wait until the allegations were cleared before taking custody of Yodel. After losing her husband, and then her son last year, the older woman wasn't sure she could handle any more.

Shay understood that more than most and promised to provide proof that she wasn't under investigation for running an illegal puppy mill.

It was item numero uno on her list of grievances, which she intended to share with everybody's favorite deputy immediately.

Item two was to have him explain how he could kiss her like that, say such sweet things, and then serve her papers in the next breath. Okay, so she'd been the one to kiss him, but he'd more than met her halfway. And it had been his decision to stoke her fire until she'd nearly melted.

Shay wasn't looking for special treatment from the deputy, but he could have recused himself and sent someone who didn't know what she brushed her teeth with.

Which brought her to item three—his easy acceptance to pretend it hadn't happened. Because it had and no amount of pretending was working. And if she wasn't able to forget about that kiss, even after he'd flashed his badge and screwed up her plans, then he shouldn't be allowed to either. Especially when it had been two whole days and her lips were still tingling.

Getting involved with Jonah was out of the question, but she'd be damned if he was the one who got to point out how ridiculous the notion was. Even if the mere thought of his mouth on hers was enough to steal her breath and send her nipples into party mode—not good since she was in one of those sports bra tops that hid nothing.

Shay was reconsidering her plan, thinking of starting with that particular grievance, when she heard a loud crash of metal cans, followed by aggressive barking. A silver ball of fur shot out from the alley beside a vacant storefront, cutting Shay off midstride. Its miniature legs pumped so hard they barely touched asphalt as it darted into the street, narrowly avoiding a kissing contest with a speeding wine truck before disappearing into an abandoned lot.

Heart in her throat, Shay took off after the kitten, bypassing the sheriff's department—Jonah and his superhero complex would have to wait—and turning toward the lot instead. She kept her eyes locked on the gray tail as it zipped under a chain-link fence, its back paw getting caught in the metal momentarily, before cutting through the overgrown brush and right up a big oak that sat at the back of the lot.

The tree was a million years old with enough gnarled branches and crannies to make the perfect hiding spot. It was also surrounded by a chain-link fence and three very visible NO TRESPASSING signs— neither of which would deter Shay.

It had been hot and dry since last week's storm, she told herself as she crawled through a hole someone had cut in the bottom of the chain links, and for a kitten as young as she suspected this one was, an abandoned construction site was not the ideal home. Not to mention she still wasn't sure how much damage the fence had done—the kitten had ripped through it so fast she was afraid it had left marks.

Shay brushed the debris off her knees and hands and slowly approached the tree, giving the kitten a good minute to calm down. It took Shay another two to catch her breath, important since the gasping wasn't helping with her *everybody calm down* agenda.

"I really need to lose the doughnuts," she panted, her hand on her side as she cautiously approached the tree.

Two wide eyes, so dilated they appeared solid black, peeked out from behind the first row of branches. Ears curled under, tail reminiscent of a duster, the kitten crouched low and gave a throaty growl—the sound about as threatening as a sneeze. Still, Shay took caution, more for the kitten than herself. The last thing she needed was to send it scurrying its furry gray butt to the top of the tree. Because then she'd have to play the retriever, and Shay hated heights more than she hated running.

"Aren't you an adorable ball of cute?" she cooed when she had maneuvered close enough to touch the bottom limb and see that the feline had ridiculously short legs. The big blue eyes only added to its adorable factor.

As though offended by Shay's choice in description, the kitten fluffed itself out even more and this time gave a hiss—also adorable and clearly a sign that it wasn't having any of her sweet talk. Which led Shay to believe he was male. That his fur was matted and she could see his little ribs poking through told her he was the missing kitten from her litter.

A litter Shay had vowed to help.

"That dog sounded scary," she said conversationally. "But I bet he was just as scared to see you in his garbage can as you were to see him." At the gentle tone in her voice the cat relaxed a little, and Shay slowly lifted her hand to rest it on the branch—as far away from him as possible. When he didn't move, other than to lower his body to the limb, she moved slightly closer.

After a moment of conversational speculation, on Shay's part, over how big the dog must have been to send a tough kitty like him running—always good to boost a man's self-esteem—she moved her hand even closer. Which was apparently one inch too close, because the kitten gave a nasty one-two swat to Shay's arm, his needle nails doing some minor damage, and took off up the tree, all the way up the freaking tree, where he tightroped out to the end of a skinny branch and resumed his puffed-out pose.

"Shame on you, Kitty Fantastic," she said in a reprimanding tone. Kitty Fantastic just peeled back his lips and showed her his teeth. "I just wanted to see if you were okay."

Obviously Kitty Fantastic was not okay, and no, he was not about to come down and let Shay give him a quick once-over. She released the bravest breath she could muster and started looking for the easiest way up.

ch🐾pter
seven

Extremely aware of the woman outside his window, Jonah tried to focus on his paperwork, telling himself he was *not* going to check on her again. Not to figure out what she was doing trespassing on an abandoned construction site within eyesight of half the town's law enforcement, nor to see if she had finally gotten smart and gone home.

Only, *damn it*, he looked. He couldn't help it. She'd been driving him crazy since he saw her tearing up Main Street about thirty minutes ago, huffing and a-puffing and dripping with pissed-off female. He'd been certain she was coming to chew his ass out. Not that he'd blame her.

Deputy Jonah had delivered a pretty shitty ultimatum the other day—part of his job, he reminded himself. But at some point he'd been off duty and instead of going over to check if Shay was okay or if she needed any help, Neighbor Jonah—who couldn't get the taste of her out of his mind—acted like a pussy and hid in his house.

Only she didn't come inside the station, didn't even report Jonah to the sheriff for allowing a report that should have been for department-eyes only to somehow wind up on Facebook. Nope, Shay, confusing as always, had perched herself outside his window, where, if he pressed his face to the glass and stretched up on his toes, he could clearly see she was chilled—or revved up. The sun had begun to set, so if a breeze had come in off the ocean, it would explain her condition. The EVERY LIFE COUNTS tank top she wore, sweaty and thin and clinging to her body as if a second skin, wouldn't help much.

Neighbor Jonah was ready to man up, go outside, and see just how cold Shay was, and after a thorough investigation, offer her his coat—or other, more creative suggestions on how to get warm. Then he'd ask if she was hurt by what the town was saying about her on Facebook and, if she was upset, what he could do to make it better.

Unfortunately, at the moment he was wearing Deputy Jonah's boots, which meant if he went out there he'd have to ticket her ass.

Fuck!

He couldn't hang up his boots for another—he checked his watch—thirty-five minutes, by which time it would most likely be dark and Shay would be gone. Then he'd go home and revert back to being a pussy, because if he knocked on her door and saw that she'd lied about how many dogs she really had—they'd all be in trouble. And if she answered it in her current attire, he'd definitely find trouble—of an entirely different kind.

Shifting back to his seat, Jonah made short order of the never-ending pile of papers consuming the west quadrant of his desk. He was starting to tackle the stack behind it when he heard a loud rustling from outside—followed by a pretty impressive string of words.

Jonah looked out the window to find his little troublemaker—*holy shit*—hugging the tree trunk. Her sparkly orange tennies were only about nine inches off the ground and that little jogging skirt of hers was about one inch from giving him the best view he'd had in weeks, but she looked determined.

He had no idea what she thought she was doing, or what she was going after, but it was clear that given enough time she would hang herself—or cut down the tree. Both of which would require paperwork.

With a sigh that came all the way from his soul, Jonah fished his cell out of his shirt pocket and dialed her number. He watched her dangle there for a long second, indecision playing across her pretty face, then with a huff she shimmied—proving that she liked to match her lace to her tennies—and dropped to the ground.

She pulled out her phone, glanced at the screen, then at his window, and frowned. All pissy and irritated and looking sexier than any woman covered in bark and dirt had the right to look.

"Sheriff." She did not sound happy to hear from him.

"Trouble." He gave a smug little wiggle of his fingers. She did not wave back—smug or otherwise. "Mind if I ask what you're doing?"

"Making friends and saving lives," she said, and even though she was back to staring at the tree, giving him a prime view of her spectacular ass, he could hear the irritation in her voice. "You?"

"Oh, you know, paperwork, red tape BS, deciding if I am going to arrest you for trespassing."

"And here I thought you sat around all day ironing your cape," she said, a tad dry, circling the tree to stare up at the branches.

"It's at the dry cleaner's."

That earned him a smile. A small one, but it felt like a win all the same.

"Why are you calling?" Moment gone, she went back to her job, examining a branch on the other side of the tree and giving him the cold shoulder. Which he deserved, he supposed. Settling on a low-hanging one, she gave it a few cautious tugs. "Can you get to the point? I'm busy."

"Right, busy making friends and saving lives," he said. "Wait. I thought that was my job?"

Shay paused midshake. Releasing the branch, those caramel pools zeroed in on him in a way that had him shifting in his boots. He didn't like the look she gave. Or maybe he liked it too much. Either way, it was determined, calculating, and 100 percent trouble. Then the line went dead.

He'd barely pulled the phone away from his ear when it rang. He looked at the screen and smiled.

"Sheriff Baudouin," she said, all kinds of professional. "I was calling to see if you could spare a few minutes to help a citizen in need?"

The answer should have been no, followed by a "you have thirty seconds to vacate the premises," but Jonah leaned a shoulder against the window frame and found himself saying, "Depends what citizen is asking."

"Me." She rolled her head to face him and smiled. He smiled back.

"Well, then, you're out of luck. I can't do a favor for someone who is illegally trespassing on private property."

She casually plucked a leaf with her fingers. "What if I am exercising my First Amendment rights?"

"Are you?"

Nothing.

Jonah closed his eyes and counted to ten. "Shay."

She dropped the leaf and huffed into the phone, and he knew he had her. "Now I am exercising the fifth, so why don't you pretend I am staging a sit-in for a rare brush turkey who has built her love nest in this old oak tree, grab your cape, and bring me some water?"

"Why don't you come on over and I can get you all the water you want? Then you can sip it while I explain what the term *trespassing* means."

"Can't. In case the nest falls out of the tree, someone needs to be here to catch the eggs."

"Brush turkeys are mound-building birds," he said, looking at the pile of reports that would still be there come morning. He locked them inside the top drawer. "Which means the male would make the nest. At the base of the tree."

"Is that so?" She sounded equally impressed and amused— something he could easily get used to.

"You aren't the only one who watches the Discovery Channel," he said, heading toward the break room. "And since we aren't in Australia, either you are mistaken about the kind of bird you are out to protect, or you're lying."

"Does it matter, since you are going to bring me the water anyway?"

Nope, he thought, looking down at the water he was snagging from the fridge, he guessed it didn't. If getting her water meant getting face time, he was game.

"You need anything else? Coffee? Tea? A stale doughnut?" he deadpanned.

"You got any tuna?"

"Uh." He searched though the plethora of to-go boxes, bags, and Tupperware, switching shelves when he got to one that had green fuzz growing up the side. "No tuna, but . . ."

He looked at his sandwich on the bottom shelf, the one he'd spent a good thirty minutes of his morning perfecting, covered in bacon and grilled peppers and a little apricot jam. The one he hadn't had a chance to eat yet but had been thinking about all day. God, he was hungry.

Then he pictured Shay being carted away in an ambulance for taking an impact from twenty feet up and sighed. "I have a chicken sandwich."

"It might work."

"I'll bring the sandwich," he said, feeling as though he was making progress. "But stay out of the damn tree."

"See you in a bit. Oh, and Sheriff, be sure to use those stealthy moves they teach you at sheriff's school."

She hung up before he could explain there was no such thing as sheriff's school.

Twenty minutes later the sun was beginning to set behind the hills, casting a beautiful orange-and-pink glow over the valley, when Shay had nearly given up. Not on the furry male, who was stubbornly perched at the top of the tree, eyeing her warily, but the sexy strait-laced one next door.

Reaching for a low-hanging branch she'd been eyeing since ending the call, Shay sent up a quick prayer, chanted "Mind over matter" three times, and gave a little jump.

Her feet left the ground, the air left her lungs, and she reached up and grabbed on—for dear life.

"Mind over matter my ass," she said because all that mattered to her mind was that she was one step into climbing a really big tree. And really big trees led to really big falls.

She hung for a long moment, waiting for the dizziness and shortness of breath to stop. When it didn't she closed her eyes and, palms sweating, repeated a quick prayer her mom had taught her, then hung for a little while longer while she recited it again. Just to be safe.

Opening her eyes, Shay swung her feet over to the trunk, ready to walk her feet up it when the gravel crunched behind her.

Shay looked between the branches as Jonah hopped the fence with the graceful ease of a man who knew how to handle himself— in any situation. He walked toward her in low-slung jeans, a blue T-shirt that did amazing things for his chest, and a brown bag dangling from his hand.

"Hey, Sheriff, where's your uniform?" she asked, because Deputy Jonah was hot, no question. But Off-Duty Jonah—*sweet baby Jesus*—that man oozed so much male swagger he could melt the panties off a woman with a single smile. Only he wasn't smiling— he was frowning.

"What happened to staying out of the tree?" he said, sounding grumpy, which was *completely* ridiculous because if anyone had the right to be grumpy, it was her.

She dropped down, relieved to be back on solid soil. "I think it took a vacation with your ability to ask politely."

There was a long moment where Shay expected him to toss back some witty retort, but he looked her in the eye, serious and intent, and in his most sincere voice asked, "Shay, would you vacate the premises?" She raised a brow and he added, "Please?" but sounded put out about it.

"Thank you for asking so politely, I know that was hard for you." She walked over and patted him on the arm. Then, gifting him with her brightest smile, snatched the bag from his hands. "But, unfortunately, I can't."

Jonah grumbled something under his breath that sounded oddly close to "a pain in my ass," but Shay was too busy digging through the peppers and lettuce to find bits of chicken and bacon for her kitty trap to pay much attention. Although she did get an impressive view of said ass when he turned around to look at the sky and mumble some more. A completely pain-free experience on her end, since his ass gave a solid showing. Not that she mentioned it, since she didn't think it would help his mood any.

"What are you doing with my lunch?" he asked.

Shay turned at the closeness of his voice and gave a little squeak when she found him standing right behind her. Arms over his chest, jaw tight, he watched intently as she destroyed what appeared to be a very impressive sandwich.

She, on the other hand, watched the play of muscles on his arms, his very long arms, and muscular legs that would come in handy to a damsel in distress.

Shay looked up at Kitty Fantastic then back to Clark Kent. She would rather die than be considered a damsel, and she had given up being distressed a long time ago, but the man had leaped over the fence in a single bound.

"I'm making a kitty trap for Kitty Fantastic."

"Kitty Fantastic?"

Shay shrugged. "I think he is the lost kitten to my litter."

"Which you'll be keeping where?" Jonah gave her an assessing look. "Never mind, I don't want to know."

He turned his attention to the tiny ball of fuzz at the top of the tree, who looked back, all puffed fur and bad attitude. She could see Jonah gauging the distance, then he looked at all five feet four of her and his face went hard. "Don't tell me you are climbing up there."

"Are you crazy? No way." She waited until he relaxed before adding, "Just far enough up so that he can smell the chicken."

Her mom used to say the best way to attract bees was with honey. Shay knew, for cats, it was all about the chicken.

And for a male, well, that was about making them believe the chicken was their idea.

"Unless you have a better suggestion."

"Now what?" Jonah asked, wanting to kick himself. One bat of those chocolate-brown eyes and he was practically offering to help her commit a crime—like adding one more pet to her collection.

"I think this is where you say you're going to arrest me."

He looked down at his jeans and T-shirt and felt a sigh of relief, because, no, he wasn't going to arrest her. Tonight that was some other asshole's job.

"I'm off duty," he said, liking how that sounded.

She stared at him as though he'd lost his mind. Maybe he had. Jonah didn't like the idea of looking the other way, but figured if he wasn't on the clock then he wasn't slacking on his duties. So he'd clocked out early, locked up his gun and badge, and made a point to leave his job at the office.

"But you're never off duty."

A problem he intended on fixing—starting tonight. Sheriff Bryant was right. Going into a new position already burnt out wouldn't do anyone any good. Just like arresting Shay for saving a stupid cat.

Plus he had a rough few days ahead of him, this he knew without a doubt. One week a year it was as though he was forced to relive it all, remember a time he'd give anything to forget. And since that week started tomorrow, he wanted to forget about everything tonight—and he'd found his perfect distraction.

"I am right now," he said and she smiled, warm and real and just for him, and he couldn't help but smile back.

"Does that mean no lecture about bringing another cat into my house?"

"Would it make a difference if I did?" She remained silent and he laughed. "Then no. No lecture. Off duty, remember?"

"Well then, Jonah." Man, he loved it when she called him by his given name. "Now we sit and wait."

Shay leaned back in the grass and made herself right at home, stretching out her lush legs, crossing them at the ankles as though she had every right to be there.

Jonah had to admit that trespassing looked good on her. Her hair was a mess of curls, her face smudged with dirt, even the tree rash on her shin looked good on her, in that tough-girl I-can-handle-myself way. But there was something about the way she was looking at him right then, with reluctant gratitude and a shy hopefulness, that had him tied in knots.

"We can wait all night, Trouble, but I don't think that cat has any intention of coming down." Just like he didn't have any intention of leaving Shay alone—and not just because he didn't trust her *not* to climb the tree the second she got impatient. There was something fragile about her tonight, a vulnerability that he'd bet the last half of that sandwich she had no idea she was showing. Because Shay didn't do vulnerable.

He'd spent the past year watching her take on one hopeless mission after another, never giving up and always managing to come out on top. No matter what. It was a testament to just how strong she was. But tonight she was showing a crack in her armor—and he wanted to know why. So he sat down next to her.

With a smile that damn near stopped his heart, she handed him his sandwich, then went back to watching her cat. Jonah took a big bite and handed it back.

She stared at it as though it were a ticking bomb.

"I didn't poison it, I promise," he said when she still wouldn't take it.

"Sharing a sandwich doesn't make this a date," she clarified, and Jonah couldn't figure out if she was telling him a date was out of the question or if she was mad because he hadn't asked her out the other night. Then she eyed *him* suspiciously and said, "So don't think this is going anywhere."

Ah, she was talking about the kiss, the one they weren't allowed to talk about according to her rules. "Thanks for clearing that up, I was afraid *Kitty Fantastic* might get the wrong impression of the kind of guy I am."

She snorted but took the sandwich.

He didn't know how much time passed, and for the first time in months didn't care. He just sat as the sun finally disappeared behind the mountains, silently passing a sandwich back and forth with *the* most complicated women he'd ever met, and yet around her everything seemed simple. Comfortable. Never once thinking there was somewhere else he'd rather be.

When the last bit of light disappeared and the only part of the kitten visible were its eyes glowing against the moon, Shay wrapped her arms around her bent knees and hugged them to her.

"I don't think the cat is into chicken bacon clubs," he said.

"Every man is into bacon. It's one of the three sacred *B*s men agree on," she argued. "Bacon, beer, and ball."

She was right; bacon, beer, and ball were all part of the bro code, but he added, "I can think of another *B* that ranks even higher."

He dropped his eyes to that top, the one that didn't require a bra. She elbowed him in the ribs.

"What? If you're going for accuracy, then it is my duty as an official card-carrying member to set the record straight." When she raised a single brow, he added, "Ten out of ten men would agree."

They would also agree, he wanted to point out, that sex ranked even higher, but sex didn't start with a *B* so he kept that to himself.

"I don't think boobs would inspire Kitty Fantastic to come down any quicker."

Jonah looked at that top again, obviously designed to drive men crazy, and grinned. "You can give it a shot."

"I like this Jonah," she said, the evening summer breeze gently rustling the few hairs that had escaped her ponytail. "Fun, flirty, and knows when to pull the police stick out of his ass and hang it up with his fancy gun."

Jonah laughed, something he seemed to do a lot of around her. Shay Michaels was unpredictable, unapologetic, and a startling breath of fresh air.

"Can you bring him around more often?"

He'd bring anything she wanted as long as she kept smiling like that.

"You bet," he said, and there it went, that thing that simmered between them. A whole lot of untapped chemistry. Only tonight it felt like more. And truth be told, it turned him on as much as it terrified him.

Mew.

The cry was small and desperate—breathless, as though it was a struggle for his little lungs to get even that out, and Jonah knew this had the potential to end badly.

For both the cat. And him.

Shay looked up at the tree, her heart in her eyes as the cat tried to move, causing the flimsy branch to sag and sway. After a moment the cat made it to the trunk and sagged his little body against it.

"He'll come down," she whispered. "He just needs time to understand we are here to help."

"What if he doesn't?" he asked softly, wanting to prepare her. He was afraid the cat needed more than time. The ratty thing was terrified to the point where helping him would likely send him leaping to his death, and if he was hurt badly enough, he might not be able to make it down on his own.

She turned her face, resting her cheek on her knee, and looked at him. And just like that, her eyes sucked him in and all that distance he'd been working so hard to maintain evaporated. "Just because he doesn't do trust . . . that shouldn't mean he doesn't deserve to be safe and loved."

There was so much rawness in that statement, it had his ribs doing a stupid viselike maneuver that pissed off his chest and made him wonder, not for the first time, just how many assholes she'd been forced to deal with in her life. Shay had a way of pulling people in with her big heart while keeping them at a distance. It was a mechanism someone used when they'd been burned, as Jonah well knew. There was no doubt in his mind that Shay had been burned badly, and that bothered him more than it should.

"I'm sorry," he said, not wanting to be one of those people in her life. "About your report being released the way it was."

"I know you didn't release it," she said, and it felt good to hear that she didn't think he would let something like that slide under his watch. "I doubt you even knew it was out there until after I did."

"Even though the report is a public document, available to anyone who knows where to look for it, it was unprofessional to have it released that way. Especially since Estella is just using it to win her stupid fight."

"Well, it's working. I am banned from Bark in the Park indefinitely, and now she has potential applicants so scared that the dogs are either stolen or from a puppy mill, they are withdrawing their applications."

He leaned in closer, giving her a little bump with his arm. "Is there anything I can do to help?" She looked at him as though accepting help was too painful to contemplate. He laughed. "Come on, I'm Mr. Fix-It, remember? Me and my cape?"

She grinned. "Okay, when you get that cape back, can you write me a note on official superhero stationary explaining that the sheriff's department isn't going to start confiscating dogs adopted through St. Paws? Then Ms. Abernathy can come and get Yodel. He's been waiting for a long time for his home, and he shouldn't have to wait a day longer."

"Done," he said, giving her another little bump, this time not moving away, so that their arms continued brushing. "Anything else?"

"Come through on that and then we'll talk."

"Following through is who I am," he said more lightly than he felt. And because he was stronger than how he'd been acting, he said, "I also wanted to apologize about the other day. I know you were caught off guard by the citation and it put you in an impossible situation."

She'd thrown him for a loop too, hiding all of those kittens, but this moment was about showing her that he was the kind of guy who fixed his mistakes. The kind of man who his father had raised him to be. He might not be the right guy for Shay, but he was determined not to be the wrong kind either.

She shrugged. "You were just doing your job."

"Yes, but I could have handled it better," he admitted.

"Or you could have let someone else handle it," she said, sitting up, and he heard a little of that bite in her voice he was so familiar with. Then, as if remembering she was mad at him, the fire in her eyes came back. "And the army of squad cars, Sheriff. Really? Talk about making Estella's case."

And they were back to Sheriff. "It was either that or let Warren go off half-cocked and take your pets away."

"I could have handled it," she argued. "Easier than having to be served by the guy who had his tongue down my throat the night before."

And there it was. The topic Jonah had been dying to bring up. Yet, hearing her talk about their kiss in direct relation to his official visit wasn't how he'd imagined it going down. Neither was the hurt he saw in her eyes.

"Ah, Shay," he said, wanting to pull her to him. "I came so you could have some kind of warning and a chance to find as many of your pets homes as possible before animal control stepped in."

"Oh," was all she said, because the truth of it was, he'd come for her. And now they both knew it.

"Yeah, oh." To him, they were two separate events from two completely separate areas of his life. But to her, they obviously weren't. And that was a big problem.

She studied him for a long moment, not shying away when he studied her right back. Nope, Shay held his gaze, never once backing down when it went way past the point of companionable silence and into something deeper, something that had heat and honesty and an intensity that wasn't going to disappear—no matter how hard they tried to ignore it.

chapter
eight

Christ, that mouth. He couldn't make himself look away.
Her lips were soft and full and a little bit naughty. And when she smiled like she was now, as if she had a secret guaranteed to rock his world right off its axis, all he could think about was being a part of hers. About kissing her again, soft and languid, taking his time to make it a real *fireworks and mind-blowing* kind of event, where thinking went out the window and all he could do was feel.

Damn it, he wanted to feel.

Being with Shay was like spinning out of control. It was exciting and terrifying and so damn addictive he'd be crazy to go there. She made him want to live in the moment, without regard for the future. And it was that exact train of thinking that had destroyed his life in San Francisco—destroyed several lives—and brought him back home.

Impulsiveness and unpredictability, even when laced with good intentions, had the potential to turn bad. Real quick. And Shay was all of those things. He had no idea why he found her from-the-hip attitude so endearing.

"Jonah," she whispered, placing a hand on his arm, and he went as still as the night. That's it. Just a simple touch and every reason he'd come up with for why this would never work between them, how they were bound to disappoint each other, didn't matter right then. All that mattered was Shay. "We're getting distracted again."

"Was there anything left to discuss?" he asked.

God, he hoped there wasn't. As far as he was concerned, there was nothing he would rather do in this moment than get distracted with a woman who, with one touch, made him feel like a man.

Jonah stared down at her for a long moment, watching how the moonlight played off her creamy skin, then leaned even closer. He couldn't help it. She smelled so damn good. Like a summer storm and the girl next door all mixed together in some crazy combination that defied logic. She defied logic. All those sharp, guarded edges surrounding that soft soul she kept hidden from the world.

She wasn't hiding it now—not from him.

Shay swallowed and scooted even closer, until she was on her knees and they were facing each other and he could feel the warmth of her breath against his mouth. And when she whispered, "Nope," popping the *P* extra hard, her lips flicked against his with enough pressure to scramble his brain.

"To be clear." He ran his hands up then back down her sides before settling them on her hips. He'd prefer her breasts, because he was pretty sure that the top she had on, efficient as it was, doubled as a bra. Meaning only one degree of separation, not two. And if he got anywhere near those full *C*s, she'd be naked in two seconds flat. And that wouldn't work because they were outside and he was a gentleman, after all. "Is this another aiming issue? Or are you going to kiss me right now?"

"You're the detective," she teased, her voice going heavy, kind of like his breathing. Her gaze square on his mouth, telling him they weren't just in sync, but that this was about to get real.

And if that wasn't enough of a green light, she placed one knee, then the other, on either side of his thighs, brought her breasts to eye level, and everything else up close and personal.

Her hands? Yeah, those went to work too, giving him all the evidence he needed, running over his shoulders and down his arms until they were interlaced with his. And just when he thought his night couldn't get any better, she took him on a tour, across her flat stomach and then down and around to—best day ever—cup her spectacular ass.

"So, Detective, you tell me."

He didn't get the chance to tell her that he wasn't a detective. *Or* the sheriff. Or even that she had the best ass he'd ever had the privilege of meeting, because he was too busy enjoying the hottest kiss of his life.

Shay kissed like she lived, wild, fierce, and taking it so far past the edge he felt free. She didn't go for soft or languid, hell no, she used her teeth and tongue to nip and tease at his lips, taking it from kissing to so-fucking-hot-he-couldn't-breathe in one touch. But who the hell cared? He had Shay Michaels, the tough, mouthy woman with the bite-me attitude, kissing him like he was her only lifeline. And in that moment, she felt like his.

Hell, she felt like everything that was right in his seriously screwed-up world.

"Christ, you feel good," he moaned into her mouth.

"I was going for amazing," she said, and without warning she slid down his body, every good part she owned scraping down his chest until she was seated fully against him, with a fistful of his hair.

"Getting closer."

"How about now?" She did this insane little roll of her hips that set him on fire. With a triumphant smile, she did it again, teasing and sweet and so damn refreshing he opened his mouth wider, taking the kiss even deeper. Taking them deeper.

"Jonah," she moaned, then let loose a sexy-like mewling sound and ground herself against him. Back and forth, creating a friction that had him making some sounds of his own because A) they were back to first names, B) she was about to go off and they weren't even naked, and C) he wasn't far behind her.

Which would be embarrassing as hell. Not to mention he still wasn't sure what she had on beneath that top, and there was no way this would be over before he had her naked. And under him.

With a new goal in mind, one which included her shouting his name, he teased at the hem of her shirt, exploring every speck of soft skin as he headed north, only to stop short when he was about to cross into heaven.

Mew.

"What was that?" Shay whispered, her hands a scant inch from where they needed to be. His were so close he might just cry, because he knew what that sound was, and *knew* what was going to go down in about two seconds—and it wasn't his fucking pants.

Mew.

"Kitty Fantastic," Shay whispered at the two blue eyes blinking up at her from the inside of Jonah's ball cap.

Yeah, Kitty Fucking Fantastic, the feline who'd already cost him his dinner and his good sense, was now using his cap for a bed and about to issue the biggest cock block in the history of bro-land.

Mew.

Two days later, Shay sat on the bed in her pajamas, contemplating her second bag of minidoughnuts. She needed it. She'd barely spoken to Jonah since the *mew* heard around the world. In fact, after they checked over Kitty Fantastic and decided the vet could wait a day, Jonah had loaded them up and driven them home, walking them to the door and wishing her a dutiful good night.

She'd texted him to say thanks for the help. It wasn't a long text, but enough to let him know how special he'd made her feel, how good it was, even for just one night, to have someone to lean on. And in the moment, Shay had felt as though he were leaning on her too—for what she wasn't sure, but she was honored he'd chosen her. Then, he'd texted her back, "Anytime."

That was it, just "Anytime."

It wasn't bad as far as texts went, but it wasn't great either. A one-worded text. Seven little letters that left no room for anything more. The last time she'd heard that word, from him, it had been thrown over his shoulder while leaving her locked in a kennel.

All Shay could come up with was that he'd changed his mind.

And that was okay. It sucked, and kind of made her belly grumble whenever she thought about it, but "Anytime" wasn't the end of the world. She'd lived through worse. At least that's what she'd convinced herself of, until yesterday when she'd received a call. Not from Jonah, of course, but from Ms. Abernathy.

Jonah had delivered on his word. Something that Shay hadn't had a lot of experience with. Not only had he stuck an official note in her mailbox as promised, he'd taken the time to call Ms. Abernathy and reassure the older woman that no one would be taking Yodel from her. Then, as if that wasn't enough, he issued a statement on the front page of the *St. Helena Sentinel* that St. Paws Rescue was not, nor were they connected with any puppy mills.

Shay didn't know what to do with that kind of gesture, wasn't used to it, and, even worse, didn't know what it meant. He hadn't stopped by or even texted to point to the awesome thing he'd done.

Sure, it was the perfect excuse for her to drop by his place, to say thanks in person, maybe bribe him with more beer and get an invitation inside, but then she'd never know if he *wanted* her to come in.

Shay popped the doughnut in her mouth and sank back against the headboard, that annoying grumble emanating from her stomach. On the outside, Shay liked to think she appeared tough, carefree, capable of handling anything life threw her way. Inside, though, she was a big scaredy-cat.

She looked at her bedroom, the lack of dogs, and felt her throat tighten, because she was also a big crybaby.

Shay had come home from work early, walked her dogs, fed the kittens, cleaned the litter box, changed her sheets, and when she couldn't stall any longer, she had to accept her reality for what it was. Yodel was gone. He was off living a happy-doggie life with his new family.

Logically, Shay knew Yodel was where he was supposed to be. All of the animals who had come through her life were. It didn't mean that it didn't break her heart, though.

Mew, Kitty Fantastic said from the carrier on the end of the bed.

"Are you ready to come out yet?" she asked the two blue slits peering out at her.

Kitty gave a long and defiant stretch, then turned around, giving Shay his back. His answer was clear with every swish of his tail.

He'd spent all day with Dr. Huntington, getting a full examination and round of shots. After treating his bruised paw and getting rid of every foxtail and burr matted in the poor thing's coat, Kitty was declared a healthy ball of bad attitude. They were sent home with antibiotics and strict instructions to remain separated from his litter for the time being.

Something Kitty still hadn't forgiven her for.

"I know you're upset, but when you're done being angry about something that can't be fixed, you can come out and have some tuna."

Nothing.

"You know you want it." She held up a plate of cat food and placed it right outside the cage.

Kitty lifted his head and eyed his dinner with serious intent, then gave Shay a scathing look that said, *Yeah right. The last time you did that I ended up in this cage.*

"Okay, I know today totally blew." Shay reached out to gently brush his tail, not going any higher, just allowing him to get used to the sensation of being touched. "Mine did too."

Kitty didn't retreat to the back of the cage as he had before, but he didn't look like he was going to come out either, so Shay moved her hand to the top of his head to deliver a little scratch. He watched her carefully, eyes full of heartbreaking mistrust, refusing to give in to the affection.

"Yodel went to his forever home today." Shay opened the Facebook app on her phone and showed Kitty Fantastic a picture of Yodel she had taken earlier that afternoon and swallowed hard. "Look, that's Yodel and his new mama, Ms. Abernathy."

Mew. Kitty Fantastic lifted his head, nudging it into Shay's hand, and she felt a simultaneous nudge on her heart. He hadn't come out, but he'd made the first step into forgiving her.

"That wasn't so hard, was it?" she whispered, then felt her eyes tear up again. "I think I needed that as much as you did." To show Kitty that Shay was willing to give a little too, and to distract herself before the waterworks got out of hand, she placed a piece of tuna inside his cage so he could easily reach it.

Whiskers in action, he sniffed it and gave the morsel a tentative lick, then another.

"There's more where that came from," she said, setting the next piece a few inches closer. "No cage this time, just a warm lap and a good old-fashioned cuddle session."

Shay could use a good cuddle today. And Kitty wasn't the only stubborn male that came to mind.

Sitting under that tree with Jonah was one of the best nights she'd had in a long time. He'd been sweet, funny, and so attentive it made her forget why maintaining distance was important. It also made her forget that he wasn't her type. Because the truth was, Jonah was every woman's type. She just wasn't sure if she was his.

And that scared her. Oh, she knew he wanted her, but for how long?

A buzzing sounded from Shay's purse. She bent over and pulled her phone out, the whole time hoping it was Jonah so she could thank him for helping with Yodel, but praying it wasn't because she wasn't sure what to say.

She looked at the screen and sighed. "Hey, Clovis."

"You gotta get down to the old barbershop," Clovis said, sounding winded. "Mr. Russell is here and he's ready to talk about leasing the space."

"Tonight?" Shay looked down at the two blue slits that studied her from the carrier, then to her attire.

"Right now!"

"I can't right now." She was in her PAWS OFF pajamas, her face was blotchy from missing Yodel, and she had Kitty to think about. She knew he was upset, but he needed to eat so he could have his next round of antibiotics.

And she needed more time. Because talking led to decisions, and she wasn't sure she was ready to make this kind of decision.

The idea of a St. Paws adoption shelter in town had merit, and so much potential she was afraid to even consider it. When the ladies had first brought it up she'd immediately rejected it, because she wasn't sure if St. Helena was the kind of place she'd want to live for the long haul. But looking now around her house, at what she'd created, the friends she'd made here, Shay began to wonder if she wasn't sure because she'd never tried it before.

When her mom passed, Shay had quickly become accustomed to switching homes, schools, friends. Every year like clockwork her life changed, leaving her nothing to hold on to, so the idea of forever with the same people was foreign to her. Terrifying, even.

But St. Helena was starting to feel different. She felt different being here. Grounded. Happy. The question then was: Was this town and were these people different enough to make it official and to lock herself into a long-term lease?

"Can we do it tomorrow?"

"It's gotta be now," Clovis said in a tone that told Shay not to argue. "Mr. Russell is heading out in the morning for the East Coast and we've got him cornered, ready to make you a deal."

Shay sat up. "What do you mean by cornered?"

"Caught that son of a bitch daisy-chaining his electricity to mine. It seems the man's also been siphoning water and heat from my shop since last winter."

Oh boy. "Me and the girls have him ready to make you an offer, but you gotta get down here before he realizes Ida's gun is nothing but a water pistol."

Shay leaped up and grabbed her jeans off the back of her chair. "Put the gun down. I will be there right after I drop off Kitty Fantastic with a sitter. Fifteen minutes tops." There was a long pause that told Shay Clovis was going to do nothing of the sort. "I mean it, Clovis. Put the gun down or I won't be doing any signings at the shop." Silence. "And I'll call Harper and tell her what is going on."

"Fine." The sound of metal hitting a table allowed Shay to breathe, but since the woman gave up so easily she added, "And he better not be tied when I get there."

She hung up and looked at Kitty Fantastic, who had paused,

midlick, to study Shay. She wondered what it would be like to come home and not have all of the barking and chew toys and chaos around her, about how quiet and clean—and lonely—her house would be.

Shay grabbed her jeans off the end of the bed. "It's not like I have to say yes. I am just getting more information."

chapter
nine

Jonah's last two calls pretty much summed up his entire week thus far. He responded to a "fight in progress" at Valley Vintage, which turned out to be two elderly residents who liked to get a little "vocal" while "canoodling," as they called it, then he chased down a punk who thought he didn't need to pay for his tab. Since the tab in question was accrued at the Spigot, a local sports bar, and consisted of a few drafts and way too much whiskey, Jonah didn't have to run too far to haul him in.

Exhausted and sweaty, Jonah walked in his front door, dropped his hat and belt at the entry, put the beer in the fridge, his gun in the safe, and headed straight for the shower. Cranking it to scalding, he stepped under the spray and rested his head against the tile wall. But no matter how long he stood there, the hot water beating on his battered muscles, it didn't wash away that heaviness he'd been carrying around all week.

Hell, carrying around for five years.

He looked up and let the water rain over his face. It had been five years and he still couldn't move on from what had happened. Didn't know how and wasn't sure, even if he tried, that he could.

"Fuck." Jonah shut off the water and toweled off. Maybe it was karma, he thought, reminding him that he didn't deserve to move on, didn't deserve to find peace.

But sitting under that tree, with Shay pressed against him, her soft skin and whirlwind of emotions surrounding him, he'd felt it. One smile from her and his world was set right.

It was strange, the woman was a wrecking ball of chaos, but around her he felt lighter. To the point when he knew the weight of his past wasn't going to pull him under and he could finally breathe. The soul-deep kind of breaths that made him feel more alive with each one he took.

Rolling his eyes at *that* thought, he dragged on a pair of jeans and a T-shirt, then smelled the pits and tossed it in the dirty clothes hamper before padding to the kitchen for a beer—or three.

He popped the top and was about to savor his first swallow when he heard a knock. He dropped his head against the freezer door.

Million bucks it was Adam, there to give him shit about not returning his fifteen calls. For a guy who was notorious with the ladies for sending them to voice mail, he sure acted like a little girl when it happened to him.

Not wanting any more grief tonight, Jonah leaned against the counter, savoring each cool, bitter sip. Adam bored easily—this was a fact. The guy was worse than a kid in church when it came to staying in one place for very long. So Jonah knew if he kept quiet his brother would eventually go away.

Only the bell rang. Three times. One after the other in rapid succession. Loud and annoying.

Ding-dong.

And clearly not going away.

Accepting his fate, Jonah swallowed the last of his beer and headed for the door.

Ding-dong.

"Keep it in your pants," he mumbled as he yanked open the front door.

Shay stood on his stoop looking too good for words in a short denim skirt, a tank top clinging to her chest that warned him PAWS OFF and showed a tantalizing little strip of skin with each sway of her body. She was also covered in enough cat fur to cause acute asthma, her hair looked like she'd been sleeping, and he couldn't take his eyes off her.

Jonah was in it deep. He knew what she tasted like now, knew what he'd been missing out on.

"Is that you trying to play hard to get?" she asked, taking in his bare chest. There was a teasing glint in her eyes, when she finally managed to look up at his. She'd been doing her fair share of ogling too—and the quirk in her smile told him she liked what she saw. "Because if so, you might want to start off fully clothed. You know, not to give off the wrong impression."

"I thought you were someone else," he said, grabbing a work shirt off the coat rack, then realized how *that* sounded and added, "I bailed on my brother and I thought you were him coming to yell at me."

"So you're avoiding him too? Whew, and here I thought it was just me." Her tone was light and teasing. The rigid way she held her body was anything but.

Yeah, about that. "I'm not avoiding you." She made a snorting sound that translated into *bullshit.* "Okay, I was, but not because of the kiss."

Her smile faded and she put a hand up. "Oh no, we agreed not to talk about that kiss."

"No, you said we couldn't talk about the first kiss, the second one is fair game," he said, loving how her breathing hitched. "And I was avoiding you because it was a tough week and I didn't want to unload on you."

Her smile turned to concern—for him. "Is everything okay?"

"Nothing I can't handle," he said.

"Right." She took a step back, sounding disappointed. "Well, I just wanted to give you this."

He took the small blue container she extended in offering and she flashed him a bright smile. Too bright, he thought, taking a closer look. Her eyes were bloodshot and the tip of her nose was pink, but everything else seemed dimmed. Fragile.

"Are you okay?"

"I asked you first and, wow, you're really good at that whole deflecting thing."

"It comes with the job." So did knowing when to let something go and when to dig deeper. "So you want to tell me why you look like you've been crying?"

"It was a rough day. I had to take . . ." She trailed off. "Deflecting again. You go first."

Jonah was torn. He wanted to know about her, get beneath the smart mouth and sharp wit. Maybe then he'd understand why he was so drawn to her. The way she was studying him, carefully and expectantly, he was pretty sure that interest went both ways. Problem was, talking it out and share-time had never been his strong suit. Just ask his family.

Jonah was more of a get-involved-without-getting-emotionally-entangled kind of guy.

"Forget it," she said quietly, and bent down to get the orange-and-white polka-dotted cat carrier at her feet. "Bye, then."

Ah, hell. He was a total and complete bastard. He knew he should have called to check on the cat. To check on Shay. But he'd barely been able to process his week, let alone what was going on between them. So he'd taken the selfish route and avoided any real interaction with her.

"Shay, wait." He reached out, placing his hand on hers and halting her before she burned rubber back across the street. The connection was instantaneous, hot and real, and she felt it too because the pulse at the base of her neck thundered. "Is he okay? The cat?"

"Kitty Fantastic?" she asked quietly, her eyes going from his hand to his face before slowly pulling away. She cleared her throat. "He's fine. Just a bruised paw and a few cuts."

"Tough little guy. Ninja with his nails, though." Jonah looked in the cage, relieved to see the cat was okay. After a hiss and a few bite-me blinks of the eyes, Jonah looked up at Shay and found something else entirely. Not a single claw out. In fact, that take-no-prisoners expression she wore like most women did perfume was absent, and in its place was a shocking amount of vulnerability. And sadness.

"Right." She pointed to the container in his hand and there went that smile again. "For you. They're freshly made. Enjoy."

He opened the lid and grinned at what was obviously store bought. "They're doughnuts."

"Fresh doughnuts," she clarified. "I just opened the bag and you're a cop, so I figured they must be your favorite. They're mine too." Which explained the bits of melted chocolate on her shirt. "I normally don't share, but I wanted to give you a proper thanks for, well, you know."

Yeah, he was pretty sure he knew, but he shook his head anyhow, because he liked watching her squirm. It sure beat the broken look he'd glimpsed a moment ago.

Her eyes narrowed and she gave him a long, assessing look. "You're going to make me say it, huh?"

He didn't speak, just crossed his arms and leaned a shoulder against the doorjamb. After years of interrogating some of the toughest criminals, he could out wait just about anyone. All he had to do was give her that silence everyone always seemed desperate to fill and she'd talk. So he popped a doughnut in his mouth and waited, biting back a chuckle when she watched him chew—her lips mimicking his. He considered offering her one, but that would defeat the purpose.

With a frustrated huff, she closed her eyes. Oh yeah, she was going to get all worked up and put herself into a mood. Sick guy that he was, he was looking forward to it. Only when she opened her eyes, they weren't lit with fire, they were suspiciously shiny.

"I wanted to say thank you," she said, clearing her throat. "For calling Ms. Abernathy. And for posting that retraction in the paper. Yodel went to his home today and it was really awesome. Then I found a new application in my inbox asking about available dogs. The family isn't right for any that I have now, but it was a relief to know people will still consider me when looking to expand their families."

She looked away and, *ah Christ*, there went the first tear. It slid down her cheek and dropped to the floor. She wiped at it as though she was just as startled by its appearance as he was.

"I don't know why I'm . . ." She pointed to her tears, which were coming faster.

"A rough week, remember," he said, setting the doughnuts on the porch rail and stepping closer, the door clicking shut behind him. "And it must be hard saying good-bye."

"It's always hard," she whispered. "I tell myself that it will get easier, but it never does."

"I know." He ran a thumb beneath her lashes, then leaned down and lightly brushed her mouth with his. He felt her eyes flutter shut and her body sway into his—amazed at how incredible she was.

What she did was hard, and tore her to pieces, but she kept doing it. Putting herself out there, setting herself up for the pain, because her belief in what she was doing was stronger than the fear of being hurt. It was a testament to just how strong she was.

But right now she felt small and fragile, her body trembling against his. Jonah could have deepened the kiss, but he knew that what she needed right then was a different kind of connection. A deeper one.

He lifted his head and watched as her eyes slowly opened and struggled to focus. Tucking a strand of hair behind her ear, he said, "Five years ago, I made a mistake and three people died."

"Oh my God, Jonah."

"Yeah." He blew out a breath. "I was on my way home from a routine follow-up when I came across this kid. Fifteen. Nervous. Obviously up to no good. Swore he was on his way home from the library," he said, remembering how scared the kid had been, and knowing he was going to bolt. Only he didn't, he stood there like a man, ready to puke, watching as Jonah dug through his backpack.

"Was he?"

"Yeah, he was. I found a biology textbook, a sorry-looking set of school supplies, and a couple of comic books. I also found a semi-automatic." No bullets, thank God.

"What happened?"

"He admitted to pinching the gun from his uncle after a few kids had tried to jump him the week before. If they came back, the kid wanted something to scare them off. I knew without a doubt he was telling the truth."

More importantly, his story checked out. Ricky was fifteen, no priors, and on the honor roll at his school—a kid from the shitty side of town trying to overcome his circumstances.

On some level, Jonah understood that.

"But instead of following protocol and bringing him in, I confiscated the gun, let him off with a warning, and gave him twenty bucks to buy a bus pass."

She cupped his jaw, her thumb gliding gently over his cheek. "Because you're a good man, Jonah, and you knew that the last thing he needed working against him was an arrest record."

"Two months later, the same kids cornered Ricky in an alley. He pulled out a different gun, this one loaded."

"Oh, God."

"Ricky and one of the other kids died." So had one of Jonah's fellow officers who had responded to the call of shots being fired.

"You couldn't have known," she said quietly, tightening her arms around him.

"I didn't have to know. That's why there are rules." They were clear and Jonah had taken an oath to uphold them. But he'd made an exception and three people died. "I send his mom a card every year on his birthday, to let her know I'm sorry. He would have been twenty this week."

Shay was quiet for a moment. "Does it make you feel better? Sending her a card?"

Jonah laughed, because it didn't. If anything it made him feel worse. But talking to Shay alleviated some of that guilt he was so desperate to cling to.

"You gonna send her one next year?" she asked, and he knew what she was really asking: When was he going to finally forgive himself?

"I don't know," he lied, because he knew he would.

They both did, but instead of telling him to move on or giving him some lame speech like his family and his fellow officers did, she gave him a gentle kiss.

"I bet she appreciates it. Ricky's mom. I bet it makes her smile that you honor his memory that way," Shay said, and Jonah wondered if she knew how much of herself she gave away when she looked at him like that.

"I hope so." A part of him always hesitated, afraid that his cards brought up painful memories for the woman, but he couldn't stop sending them.

As if reading his mind, she said, "When my mom died I remember feeling sad and alone. If someone sent me a card, letting me know I wasn't alone in my loss, it would have meant the world."

He wanted to know more about her world, wanted to know what it took to be a fixture in it. From what he'd noticed, Shay didn't let people in. Oh, she had a bunch of people fluttering around the periphery, but very few, if any, seemed to actually make it in—and stick.

"A card isn't much, but I don't know what else to do and I need to do something."

"And one day, that need will become a want and then it won't hurt so much."

"I hope so." He was looking forward to that day.

Shay put her arms around him and burrowed in as close as she could get. "I know so."

She ran a hand over his back, as if trying to offer comfort and ease some of the tension he felt building, to let him know she was there. Unable to help himself, he pressed his face into the curve of her neck, breathing her in, and doing his best not to notice how damn good she smelled—she felt even better.

"Thank you for listening. And for sharing," she said, sliding her hands in his hair and moving against him and yeah, she was ready for a change in topic.

"Want to come in and share some more?" he said, and before she could answer his lips were on hers because he too was done spilling his guts. To prove it he gave her a little nibble.

She groaned and her head tipped back, a clear "go" when it came to *other* forms of connection. He sucked and kissed all the way down her neck, taking his time and showing her just how ready he was.

"I can't," she said, pulling back, her gaze running the length of him while indecision and hunger played across her pretty face. "I want to. Like *really* want to, but—"

He placed a finger on her lips, because he could work with want. He could also work with the need he saw in her eyes. "Thank God, because I was afraid you were making up some reason to leave."

"I am." Suddenly her hands were on his shoulders and she was stepping back, right out of his arms. Connection broken. Any hope he'd had for taking this into the bedroom—or to the nearest flat surface—was broken. "But it's a really good reason."

As far as he was concerned it better have something to do with a speeding meteor or zombie invasion, because there was nothing that needed more immediate attention than what was going on between them—and in his pants.

"I am supposed to meet Mr. Russell at his store in . . ." She looked at her watch. "Shit. Four minutes ago. You distracted me."

She sounded pissy, but if anything it made him flex his chest a little. He liked being her distraction, liked that he was good at it. He wanted to prove he could be even better if she stayed. So he slid his arms around her waist and pulled her against him so she could see what kind of distractions he had to offer. "Call him and reschedule."

"I wish I could." This time her hands came between them, but they landed on his chest, which proved difficult for her, so she crossed them in front of her, creating a wall. "He's willing to cut me a deal on renting his store. A store, Jonah, where I can bring all my animals."

"That's great." He wanted her to get a store. He really did, but he also wanted her naked and moaning beneath him. But she was already in rescue mode, and she wasn't out to rescue him anymore.

"I need a favor." She looked at the carrier and Jonah had a sinking feeling that he was about to get screwed—and not in the way he'd been hoping. "Kitty Fantastic needs his meds and to eat dinner and I can't get him out of his cage. And I can't bring him with me."

"Oh no," he said, backing up, because from the growling emanating from the cage, Kitty Fantastic needed a complete attitude adjustment. And Jonah wasn't the guy to do it. "I don't have it in me to take care of a cat tonight."

"You just need to give him his meds." She picked up the carrier and handed it to him. He noted that it had a little squirt bottle hanging off the side. "Plus, he's here to take care of you. Thanks, Jonah," she said, making her way down his front steps, leaving him no way out. "See you later."

A paw came through the cage, claws out looking for blood, and swatted at his leg. Jonah walked farther onto the porch, nearly tripping over a dozen cans of food, a litter box, and a twenty-pound bag of litter. "When is later?"

Shay turned around to face him but didn't stop walking. "I think it's right after 'anytime.'"

ch🐾pter
ten

Carrier in hand, Jonah shut the door behind him, the low hiss the only warning before five razor-sharp needles tore into his hand.

"Not cool." He lifted the cage and looked the cat in the eye, letting him know just who was in charge. "You have nails, but I have a squirt bottle." He held it up to show him just how serious he was. The cat yawned. "If that doesn't work, I'll pull out the hose. Got it?"

A little uncertain, the cat sat down in his cage but didn't sheath his claws. "Now, for the house rules. No scratching me or my stuff, no peeing anywhere except the box I will put out for you, and no shedding. On anything. Understand?"

"Make sure you tell him about your coaster rule. The one you get all menstrual about."

Jonah looked up to find another stray in his house and swore. Adam must have come in the back door—never a good sign—because he was sitting on Jonah's couch watching ESPN. His feet on the coffee table, making himself right at home, and drinking Jonah's beer—the one Shay gave him. No coaster in sight.

He set the carrier on the table, gave the cat one last hard *I mean business* look, and opened the cage door. The cat licked his paw as though not intimidated in the slightest.

Satisfied that he'd set the boundaries, Jonah snagged Adam's beer and sat in his recliner.

"I was drinking that," Adam said, sounding put out.

"Funny since it was in my fridge." He took the remote and flicked it from baseball to soccer.

"I brought a six-pack. It's in the fridge," Adam defended, grabbing for the remote. Jonah held it out of reach.

"Good. Then go grab it and take it home."

"You're in a mood." Adam stood, making one last play for the remote. Jonah stopped him with a single glare and he gave up and walked into the kitchen.

"See that," he said to the cat. "He's twice your size and knows not to screw with me."

When he looked back up, Adam was standing there smirking at him for talking to the damn cage. Jonah shot him the finger, and Adam sat down with enough chips, salsa, and beer nuts for ten. The beer, though, was one bottle—not the six-pack.

Adam set the spread on the table, then his feet, then the beer—no coaster. Jonah picked up the water bottle off the side of the carrier, aimed, and fired. "Off."

Adam sprang up. "What the hell?" He wiped his arm over his face, pouting the whole time. "What did I tell you?" Adam said to the cage. "Menstrual."

"I thought you were going home," Jonah said.

"Can't." He pulled a coaster out from under the coffee table and obediently set his beer on top. "Frankie's camped out on my porch, waiting to chew my ass out for missing Blanket's first birthday last night."

"That was last night?" Jonah sat up to look out the window, checking for his sister's car.

"Yup." Adam leaned back, this time sprawling his long body across the entire couch.

Jonah watched as Adam dug into the bag of chips, raining little crumbs all over his leather couch. He held up the squirt bottle and Adam obediently cupped his hand under his mouth as he finished chewing.

"So you came here?"

"Snuck in the back. Figured if we stuck together we stood a better chance."

Their sister didn't have kids, she had alpacas. A family of them, with their own luxury habitat complete with a playroom, splashing pool, and library. Frankie was also a straight-up ballbuster—with impeccable aim and a mean streak as wide as the valley. And when it came to her newest baby, Blanket, she could get a little intense. Which was saying a lot for a woman who had kneed her own husband in the nuts twice before getting around to telling him she loved him.

"I'm good," Jonah said. "I sent a present and a card last week on Blanket's actual birthday, so you can leave and face Frankie alone."

"Aunt Lucinda sent that present. Picked it out, too." Adam smiled, slow and smug, because he knew what Jonah knew. Frankie was a master BS detector. She had to be, growing up with three older brothers who dragged her into their schemes, then left her holding the bag.

If she thought for a second that Jonah didn't pick out Blanket's present, which he did not, and passed it off as his idea, which he had, then he'd better start wearing a steel cup when he left the house.

"Total Dad move by the way," Adam said, and Jonah wasn't sure how he felt about that. "He used to have Aunt Luce pick out all of Phoebe's presents."

After Jonah's mom passed away, his dad quickly remarried the free-spirited Phoebe, hoping to fill the void in his own life as well as his sons'. Phoebe was fun, whimsical, and a much-needed breath of fresh air for Jonah and his brothers.

His dad, not ready to let go of the anger of losing his true love, never accepted Phoebe's passion for life or forgave her for it. David wasn't a bad guy, just misdirected, and normally Jonah didn't mind the comparison, but in this case he did.

"I'll send her something else." Maybe he'd even stop by her house and visit. Frankie'd like that. Ever since she married into the largest Italian family in town, she was all about sibling bonding, throwing BBQs, and all the things that made Jonah's eye twitch.

"Let me know how that works out for you," Adam said, then pulled out his cell and started swiping.

A few seconds later he flipped it around and there was a picture of Frankie with Blanket. They were standing in front of a HAPPY BIRTHDAY banner. The alpaca was making mincemeat out of the book Jonah had gifted the weed-eater, and his sister was wearing a black T-shirt and the finger.

Jonah grabbed the phone to get a better look. The finger was a no-brainer, Frankie was just saying hi in her own special way. The shirt, however, looked like it had—

Jonah sat up. "What the hell is she wearing?"

"A WARREN'S GOT BOOTY tank top," Adam said, flipping back to the baseball game. "They're all the rage. Saw two ladies jogging in WARREN'S GOT BOOTY shorts on my way here."

"Look, I don't care about who the women of St. Helena have on their butts," he said. He just cared who Shay wore on her butt, and wondered if she was voting for Warren like she'd said a few weeks back.

"You better check Facebook before you say that."

"I'm not on Facebook."

Adam froze, his expression going completely serious. "Don't admit that, man, it makes you sound old. What's your personal e-mail account again?"

"Why?"

"I'm making you a Facebook account. Never mind, I remember it," Adam said, picking up his phone, his fingers flying over the screen. "I will even friend you, but don't go posting pictures of your cat on my wall. It's not cool."

"It's not my cat."

"Whatever you need to tell yourself." Adam looked over the screen of his phone, long and hard. "And cat pictures are never cool, got it?"

Jonah gave him the *whatever the fuck you need to hear, bro* shrug.

"Your password is BarneyFife82, as in how old you pretend to be." He hit a final button and smiled. "As for what women have on their butts, you should always care. Especially if you want to win the election."

"People aren't going to vote for Warren because he looks good in a calendar."

A few swipes to the phone later and Jonah actually cared who women had on their butts. Because lots and lots of women were sporting WARREN'S GOT BOOTY merchandise, and what had looked like a sheriff's race slam-dunk for Jonah seemed to be shifting—in Warren's favor. Not enough to make Jonah scared, but enough to have him taking notice.

"What's that?" He pointed to a link on Nora's timeline that read "Which Sexy Candidate Fills Out the Uniform Best?"

"A Facebook poll that Nora is hosting. Oh, and in case you're wondering, yes, the guys at my station are going to give you so much shit when they see you next." Adam laughed and then scrolled down. "You have the Boy Scout and Quick Draw categories in the bag, but Warren is smoking you in the Does Boot Size Matter?, Best Booty, and Where's the Beefcake? categories."

"Where's the Beefcake?" Jonah sat back in his recliner, no longer concerned. They couldn't be serious.

"Yeah, whenever a sheriff hopeful is spotted around town, making connections and securing votes, people snap a photo and post it here." Adam held up the phone and scrolled slowly, showing Jonah a continuous stream of photos—all of Warren in his uniform, while he was on duty, shooting the shit with citizens all over town.

Jesus, no wonder why response times had gone up. The prick was using county time to patrol for votes.

"How long has this been going on?"

"Couple days," Adam said, putting the phone away. "So if you want this job, then you need to loosen up a little. Maybe call that hot girlfriend of yours. It's too late to get in on the calendar, but maybe she could put you on her blog."

"First off, I am running for sheriff, not for most popular in the class yearbook."

"Aren't they the same in this town?"

"And second, Shay isn't my girlfriend." Sure, they kissed, and if the cat hadn't sounded his alarm they would have done more. But that was a far cry from being his girlfriend.

"Thank God," Adam said, his eyeballs on Jonah. "Because I've been thinking of asking her out, and it would be weird to sleep with some hot chick that my brother is secretly picturing naked."

"Fuck off," Jonah shot back, but Adam just laughed. "And we're just friends. She asked me to cat sit Kitty Fantastic."

"Kitty Fantastic?" Adam's lip twitched. "Is that some kind of new slang, because last time I checked, when a chick stuck her tongue down my throat like that, friend wasn't the *F* word she was looking for."

"It's complicated."

"Well, then let me uncomplicate it. You've been walking around all summer with your dick on your sleeve. And people are talking."

That got Jonah's attention. "About me and Shay?"

Adam snorted and grabbed a beer—Jonah's beer. "The only person in town who doesn't know there is something going on between you and Shay is you. So do us a favor and invite the girl over for a pillow fight. In your bedroom."

Shay cursed her sandals as she ran up Main Street toward the old barbershop, wheezing as if she was about to go into cardiac arrest. She was only nine minutes late, but Ida had a gun—and who knew if it actually held water or bullets—so nine minutes could be the difference between life and death . . . for Mr. Russell.

And for Shay getting that storefront.

Shay burst through the front door of the shop, the bell jingling wildly in her wake. Bending over to catch her breath, she noticed there was no Mr. Russell in sight. However, there was a gun on the counter of the first station—water, thank God—and a set of red leather cuffs dangling from the barber's chair.

Shay had either missed her chance—or the grannies were hiding the body. Either way, she wouldn't get the shop, which was more upsetting than she'd anticipated because even though it smelled vaguely of mothballs and hair tonic, the place was perfect. The deep bay windows lining the front of the shop would lend themselves to the vintage pet-shop feel Shay was going for. It was easy to picture her kittens wrestling in newspaper strips while families stood on Main Street and looked inside.

The crown molding and abundance of natural light filtering in through the beveled windows made it feel more like a home than a shop, and the two stations and barber chairs were visible from anywhere in the store. Shay could groom her animals before sending them home to their families—a little glamour station of sorts where they would don their kitty couture and doggie allure . . . all of which she would make available to customers for purchase. And if she tore out the shelves on other side of the room, it would make it wide enough to have animal-friendly cages spread around the store so her babies wouldn't be stacked on top of each other and people could interact with each animal individually.

"Ida?" Shay called out, her voice bouncing off the walls. "Mr. Russell?"

"Back here," Ida returned.

Shay followed the sound into the back room, which would make the perfect meet-and-greet area, and down a narrow hallway that led to—

"No way," she whispered, taking in the beautiful arched cast-iron fence that bordered the entire perimeter of the space. "It's beautiful."

She couldn't believe it. Unlike the Paws and Claws Day Spa, and many of the other shops on Main Street, this shop had a yard. Not large by any standard, but cozy and peaceful, completely draped in pink and orange bougainvillea and what appeared to be a million twinkle lights. It was as though she was walking into the pages of *Pride and Prejudice.*

"I don't want to touch it!"

At Mr. Russell's bark, Shay walked farther onto the patio, shocked to find a table covered in enough silk and lace to pass for the biggest panty raid in Napa County, and four guests already gathered around. Well, three guests digging through neon-rainbow G-strings, a duck with a bone in its beak, and one reluctant host sitting at the head of the table.

"Mr. Russell," Shay said, going over to check his wrists for restraints, only to find a box of battery-operated equipment in his lap. "Are you okay?"

"Of course he's okay," Ida said, picking up the teensiest pair of panties Shay had ever seen and rolling them into a ball. A quick flick of the wrist later and it looked like a rose.

"I most certainly am not," Mr. Russell said, taking the box off his lap and slamming it on the table. A muffled hum echoed off the wood surface. "They told me that I couldn't leave until I priced each and every item in there."

"If he thinks he can help himself to my electricity," Clovis spat, "then he can help with the merchandising as well."

Mr. Russell was squat, with owl-like eyes and more hair on his face than his head. He was also looking at the latched gate in the back, as though judging the most direct path between him, the panty raiders, and freedom.

Norton flew up on the table and waddled right up to him and flapped his wings as if to say *Go ahead and try it.*

"Thank God, you're here," Peggy whispered, clutching a pair of vinyl panties to her chest so tightly that the fabric looked ready to burst at the seams and send the little metal studs scattering. Peggy looked ready to come apart too. She obviously wasn't big on kidnapping and blackmailing.

"Without the restraints I didn't think we'd keep him here much longer. Then he started hollering for the sheriff." Peggy leaned in and lowered her voice. "I was afraid Ida was going to tie him up with some unmentionables and then gag him with one of those balls Clovis sells in her shop."

This was not good. There was no way a man who'd been tortured with unmentionables for the past hour was going to cut Shay any kind of deal. And she felt that familiar panic, the one that always came when everything was about to change, well up inside of her and take hold.

It was silly. An hour ago Shay wasn't even sure she wanted to open a shop, but suddenly she wanted this shop with all of her heart.

Wanted to try on St. Helena and see if she fit.

Wanted to see if maybe she could find what she'd been searching for here—maybe even with Jonah. Mostly, though, she wanted to see her animals find good homes. In order to do that she had to take the plunge.

Only she didn't think Mr. Russell wanted to plunge into anything. Not with Shay. Not today. Maybe not ever.

"Mr. Russell. I am so sorry about this." Shay took his arm and Norton started acting cagy, pacing back and forth, not sure if he should attack or retreat. "If you'd like me to walk you back inside, maybe we could talk about the lease sign hanging in the window."

"The man isn't going anywhere," Clovis said, resting a hand on his shoulder and shoving him back in the chair. "Tomorrow I'm having my Toys of the World half-yearly blowout. I've already priced those ones over there, so that means he's got one box left."

Meaning Shay had about five minutes to explain her situation, get him on board, and negotiate terms that would have to be well under the asking price, all while the man was putting stickers on— she looked at the box—Down Under vibrators.

"Or you can just let the girl have the space and we'll call it even," Clovis said, pulling out a Wom-Batter and setting it on the table directly in front of Mr. Russell. She activated the On switch and it vibrated toward Mr. Russell, sending pink and purple strobe lights flickering off the fence and leaves.

Quark!

Norton, feathers in flight position, took off chasing the lights. Every time it buzzed, Norton responded.

Buzz. Buzz.

Quark! Quark!

"You people are insane." Mr. Russell stood right before the Wom-Batter would have jiggled itself into his lap. "Fine, she can have the space. Two-year lease, no more, no less. If it works out, we can renegotiate the terms then."

"Thank you, Mr. Russell," Shay said, afraid to ask what that two-year lease would go for. Even though the place was perfect in theory, getting it to work as a functioning shelter would take time and money. She was pathetically short on both. "What kind of terms were you thinking?"

He threw out a number that was on the high end of what she was hoping, but she had enough to last her three months. Making rent after that would be a stretch, but if she got creative and started selling Cuties with Booties merchandise, it was a number she could work with.

"You're responsible for all utilities, tenant improvements, and you can move in as soon as you get me the security deposit, which is equivalent to two months' rent—ow!" He looked at Clovis, who was holding her cane and smiling angelically.

Mr. Russell rubbed his shin, then continued, one eye on Clovis, the other on her cane. "No security deposit." The cane lowered. "But first and last months' rent, plus the utilities and all tenant improvements are her responsibility."

The three panty raiders looked at Shay expectantly—although Clovis was swinging her cane like a billy club. It was clear; they were there for her, willing to do whatever it took to help her make this a reality. And that alone made Shay's heart roll over.

"Then we have a deal."

ch🐾pter
eleven

At the time Jonah's alarm clock was supposed to be going off, he found himself standing at the foot of his bed in full gear, tired and pissed off. Tired because A) it was dawn and B) he'd had one hell of a week. The pissed off part was because all he wanted was to crawl into bed and sleep for the next twelve hours, but he only had six before his next shift started—and he'd just come off a double.

There were barely enough guys to cover the required shifts, so when someone took a personal day it meant someone else had to step up. Last night, that someone had been Jonah. So instead of his normal ten-hour haul, he'd pulled two tens, back-to-back. If he planned on being any kind of useful, he needed sleep.

Too bad his bed was currently occupied by a two-pound fleabag and every pair of dirty socks he owned. The socks were now snagged and punctured like dead carcasses, and the cat, he was on Jonah's favorite pillow, faking sleep.

"We talked about this yesterday, the bed is off-limits." They'd talked about it again last night when he'd swung by to give the shit his meds and found him burrowed at the bottom of the bed, Jonah's sheets a tangled, lumpy mess.

Jonah had called Shay. She'd sent him to voice mail. So he'd made it more than clear that he needed to know when she was going to pick up her cat. She'd texted back, "Soon." That was two days ago.

Obviously no one took him seriously.

Jonah grabbed the squirt bottle and aimed. "I mean it. I used to be SWAT. Still hold a few records for accuracy and distance." Kitty Fantastic opened one eye, then closed it. "Fair enough. One. Two." Squirt. "Fuck!"

Even though Jonah was rated out to a thousand yards, the cat outmaneuvered him, moving at the last second to God knew where. All Jonah had accomplished was getting his pillow soaked. But at least the cat was off his bed.

So spent that standing was too much, he hung his utility belt on the hook by his nightstand, his uniform went on the floor, and he fell into bed. He didn't bother to pull the sheets back or remove the forest of mangled socks. He just flipped his pillow over to the dry side and closed his eyes, groaning at the sensation of not being in motion.

The next time he opened his eyes, his room was light, his body felt like he'd been hit by a semi, and something was sticking him in the leg. Sitting up, he found a shredded frond from his potted palm resting against his thigh, little soil paw prints marking the entire perimeter of his comforter—and pillow—and Kitty Fantastic curled up asleep in his gun holster.

How he'd managed to get up the utility belt and wedge himself in there was beyond Jonah, but he was pretty sure the little fucker had used his claws—with glee.

Knowing it was still early, but not caring, Jonah threw on jeans and a T-shirt and marched across the street. He rapped on Shay's door, surprised when she answered so quickly.

She wasn't in her pajamas, looking like he'd just awoken her from the best sleep of her life. Nope, Dr. Dolittle was in another one of those skirts she was so fond of, this one white with a little drawstring, and a bright yellow top that tied behind her neck and did incredible things to her cleavage. Hair pulled up into a ponytail, lips glossy, no shoes.

"I got it," she said, bouncing on her toes and twirling in place. Her skirt didn't have enough give to fly up, but it caught enough wind to make him forget why he was angry. "Mr. Russell sent over the lease and keys last night. Keys," she said, her face lighting up, "for my own place."

She closed her eyes and paused as if letting that statement settle, and he felt something else entirely settle in his chest. Something warm and heavy that scared the shit out of him.

"I am meeting with the contractor in thirty minutes to see what needs to be done."

"That's great. Congratulations." Jonah didn't know what shocked him more, that Mr. Russell had agreed to finally lease out his shop or that Shay was taking a bold step that would keep her here, in St. Helena. He wasn't sure how long she'd stick, or how he felt about that.

Her smile faded. "Wow, you look awful. Like you should go back to bed."

"That's why I'm here. I seem to have a bit of a problem in the bedroom."

Shay choked back a laugh and it came out sounding like a snort.

"Jesus." He ran a hand down his face. "I meant that Kitty Fantastic isn't so fantastic. In fact, I haven't slept in three days." Okay, part of that was the job and part of it was thinking about Shay, but the cat wasn't helping matters. "I woke up to half of my palm tree in my bed."

The other half he'd spotted on his recliner.

"That is so sweet," she cooed, her hand on her heart.

"Sweet? The damn thing tracked soil all over my bed."

"It was a gift, his way of saying he accepts you as part of his family."

Jonah had enough family, and spent a good deal of his time avoiding them. He didn't need to add one more to the mix. "I need to sleep, Shay."

"Of course you do." With a serene smile, she clasped her hands in front of her and pitched her voice as though talking to a six-year-old. "But keep in mind, palm tree branches are like a toy to your cat."

"You mean *your* cat."

There went that smile again. "I can't have any more cats, remember, Sheriff? At least not until I get St. Paws opened."

"It's not Sheriff or Detective, it's Deputy. And how long will that be?" She opened her mouth to respond and he added, "And don't say soon."

She closed it.

"I need a time frame, Shay."

She considered him and the situation for a moment. "Well, *I* need a full month to get the shop up and running, but unfortunately I only have twenty-three days left to find homes for my current fosters. That's the downside of being a repeat offender over the legal limit." She looked him in the eye and he felt the warm morning air press in around him. "So my final answer is twenty-three days."

Hell no. He stepped back. "I can't do this for twenty-three more days." He couldn't do this for twenty-three more minutes. The only quiet place in Jonah's world was his house. And that cat was the antithesis of quiet. As far as Jonah was concerned, Kitty Fantastic was the Antichrist cloaked in fur.

Shay stepped out onto the porch and rested a hand on his chest, and he admitted, silently to himself, that she was also his quiet place. She was also staying, apparently, which added a whole new level of complication to their already complicated situation.

Knowing she was a tumbleweed at heart, who would eventually roll herself right out of town, made it easier to maintain his distance. Knowing she was staying? Well, that changed everything.

"Of course you can't," she said, sympathetically. "Nobody could."

He was pretty sure Shay could. The woman shied away from nothing—except him. Which was why he'd come over here thinking that this was going to be a battle. Relieved to see that it wasn't, he stepped back and was about to offer to go and get the cat when she said, "Hang on," and shut the door in his face.

He waited a good long minute. When she still didn't come back, he knew he'd been played. She was probably running out the back door, bolting for freedom as he stood there on her porch in bedhead and potting soil. Then the door swung open and Shay stuck a stick in his hand. It was about a foot long and had a couple of colored feathers attached to an elastic string.

"What's this?" He shook it and it jingled. From inside the house a dog barked.

"A bonding toy. It will make him feel as though he belongs in the space."

"He doesn't belong. It's my space."

"Before you go to sleep, wiggle this around on the bed for about ten minutes," she said, undeterred. "Kitty Fantastic will be so tired he'll curl right up and pass out." She leaned up and gave him a quick peck on the lips, nothing big but it still left him rocked, which was how she was able to say, "Gotta go. Call if you have any questions, and good luck," before closing the door in his face again.

This time she didn't come back. Even when he rang the bell three times and knocked twice, sending the dogs into a barking contest. On the last rap, Ms. Pricket poked her head out the upper window. Even though she was in a bathrobe with curlers in her hair and toilet paper wrapped around her head, she sent him a scowl as though he was the one violating the morning.

He looked at Shay's front door one last time and sighed.

"Rookie mistake," he mumbled, walking back across the street, the feathers dragging on the asphalt, a jingle sounding with each step he took.

He should have brought the cat with him.

Later that night, Shay sat in the barber chair and stared down at the plaster and dust covering her skirt—her favorite white eyelet skirt. It was less depressing than looking at the contractor's estimate Peggy had brought over. There was no way she could get all of this done with her limited funds.

"I've got a few bucks saved for a rainy day," Peggy offered, placing a gentle hand on Shay's.

"I can't take anything else from you," Shay said. The older woman hadn't even batted an eye when Shay explained that she might need to break her lease and move out of Peggy's rental if this was going to work. She gave Shay a hug, then offered to lower the rent until Shay got the rescue up and running. "Maybe it's not too late to call Mr. Russell and tell him I changed my mind."

"It can't be that bad." Harper set down her gyro—compliments of Emerson and the Pita Peddler—and picked up the estimate. Her only response was a low whistle.

"Not helping," Shay said.

"Right, sorry." Harper put on her best *let's get down to business* face and really looked at the numbers. "Okay, well, if we do all of the demo and painting ourselves, it would save us," she closed her eyes and mumbled, "nine, carry the one, add the six." She handed Shay the paper back. "Just over two grand."

"And I bet with your girls' help, we could get it done in three or four days," Peggy said, looking around the room, assessing it with the eyes of someone who had done a remodel or two in her lifetime.

"When did St. Paws become a 'we' and an 'us'?" Shay asked.

Emerson snorted. "For Harper, it was the second she said hi and you said hi back. One semismile and she becomes a barnacle of friendship and rainbows. You collect strays, she collects people. You'll get used to it, cat lady." She shrugged.

"I can never say no to a worthy cause," Peggy said and Shay wasn't sure if it was because, like her, Peggy couldn't say no to an animal in need, or if she meant that Shay was the worthy cause. Either way it warmed her heart.

"As for the demo," Emerson said, double-fisting a crowbar and a baseball bat she'd dug out of her truck. She gave the frame a little whack, then kicked it with her boot. Hard. The old wood was no match for her steeled toes and came loose at the bottom. "I bet we can get it done by the end of the weekend."

Harper clapped her hands once, then looked around the room. She located a piece of cardboard in the far corner and, with markers that materialized out of thin air, got busy. Two seconds later she held up a stellar drawing of a giant thermometer with twelve lines—the first two already colored in.

"See, two grand closer to the goal. And to be clear, I only attach myself to awesome people." Harper leaned into Shay and gave her a big hug. Then she moved on to Emerson, who just accepted it with her hands at her sides.

Not sure about the awesome part, Shay busied herself looking at Harper's handiwork. It was like one of those fund-raising growth charts that would hang in a third grade classroom and had a cartoon trench coat with a scarf and dancing limbs.

"Well, when I add the cages, pet supplies, and carry the nine," Shay said, adding another two lines to the thermometer, "it seems that we have to find another ten grand before we reach the big smiley trench coat at the top."

"Oh, we're going to reach the Coat Crusader," Harper said, totally convinced.

"Coat Crusader?" Shay asked.

"Oh yeah." Harper nodded.

"Oh God." Emerson thunked her head against the wall.

Harper ignored this. "Every year the Coat Crusader helps the Fashion Flower gather enough donations and money to supply winter coats for kids in need. And he wants to help you, Shay."

"Great," Shay deadpanned. "Can the Coat Crusader help me raise eight grand? Because after giving Mr. Russell first and last months' rent yesterday, and making sure I leave enough in my account for the next couple months, that's how much I'll need."

Harper said nothing, just filled in the next two lines, then stepped back to admire them.

"Oh, don't forget Ida and Clovis have offered to donate some cages," Peggy said, catching the spirit and taking the pen from Harper, shading in another two lines. "And you still have Warren's Cuties with Booties calendar signing at my shop next Wednesday."

A signing with Jonah's biggest rival. How had she forgotten?

"Look at that, day one and already six lines closer," Harper said, completely ignoring the other six left to go.

Shay opened her mouth to point this out, but Emerson held up a hand. "Don't. Just let her go. She will find the money somehow, even if it means offering to clean out every garage and storage closet within city limits in search of old jackets and spare change. It will happen."

"We found enough jackets to keep three hundred kids warm in one weekend," Harper defended proudly. "And last year I got the local preschool to pitch in, and the kids did a walk-a-thon and raised eleven thousand dollars for new coats."

"Eleven grand?" Just for walking? Maybe Harper was on to something. "But how many preschoolers are there? I mean, there are only four of us and like a thousand of them."

"Ninety-two," Harper corrected. "And how many pet owners do you think live in St. Helena?"

Suddenly the doom and gloom lifted and Shay started to see this as a real possibility, that maybe this could all work out, and that with her friends she could make a success of St. Paws.

"People are going to pay you so they can walk their own dogs?" Emerson asked.

Harper shrugged, not concerned in the slightest. "We just need a good cause and a hook and people will open their wallets. We have the first one already. What's more endearing than puppies and kittens?"

Nothing, Shay thought. She was proof of that. Not much could penetrate her carefully constructed walls, but a button nose with soft paws and floppy ears, and she became a big ball of mush.

"That's it," Shay said, looking at the wall she'd planned on turning into Couture Corner. "What if we make it a catwalk event, where everyone gets to show off their pet?"

"I can pull out the Halloween inventory left over from last year when it rained," Peggy added.

"I like this," Harper said. "We can charge people an entrance fee and let them get sponsors for the walk if they choose. I bet you we'll have enough to do all of this and have leftovers to spay and neuter the new pets you will bring in."

"If we start the walk at town hall then head up Main Street it can end in front of the new St. Paws," Shay said. "To introduce people to the new shelter."

"I can park my cart out there and offer all kinds of human and pet-friendly foods," Emerson offered. "All the proceeds could go into the Coat Crusader's pot."

"I can't ask you to do that," Shay said, completely humbled and overwhelmed by the generosity in the room.

"You don't have to ask. I'm offering." Emerson's look told Shay that her mind was made up so Shay could get on board or get out of the way. "Plus, who knows? Maybe I will be able to book a few gigs that don't demand chicken tenders and clown shoes."

Shay didn't know a whole lot about Emerson's past, but she was pretty sure that when Emerson came home from culinary school in Paris, she'd had bigger plans than owning a refurbished hot dog cart and catering birthday parties and bar mitzvahs. But with a kid sister and dependent father to take care of, Shay thought Emerson was doing the best she could. So her offer to help meant a lot.

"I want to make sure it doesn't cost you anything," Shay said sternly.

"Fine." Emerson shrugged. "All of the money minus expenses."

"Count me in for a case of wine and some of my chocolate-dipped exotic fruits for the winner," Ida said from the doorway.

"And I have a bunch of boas left over that I'd love to donate. Can't have a strut without boas," Clovis said.

"Prance," Peggy clarified. "Animals prance when they feel glamorous."

Shay stood up. "The Prance for Paws Charity Pet Walk!"

"It's perfect," Harper said. "Every animal lover in town is going to turn out."

"Especially if we sweeten the deal and offer a prize," Emerson said. "People would totally turn out for pets and money."

They would, Shay thought giddily. And all of her fosters would be right there, front and center, glammed out and looking adorable. Who better to adopt her babies than an animal lover? It was like she was creating an event that gave them the best shot of finding their families. So even if Shay was a day or two late on opening her shop, her dogs would be safe.

"You could do this every year," Peggy said. "Since Bark in the Park has been moved, you can have your prance the third weekend in August."

Shay thought of all of the other shelters and foster parents who lost out because of Shay and Estella's spat. She could offer them a discounted entry rate so they too could showcase their pets.

"It's perfect," Clovis said.

Yeah, perfect, Shay thought, taking in the five women who had come to offer their support. Shay hadn't called them, hadn't asked for their help, yet they'd shown up anyway with Pita Peddler to-go bags, a case of wine, and something that Shay hadn't had since her mom died—a sense of belonging.

ch🐾pter
twelve

The cat was driving him insane.

It was 6:09 in the morning, on Jonah's one day to sleep in, and Kitty Fantastic had been staring at him for the past twenty minutes. So close Jonah could smell last night's tuna on his hot breath.

To be fair, Kitty Fantastic always got his breakfast and meds at five forty-five, right before Jonah left for work, but today Jonah was on late shift and really wanted to sleep until noon. Kitty wasn't having it.

He sat on Jonah's chest, flicking his tail. At least he wasn't on the bed or the pillow.

"Mew."

Jonah opened his eyes. "You've got kibble."

Kitty Fantastic wanted tuna.

"Sorry buddy, if I feed you wet food, you're going to fill up the litter box." Something Jonah wasn't tolerating. He wanted to sleep a silent, smell-free slumber. "Go back to sleep."

Kitty hopped off the bed, and Jonah, with a soul-deep sigh, closed his eyes, enjoying the quiet. His breathing slowed and he started to drift off.

Jingle. Jingle. Jingle.

Great, the cat had liberated the stick toy from the bottom of Jonah's underwear drawer—which meant he'd probably liberated all of Jonah's underwear in the process.

Unconcerned with any of that, since *he* wouldn't be cleaning it up, Kitty Fantastic perched himself on Jonah's stomach—and the stick on Jonah's nuts. A furry paw darted out and tapped the feather, which was on Jonah's face.

Jingle.

"Yeah, jingle, jingle." He leaned up on his elbows, his eyes so gritty everything took a few minutes to focus. "Do we really need to bond before—"

Jingle jingle.

Kitty hunched down low, going as flat as a piece of plywood, his eyes big, tail flicking in anticipation.

"Right." Jonah ran a hand over his face, then picked up the stick and wiggled it. The cat jumped back, arched up, and did a weird side-walk thing that made his hair look as though he had gone through the dryer without a fabric softener.

When he wasn't stringing the toilet paper from the rafters or using the recliner as his own personal scratching post, the thing was kind of cute.

Jonah flicked the string again and the cat went apeshit crazy, darting back and forth across the bed, swiping his paw at the feather, then batting it dead. This went on for a good ten minutes until Kitty Fantastic lay on his side just watching the feather whiz by. With one last flick of the paw, his eyes finally slid closed.

Thank Christ. It actually worked. Jonah lay back down and, deciding to overlook the fact the cat was on his bed—two inches from his pillow—he too closed his eyes.

Then the cat started snoring.

Several hours later Jonah was back at work, trying to keep his mind on the problem at hand, which wasn't easy due to the headache forming behind his right eye. Jonah jotted down detailed notes as Clovis explained the ongoing situation with Giles as though Jonah were a detective working a case when, in fact, he felt more like a receptionist.

He had no idea how he'd managed to get stuck on front desk duty and handling this case. Except, oh right, Warren was too busy running for sheriff to do his damn job.

"That man should be arrested in violation of penal code three fourteen."

Jonah dropped his pen. "So you're saying Giles exposed himself?"

"I would call wearing a man-hammock to show off his swizzle stick in a public pool all kind of indecent exposures. Wouldn't you, Deputy?"

Jonah wanted to tell her that just hearing her complaint was violation enough. "Where did this happen?"

"At Valley Vintage's pool."

Jonah stopped scribbling and looked up. "And what were you doing there?" Because he knew every resident of the senior community, and Clovis wasn't one of them. She lived downtown, a good five miles from the place of the supposed incident.

Clovis stopped, her face going a little flushed. She recovered in record time and flapped a dismissive hand, as though she were the expert on the matters of penal code violations. "That's irrelevant."

"Uh-huh." Jonah stared at her.

Clovis stared back, her wrinkles rippling at the expression she adopted. Moments passed, along with a few silent challenges.

Finally, with an exasperated huff, she plopped her enormous purse on the counter to dig around inside. "I have pictures somewhere, if you need them as evidence for the warrant."

Jonah wasn't buying it. "When did he, uh, expose himself to you?"

"Not me," Clovis snapped. "It was that swim teacher."

Pausing, she glanced at the other people in the station, then leaned in and lowered her voice, and Jonah was beginning to see the real problem. "Giles has been paying her twenty-five dollars a pop for 'lessons' so he can watch her flotation devices up close. Only this week he got bold, faking that he couldn't swim, and started flapping around. His man-hammock, which he bought at some fancy out-of-town shop, swayed with the current, if you know what I mean."

Clovis signaled with her eyes to her lower regions and Jonah threw up a little in his mouth. There was nothing about his uncle's man-hammock that he was remotely interested in knowing. Although the only reason Giles would go out of town to buy a man-hammock—and there went another gag Jonah had to suppress—was if he was too embarrassed to buy one in town.

One of the most important rules for getting to the truth of the matter, Jonah knew, was to ask the *right* question. "Now, Ms. Owens, does this have anything to do with his Pinterest page?"

A page that was becoming the bane of Jonah's existence.

"It's not a *page*, it's a *board*—his Sexy and Single in St. Helena board—and no." Clovis folded her arms over her chest—rather under because her arms weren't long enough to go over. "It most certainly does not." Although her pained expression told a different story.

Jonah didn't argue. He just stood quietly until Clovis's beady eyes got even beadier, trying to intimidate him into submission. Only Jonah didn't intimidate easily. Growing up with a sister and great-aunt who weren't afraid to fight dirty—to use fists, knees, any sharp body part that could do damage—gave Jonah a leg up on the older woman. Unless she was concealing a weapon inside her bag, or aimed her cane at his boys, he wasn't caving.

"I think you should bring him in for questioning."

Jonah closed his notebook and put it away so he could put his hand on Clovis's, and softened his voice. She wasn't mean or vindictive, just a lonely woman with the misfortune of having feelings for a man who was blinded by the latest and greatest model in sweater-kittens. "Maybe instead of trying to get him arrested, you should tell him you want to be friends. Cook up one of your famous lemon-iced fig cakes and take it as a peace offering."

"He wouldn't invite me in," she said.

"I don't know a man in town who could turn away one of your cakes, Ms. Owens."

"Oh." She looked away, shy and nervous—and soaking it all up. "I don't know about that. Plus, we'd start arguing before we even cut the first slice."

"Don't bring up the *board* or Celeste, just be yourself. Show him that flotation devices eventually deflate, but an evening with a charming woman who has a big"—Jonah smiled until Clovis was good and flustered—"heart and a wealth of life experiences is a night well spent."

"My fig cake," she said with a shaky nod and collected her cane. He wasn't sure if she would take his advice, or if he'd solved the problem, but at least the real issue was out in the open.

He watched her slowly make her way toward the exit and wondered how much energy the older woman expended on covering up the fact that she was lonely.

A lot, he decided, thinking about his work schedule. A whole hell of a lot.

"You just earned my vote," a sweet voice said from the other end of the counter.

Jonah turned to find the best set of sweater-kittens he'd ever seen in a bright blue sundress held up by tiny straps. The neckline was clearly made to mess with his mind. It fell down into a deep

V, and there was just enough fabric to cover her without covering everything. He couldn't tell if the dress went to the knees or flirted around her thighs—the counter was in the way—but he took his sweet time imagining the latter. Then he imagined a big gust of wind blowing through the door and smiled.

Desk duty wasn't looking so bad after all.

"Well, if doing my job is all it takes to get votes, then maybe there is still hope," he said, glancing at the woman waiting at the ticketing counter in a WARREN'S GOT BOOTY tee.

Shay looked over her shoulder and chuckled. "Warren's the pick of the week, a passing phase."

He eyed the woman again and wished he could say he agreed. A few days ago, it wouldn't have even crossed his mind that a slacker like Warren could wind up as sheriff. Now, he wasn't so sure. "I hope it passes before the election."

She placed her hand on his. Everything about her in that soft dress, with those soulful eyes, called to him. "He needs a badge to prove he's sheriff quality, a leader. You're already that man, Jonah, and the town knows that."

Jonah looked into her warm eyes and found himself hoping that she included herself in that statement. For some reason, the idea of disappointing her or, worse, being a passing phase in her world, didn't sit well.

"And that wasn't you doing your job. That was you taking care of someone." He rolled his eyes and she laughed. "What? I think it's sweet."

"Sweet?" he choked. Then to be sure he was clear, he said, "I am not sweet."

Sweet was a word someone used when describing a basket of puppies, not someone who carried a Glock and was trained to kill with his hands. It most certainly did not pertain to someone she had X-rated dreams about.

And that was a problem. Jonah didn't want to be just another one of Shay's strays, another lost soul she felt the need to rescue. He wanted to be—well, he wasn't sure, but it was nowhere near *sweet*.

"You so are," she laughed, then leaned in, showing him a little slice of heaven encased in hot pink lace. "It's one of your best-kept secrets, Sheriff. But don't worry, I won't tell anyone."

He liked the idea of sharing a secret with Shay, as long as she was willing to be a part of that sharing. Secrets were about give and take and usually led to common ground. And common ground would hopefully get him more sure footing so he could go behind enemy lines and demonstrate just how far from sweet he could be.

"Thank you," he said, leaning in and lowering his voice. "Now it's only fair you tell me one of yours."

He was hoping for the secret that led to getting in her panties, because so far he was oh-for-two in that department. But more than that, he wanted to understand how a woman could give herself so completely to her flock of animals but hold herself distant from everything else life had to offer.

"I don't have any secrets. I'm an open book."

Now it was his turn to laugh. Loudly. "Trouble, you are like Pandora's box." She pressed her lips tightly together and raised a brow. "Fair is fair."

She thought about this, then gave a slow nod, her eyes serious as she leaned in and—*hello*, that neckline went from V to plunging. So he leaned in too, his chest all kinds of serious as she cleared her throat and made a big deal about lowering her voice.

"I'm here to get your signature."

He liked the sound of that. According to Adam—and Facebook—getting a man's signature in St. Helena was woman-speak for *I'm interested if you are.* He looked down at her cleavage again—how could he not?—and grinned, because, yeah, he was interested. "Where would you like me to sign?"

"Right here," she said, pulling a form out of her purse and setting it on the counter.

He could tell by the color and size that it was a permit from the city, and his right eye twitched.

Impatient as ever, she pushed the permit closer for his viewing ease and he subconsciously stepped back. He looked behind him, disappointed to find not a single other deputy around to hand this off to.

"You haven't even read it," she said, crossing her arms.

"Don't need to." The second he touched it, gave it even an ounce of consideration, he'd be sucked into one of her schemes. "I don't do permits. Shirley, the secretary, does though, and she'll be back from her break in about ten minutes."

"I know," she explained. "But the lady at town hall said it usually takes her a few weeks to process these kinds of requests and I don't have a few weeks. So I'm asking you." She swallowed—hard. "As a favor."

"Last time you asked me for a favor, I ended up with a cat."

She patted his arm. "And see how well that turned out."

Jonah felt his gut tighten because he knew this favor was going to bite him in the ass—and he was going to say yes anyway. There was something about Shay that had him making bad decisions, and his gut was telling him that nothing about this favor was going to be easy—or smart.

His heart, though, was reminding him that Shay didn't ask for favors—ever.

She gave a long-suffering and somewhat nervous sigh and he picked up the form. "To be clear, my taking the paper does not mean I am agreeing to the favor."

"Oh, you'll agree," she said, her excitement bubbling from her every pore. "I am throwing a charity walk."

"A walk, huh?" He scanned the permit.

"More of a prance. I'm calling it the first annual Prance for Paws Charity Pet Walk. I hope to raise enough money to get my shelter up and running before the deadline."

"Is that how you got these?" He set the paper down and picked up her hands, tracing the scratches marring her palms and forearms with his thumb. He felt her shiver.

"Demo was two grand, so to save some money, me and my crew—"

He smiled. "You have a crew?"

"Why do you look so surprised?"

"I'm not."

"Well *we*"—she put fancy air quotes around the last word—"demoed the entire first floor of the shop over the weekend. By ourselves."

"Impressive." And sexy as hell. Oh, he knew Shay was a hard worker, that she would build the shop from the ground up with toothpicks if she had to, but the image of her wearing a tool belt and swinging a sledgehammer turned him on.

"I know, right?" She bounced a little on her toes and it took everything he had to keep his gaze on her face. "And since I learned my lesson last time, I am here to get the appropriate paperwork completed. Apparently I have to get someone here to sign off on it before the city will consider granting me the permit."

She was quiet, waiting for him to read. He picked it up again, loving how her eyes followed his every move, proving that she was as impatient as a kid on Christmas morning.

When she was one flip of the permit from reading the thing to him herself, he gave it his full attention. The first part of the permit was doable, but when he got to her desired location he knew it was a no-go. "You want to close down Main Street?"

"Where else would I have a walk-a-thon?" He could think of a lot of other places that didn't include closing down the main thoroughfare in town. "It's the same few blocks as the farmers' market."

"Closing a street off requires traffic and crowd control. The farmers' market has to request enough officers to handle that kind of event."

"Okay," Shay said, undeterred. "Is there a request form I can fill out then?"

He wished it were that simple. "Yes, but the officers have to be off duty and they have to be paid the union minimum." Jonah quoted her what that was and he could tell by her expression that the woman at the permit department had done a piss-poor job of explaining to Shay what she was up against. "And the county doesn't have the funds to pay for this kind of event. It has to be covered by the event host."

"So I'd have to come up with the money?"

"Yes," he said and could tell Shay didn't have an extra fifteen hundred dollars in her budget. "But even then, I don't think I could find enough guys on this short notice willing to work it. With Bark in the Park the weekend after, and the department cutbacks leaving us short staffed, my men are overworked. Which means I can't sign this form."

"I can't make St. Paws work without it, Jonah. I need this permit."

"And I want to give it to you." He really did. Shay had done everything right this time, followed the rules, put her heart into turning a bad situation into something amazing, and she was still getting turned away. That pissed him off. But his hands were tied. "I can't force guys to work off hours, though."

"I get that," she said, accepting the big turd he'd just handed her with a graceful resignation that could only come from a lifetime of nos and letdowns.

Jonah didn't want to be one more letdown in her life. He wanted to be that guy who showed her just how easy she was to say yes to. He picked up the permit and folded it, tucking it in his shirt pocket. "I can't sign this until I have a verbal commitment from the guys, but let me see what I can do."

"I appreciate it," she said, and then with a smile that was shy and uncertain and unlike any smile she'd ever sent his way, she leaned in. "As for that secret I owe you, I've never had a lemon-iced fig cake, but it sounds like something I would love to try."

With a look that said she was talking about more than icing a cake, she grabbed her purse and headed out the door, her hips swishing like she knew he was watching. And he was. He watched as the cute curve of her ass walked out of the station. He groaned with every step she took because the bottom of that dress teased at her thighs, just like he knew it would, showing off those amazing legs of hers.

When her car pulled out of the lot, he fished out his phone and dialed Adam. "'Sup."

"What's the password for that Facebook account you set up for me?"

"BarneyFife82," he said. "Why?"

"I need to make somebody my friend." Isn't that what he'd told Clovis to do?

"Jesus, it's called *friending* someone."

He didn't care what it was called. He was going to do it.

With extra icing.

ch🐾pter
thirteen

Two days later, Shay looked out the window of Paws and Claws at the excited mass of women waiting to come in and wondered if she should call the cops.

They weren't women—they were more like ladies. Senior ladies. Some of them so old they predated Christ. And they all wanted a piece of this week's Cutie with Booty.

"I still think we should call for backup," Shay said, now understanding why Jonah had placed so much emphasis on crowd control. One wrong move, like say, forgetting to pack all the limited-edition Warren trading cards she'd advertised, and she'd have a riot on her hands.

"I'm all the backup you need," Warren said smoothly, and Shay rolled her eyes.

Sure, the deputy was doing her a favor. And sure, he was so good looking he was hard not to stare at, but Shay knew his type. Had dated his type. In fact, her life was full of his type. Witty, charming, always around, ready to lend a hand—until she really needed one.

"I don't think you stand a chance," she said and Warren laughed, sure to flash his perfectly white teeth her way.

"This isn't Kevlar under here," he said, puffing out his chest and running his palms over his pecs to prove it. "This is hard work. Want to feel?"

Shay did not want to feel, she wanted to call Jonah. There were so many large handbags and walkers that could easily be concealing weapons—or be used as weapons—she knew that this event was one line-cutter away from getting out of hand.

"Maybe they would understand if you explained the situation," Peggy said, coming up beside her, and Shay shot her a *yeah right* look. "Then how about I stall? I'll say we are getting the dogs ready for their big day. Every woman knows that sometimes primping can take longer than expected."

Woof, Jabba said, pressing his already groomed face to the window and panting excitedly at the growing crowd. He was joined by two of her other fosters: Socks, a cupcake-sized Maltipoo dressed in pink bows and a tutu, and Boss, a five-year-old basset hound who was looking good and showing his best side to the waiting ladies.

"Well, that option is out," Shay said, giving her mutts a pat on the head. "I can always run home and grab the cards."

"I've got my booty buttons," Warren offered, sitting back in his chair as though he didn't have a care in the world. As though there wasn't a crowd of demanding, impatient—and sometimes mean—old ladies all lined up to get their signed Deputy Booty trading cards.

Peggy looked out the window, then back to Warren and Shay and admitted, "Or maybe I should just call Jonah."

But it was his day off. Shay knew this because she'd watched him mowing the lawn this morning from her kitchen window—while enjoying a cup of coffee.

Okay, she'd been spying. But the man was in flip-flops, cargo shorts, and no shirt, looking relaxed and ready. For whatever came his way.

If she were being honest, though, the real reason she'd hesitated was that she didn't want to explain why Warren was there. This signing had been scheduled for weeks, and flyers had been displayed all over town since the calendar release, but a lot had changed in that time.

Namely, they'd kissed.

Three times.

Having Warren here with his BE THE BOOTY, VOTE WARREN FOR SHERIFF buttons, giving him the added publicity right before the election, felt like she was endorsing the wrong candidate. Even worse, she felt like she was betraying Jonah's friendship.

"Well, would you look at that?" Peggy said, her eyes big with awe. "They're lining up so orderly it's like they're at boot camp. And they're doing it without a riot squad or the fire hose."

That was because while most officers of the law carried their backup in their holster, Jonah carried his in the easy gait and stride he possessed. He didn't need to show he was packing, didn't even have on his uniform. The sheer amount of testosterone and bad-assery rolling off of him as he walked down Main Street in his shorts and ball cap was enough to send even the most dangerous criminals cowering.

That he did it with a smile was even hotter.

Jonah strode to the door of the spa and reached for the handle. It was locked.

He raised an amused brow at Shay. "You going to let me in?"

"Are they going to storm the shop?" she asked.

His confident look said everything she needed to know. She unlocked the door, and the sound sent Socks darting across the room and under the designer food bowl display.

With a grin that had her heart cheering and her lady parts sighing, Jonah stepped inside and handed her a box. Not just any box, but *the* box. The one from the printer that she'd been too distracted by his morning strut around the yard half-naked to remember.

"The Deputy Booty trading cards," she said, pressing it to her chest. "How did you even know I forgot them?"

"Peggy called and said there was about to be a problem."

"After I specifically told her not to bother you on your day off?" Shay looked for Peggy, who was too busy organizing the already organized cat collars to look up.

"Thanks, man," Warren said, stepping over to grab the box, putting his arm around Shay in the process. "The day would have been a bust without these. Want one?"

"I'll pass," Jonah said, then looked at Shay. "You all good?"

"Yes." No, she was so far from good it was making her palms sweat. "Warren, why don't you start signing those?" She moved from under his arm and ushered him to the opposite side of the shop.

When he was out of earshot, Shay said, "I'm sorry, Jonah."

Jonah looked at the guest of honor, sprawled out under a WARREN FOR SHERIFF poster, then back at Shay and gave a nod. One single nod that no matter how hard she tried she couldn't decipher.

"That's why I didn't call you," she admitted. "I didn't know how to explain this. I thought about canceling, but then realized how many cards and calendars I could sell. And the dogs really need the exposure and I . . ."

Jonah's face softened and he became the off-duty guy who made her belly flutter, and suddenly everyone else disappeared. "Nothing to explain. I knew what today was. I saw your post on Facebook."

"You friended me," she whispered.

"You accepted."

Duh, as if she'd pass up the chance to stalk him in a socially acceptable way. The second she saw the request she accepted then went to his page to rifle through his photos, check out his history. All she got was a profile picture of him on his porch—drinking a beer and looking fine—no posts, no hobbies, and no other friends.

She wondered if the other people hadn't responded yet. Or if he'd opened an account for the sole purpose of friending her. Both ideas intrigued her.

"So you knew and came anyway?"

"I knew today was important." That was it. Five simple words, spoken with a warm intensity that was as wonderful as it was overwhelming.

"I don't know what to say," she admitted, beyond humbled. Jonah had brought the cards for her, even knowing they could inadvertently help his opponent. "Wait. How did you get the cards?"

He smiled, loose and easy, and—*good Lord*, was that her heart melting? "You might want to hide your key somewhere other than under the doormat."

"Did you break into my house, Sheriff?"

"Jonah," he said, his name a low rumble on his lips, making it clear who was before her today. Badge or not, she decided, he was her hero. "And technically I had the owner's permission. Why, Trouble? You want to press charges?"

There were a lot of things she wanted to press right then, but none of them included charges.

"I want to say thank you," she said and realized that she was swaying. *Swaying.* Shay didn't giggle or blush and she most certainly didn't sway. She looked at the ground, saw it move side to side, and sighed. Definitely swaying. "But it will have to wait since you know how my thank-yous can be."

His gaze dropped to her lips, then the neckline of her dress, and she shivered. "The cat needs his meds soon, I'd better go. Good luck with today. Call if you need anything."

"We're fine," Warren said, walking over to sling his arm around Shay's shoulder again. "I got this. In fact, I was just telling Peggy that I could work your charity walk, Shay."

"No need," Jonah said and, wow, if he'd sent that look her way she'd wet her pants. "I actually came down to let her know that I already got a team together. Permit is signed and ready to submit."

"You did? It is?"

"I did," he said, all authoritative and sheriffy, but she could see the softness in his eyes. "And it is."

"You did all that on your day off?" Warren asked, the bullshit detector clear in his voice. "That's some kind of dedication."

Warren did not mean it as a compliment. In fact, the *what a loser* look he sent Shay made her ears burn with anger—and ignited a protectiveness she hadn't felt over another two-legged friend in a long time.

"That's called being sweet," Shay said, untangling herself from Warren. She leaned up and gave Jonah a kiss on the cheek, then stepped back and said, "And I am a sucker for sweet."

At that, Jonah smiled big and wide. "It's at my place if you want to stop by after work and pick it up."

"I have to stop by my shop first. My new couch is being delivered later today." It was big, durable, and comfy in that have-a-seat-and-stay-awhile kind of way. It was also the most important piece of furniture she'd purchase for the shop. She couldn't open without it. "It might be late."

"Anytime," was his response, but the secret smile he gave said it was more of a *tonight you're mine* kind of invite.

Shay nodded. She couldn't speak. Jonah was in his element, being large and in charge, and he'd just invited her back to his place—after hours.

Anytime had suddenly become her favorite word.

Jonah hadn't walked into the pet spa with the intention of starting a pissing match.

Okay, he'd totally gone into it with that exact intention.

When Peggy called asking him to bring down the box on Shay's kitchen table, he'd thrown on his superhero cape and raced on over, wanting to save her event. Only when he'd arrived, he discovered she already had a superhero. Not that Warren was anywhere near superhero level—he was more of the bumbling sidekick—but he put on a good show. That the show was for Shay pissed him off, thus the match.

Lying about the permit had been a rookie move, one that Warren could prove in a single call. But there had been something about the way Shay looked up at him when he walked in, as if he, not Warren, had just made her whole day, and Jonah made a snap decision. One he had to fix.

Good thing he excelled at thinking on his feet. He knew the only officers not working that day were Warren and another deputy who was going to a wedding. And Warren spending all day with Shay, at her charity walk, was not going to happen.

Once outside, Jonah gave a final stern smile to the line of women, then pulled out his cell and dialed his boss.

"It's your day off, Baudouin," Sheriff Bryant said when he answered. "So if you're calling me it means you need to get a life."

"Working on it, sir," Jonah said. "It's actually what I need to talk to you about. I'd like to take a personal day the Saturday after next."

"I'm glad you're finally starting to think long term, use up some of those vacation hours before they expire, but Saturdays are hard."

Jonah peered back through the spa's window at Warren sitting next to Shay, looking a little too cozy for his liking, signing those damn cards, which were as good as votes.

"I bet Warren can take the shift," Jonah said. "He hasn't worked a Saturday in over a month. He wants to be sheriff, the guy should know what he's getting himself into."

The sheriff chuckled. "I agree. I'll let him know as soon as you fill out the request. But if you're taking the day off to work that walk-a-thon, know I can't spare anyone else."

"Understood." Jonah disconnected and dialed in the next favor on his list.

"Are you calling to explain why you haven't accepted my friend request?" Adam said by way of greeting.

"No, I'm calling to see if any of your guys are looking for some overtime the Saturday after next."

It was usually the sheriff's department that handled this kind of town event, but it wasn't unheard of to reach out to other qualified county departments in a pinch. And since Jonah was officially heading up the team, he could use his discretion.

"Is this for your pretty neighbor's charity event?"

"How did you know about it?"

"Facebook, man. Facebook." He could practically hear Adam shaking his head. "Nora posted that Shay's wearing something from the Boulder Holder in the walk-a-thon, so count me in."

"You're not invited," he clarified. "But I need three guys." Jonah thought of Adam's friends: smooth, good looking, even better with the ladies. "Three of the fattest, oldest guys in the house. And they have to be married."

"Since when is 'married' a requirement?"

"Since now. You going to help me or not?"

"You going to accept my friend request?"

After getting the names of a few guys Adam thought might need the extra cash, Jonah hung up, then went to Facebook. He accepted Adam's friend request so he wouldn't have to hear him whine like a little girl, then posted a picture on Adam's page of Yodel in a tutu that was taken from behind and typed, *It's not a cat.*

Look at that. His first post.

ch🐾pter
fourteen

It was nearly five when Shay ushered the second-to-last of the fans out the door. The day had been a success. Warren had drawn the crowd, but it was her dogs that were the stars of the event, winning over the hearts of the ladies. One lady in particular.

Mrs. Moberly sat at the back of the shop, where she'd been for the past twenty minutes petting and talking to Boss, with his floppy ears and melt-your-soul eyes. Boss was a sucker for naps but at times craved being in the thick of the action and life. Shay had been holding out for a family with older kids. Placing him in a home where he'd be left alone during the working hours wouldn't work with his personality. And although Mrs. Moberly would make a great doggie mommy, as the town's head librarian, she worked long hours.

"Boss doesn't do well with being alone for long periods of time. He's a cuddler, needs constant companionship," Shay explained, because it wasn't about placing an animal with a family. For Shay, the process went deeper. It was about matching the needs of the animal with the lifestyle of the family, being sure to make a successful pairing.

St. Paws was eHarmony for the furry and four-legged.

"I was thinking that Boss could come to work with me," Mrs. Moberly explained, pushing her glasses higher up on her nose. "Most libraries have cats, but I think ours could use a dog, one that's good with kids."

Mrs. Moberly could use a dog in her life too, Shay thought, watching the way she gravitated toward Boss, leaning her body into his. Boss, being one of the most intuitive dogs Shay had ever fostered, leaned back, giving the woman what she needed—affection. Uncomplicated, unconditional affection.

"I have an application if you'd like to fill one out—wow, okay," Shay said as Mrs. Moberly pulled an application from her handbag and handed it over. It was completely filled out, with a list of references attached to the bottom, and *Boss* written next to *Pet of Interest*. "This looks great. If you want, we can set up a time to meet somewhere neutral, like the park. It will give you a chance to see him in action and I can see how you two interact."

Because sweet as he was, Boss was not a dog that would chase a ball or roll over on cue—he wasn't built to roll and moved like molasses. Then again, Mrs. Moberly was nearing retirement age and walked like she wore slugs for shoes.

"If that is how this works," the librarian said, looking down at Boss. "But I pretty much knew the second I saw him in the calendar that he was mine. It's the eyes, they remind me of my husband." She gave Boss a scratch behind the ears and he let out a groan of ecstasy. "I've been waiting for you to bring him to an event so I could see if he felt the same."

And Shay knew right then that she didn't even need to read the rest of the application. Mrs. Moberly had just told her everything she needed to know.

"I need to come by and do a house check," Shay explained.

Mrs. Moberly smiled. "Well, I'll be sure to have some tea ready."

Shay said she'd drop by later in the week, and with one last hug, Mrs. Moberly left the shop, Boss whining when the door closed.

"Well, look at that," Shay said. "Impressing the ladies with those big eyes." Eyes that looked up at Shay and hit her straight in the gut. Another good-bye so close to the last was going to make this a hard week.

Suck it up, this is your job.

With that reminder, she locked up the shop, leashed her pack, and walked to the soon-to-be St. Paws Rescue. She wanted to tally up her daily earnings and account for it on the Coat Crusader's chart before the couch arrived.

It was silly. She'd estimated that she only pulled in around four hundred bucks today, but that was four hundred bucks more than she'd had this morning. It was also a quarter of a line that she got to fill in, taking her one step closer to high fiving the Coat Crusader —and to becoming a real St. Helena resident with staying power.

Shay slid the key into the lock and smiled as the bells jingled on the front door. Signing on that dotted line for the lease had been a terrifying thought, but now that she'd done it, she felt free. It was hard to explain, but somehow forcing herself to stick around gave her the courage to believe that she could make a life for herself here.

She unleashed her brood, and they took off running in different directions—except for Boss, who moseyed over to the first chair and plopped down beneath it to watch Jabba shove Socks out of the way to get the leftover kibble at the bottom of the bowl Shay had brought over.

The shop still needed lots of work, but it was slowly coming together. The walls were now a playful yellow and the trim, which she'd stayed up last night finishing, was a crisp white.

Woof. Woof. Jabba alerted Shay to the dire emergency at hand— the bowl was seriously short on kibble. Then he eyed Socks as if to pass the blame on to the five-pound ball of powder-white fur, who looked more like a Shrinky-Dinked Ewok than a dog.

"Uh-huh, and I bet you had nothing to do with it disappearing," Shay accused, picking up the bowl. Jabba snorted his innocence. "I've got more in the back."

With a quick pet to the dogs, she strode into the back room and gasped.

Her couch was already there—and it was perfect. Big enough to hold an entire family of four, yet its *L* shape hugged the wall in the new meet-and-greet room and left plenty of room for floor play. It was also currently occupied.

Jonah leaned against the cushions, his arms casually strewn across the back of the couch as though he owned the space. And the man looked good owning her space. Dressed in a pair of loose-fitting jeans, a soft-looking blue collared shirt that had the sleeves rolled to the forearms, and a little sweat from the hot afternoon, he looked like a magazine ad for sex.

"What are you doing here?" Shay asked, hoping that he said sex, because now that she'd seen him on her couch, she couldn't think of anything else.

She followed his gaze to the counter to her right. And there, sitting on a crystal platter, three tiers high with yellow creamy frosting smoothed over the top and sides, was the most amazing lemon-iced fig cake she'd ever seen.

"You made me a cake?"

He sat forward, resting his elbows on his knees, and chuckled. "No. I *brought* you a cake. Clovis made it. After three failed attempts, and one visit from the fire department, I bribed her into making me one."

Shay walked closer, stopping a few feet from the edge of the couch—and him. "And did you bribe her to let you in?"

"No, I was dropping off papers across the street when I saw a couple of delivery guys trying to navigate this mammoth in through the door." He patted the seat of the couch and she wondered if he was asking her to join him—for sex.

Hot couch sex.

"And since Clovis was harping about not scratching the walls, and unlawful entry isn't my thing, I offered to help." Shay watched as he considered that for a moment and seemed to give extra consideration to the tie at the waist of her wraparound dress. "But with you I always seem to want to ignore the rules."

She liked the sound of that. A lot. "Ignoring the rules can be fun."

"They can also lead to trouble," he said and then smiled.

"Trouble can be fun."

Fire flickered in his eyes, telling her she was the exact kind of trouble he was looking for. Reaching out, he cupped her hip and slowly drew her toward him. He parted his legs to make room for her and—pow, all she could think about was hot couch sex.

The kind that led to naked bodies sticking to the leather.

To each other.

And more than anything she wanted to stick with Jonah. Stick to him all night, well into the morning, and maybe for longer. His always-ready attitude and attention to detail would make him the rock star of hot couch sex, but the way he touched her as though she were special, someone to be treasured, made her want to be the kind of woman Jonah would stick with.

"Do you know what this couch is for?" she asked.

He shook his head, his palms moving from her hips to her lower back, scooting her closer.

"It's the wishing couch," she explained.

"Wishing couch?" he asked but there was no mockery in his tone, just a deep interest in her answer—a deep interest in her.

"Most people come into a shelter with a pretty good idea of what they are looking for in a companion, but then they gravitate toward the one that has the highest cute factor, never once taking into account what that kind of companion needs." She'd seen it a thousand times, and it never ended happily—for anyone. "Let's say someone comes in looking for a lap dog to keep them company at night and maybe go to the park with them on the weekends, but then they see a cute terrier in the window and instantly fall in love. They don't care that terriers were bred to be herders or that they love to climb and are by nature in constant motion. All they see is small and cute."

"And they want the terrier."

"At least they think they do," she said quietly. "But one too many times of coming home from work to find their shoes chewed to bits or their couch destroyed, the cute starts to fade, and eventually something has to give." Sadly, it usually led to giving up the dog. "Because no matter how much that couple wants their terrier to be a lazy lap dog, they'll never be one."

"Because the dog is a terrier, and even though he never pretended to be anything else, he loses out," Jonah supplied, and suddenly Shay didn't feel like they were talking about the terrier anymore.

"So to help eliminate any potential buyer's remorse, I bought a wishing couch, where people sit and tell me what they are looking for in a pet. Not on the cuteness scale but on the compatibility scale. I listen to what they are saying, and more importantly what they aren't saying, then I assess what pets I have that they'd be a good match for. And one by one I bring them in and have a little get-to-know-you session without all the pressure of the adorableness that happens in the front room."

"Smart." His gaze met hers in a way that left her feeling completely exposed. "And takes a lot of time on your part."

She lifted a shoulder, her hands fidgeting with the collar of his shirt. "It cuts down on returns."

After the lives they'd had, Shay wanted to make sure that none of her pets ever felt unwanted again.

"I'm sitting on the wishing couch, Shay," he said, his hands spanning each hip as he ran them down her thighs, stopping at the hem of her dress, then back up and—*oh my*—under. His rough skin on hers gave her a head-to-toe shiver. "Aren't you going to ask me what I want?"

"What do you want, Jonah?"

"You," he said, his voice so raw and honest, Shay didn't know how to respond. Flirty, casual, that's what she had expected. But Jonah had just taken this to a place she wasn't sure how to navigate. "I want you."

It was those three words she'd felt like she'd waited a lifetime to hear. Sure, there were the other three words that also started with *I* and ended in *you*. But even though she walked around with her heart on a plate when it came to her pets, Shay was a realist when it came to herself and had accepted long ago that she didn't have the love-you gene when it came to people.

Not that Jonah was looking for love, or even if he was, that he'd find it in her, but he was looking for something that she could relate to—connection.

A way to ease the loneliness. And that she could handle.

"How do you want me?" she teased, trying to bring a lightness to the moment, bring it back to safe. Her hands went to the tie of her dress, dancing over the knot.

Jonah reached out and stilled her hands, drawing her close. He met her gaze, his serious and heavy. "Exactly how you are."

Shay stilled, her heart stopping right there in the meet-and-greet room, afraid to beat because she'd heard it all before. But Jonah said it with so much conviction, she wanted to believe him. Wanted to find the courage to ask him the one question that, in the past, hadn't worked out for her so well.

Over the years, lots of people had wanted Shay for lots of different reasons, but the only person who had ever wanted her for who she really was had been her mother.

And Shay desperately needed to remember what being wanted felt like, without the fear of being returned. At least for one night.

"Are you sure you know what you're asking for?"

"Oh, yeah," he whispered without hesitation. "I've never been more sure of anything."

Shay didn't know what to say, not that she got a chance to respond. One minute she was standing and the next she was using his lap as her own personal seat, her knees straddling his thighs as he kissed her.

And kissed her.

And, *oh my God*, the man had lips that could make a grown woman cry. Or maybe it was the gentle way he cradled her face that made this grown woman want to cry. Because even though she was flush with him, all their good parts pressed together, right there for the taking, he didn't shift course, didn't cop a feel or go straight for the goods. Nope, Jonah took his sweet time to gently caress, explore her lips, as though he was trying to tell her she was worth his time, worth getting to know.

He held her in a way that was completely unexpected, and it took her by surprise. It was sweet and slightly erotic, and felt so right a small burst of hope welled up in her chest and spread, because Jonah was taking the time to show her that she was special.

To him, in this moment, Shay Michaels was special.

Ignoring the warning bells going off in her head, Shay gave herself over to the experience. Let the what-ifs and fears of tomorrow be left for tomorrow and gave herself wholly to this moment. To this man.

Jonah must have felt her change, felt the shift in her body, because with a groan he tightened his arms around her and slid his tongue across the seam of her mouth. She opened to him immediately, opening everything to him, including her heart.

"I want you too," she admitted against his lips, breaking the kiss.

"How do you want me?" he asked, his forehead to hers, and for the first time Shay heard doubt in his voice. Jonah was as nervous as she was. She'd never thought about it, but Jonah hadn't dated all that much since she'd moved to town. In fact, she couldn't remember a single girl who stuck around for more than a few weeks—and she'd been watching.

Having a job that demanded everything one had to give, and being on call 24/7 couldn't be easy on relationships. It would make for a very lonely road—and that was something Shay could relate to.

"I want you however I can get you," she said, meaning it. His job was as much a part of him as her animals were to her. It was one of his most appealing traits—the level at which he gave of himself to his town. "Although I'd prefer you naked."

"You first." He smiled, his hands giving a gentle tug on the belt at her waist. The fabric untwined itself and the dress parted right up the middle, exposing a strip of bare skin, but Jonah held it there, staring at a hint of flesh and black lace.

The longer he looked, the harder he became beneath her, and the hotter she got until she was sure she was one breath away from an orgasm. An orgasm she desperately deserved.

"Jonah," she said, her hands going for the edges of the dress.

"Give me a minute," he begged. *Begged*. "I only get to do this once."

He wasn't going to get to do it at all if he didn't move along. With a long exhale, he slowly pulled the dress open, and the look on his face was worth it.

"Holy Christ, I knew you were . . ." He traced a finger over the lace edging and to the clasp in the middle. "Damn, Trouble. This is better than I imagined. And trust me when I say I've been imagining so much lately that I am afraid this might not last long."

"Then I guess we'd better get to it," she said, giving a shimmy of the shoulders and sending the dress puddling to the floor.

"Yes, ma'am."

In one breath his hands were on her ass, pulling her to him and flipping them around until she was on the couch and he was on his knees before her. Looking his fill while completely clothed.

"What are you doing?"

"Getting to it," he said firmly, and before she could object, his shirt was on the floor, his pants unzipped, while his gaze roamed up her body, locking on hers. "Now, you going to let me do my job? Or do I need to pull out the cuffs?"

The only answer he got from her was a moan, low and throaty, and so needy she would have been embarrassed if that talented mouth of his wasn't doing an insane little nip and flick combination a scant millimeter above the little bow of her panties.

His hands skimmed up her legs to her thighs, pressing them wider so he could maneuver himself into place. Shay knew that he didn't need cuffs, Jonah could control every inch of her body with a single touch. He knew how to touch her in a way that had her heart waving the surrender flag.

"Jonah," she whispered, because all of this warmth collecting around her chest wasn't part of the deal.

"I got ya," he said and then his mouth was on the move, going lower and lower and lower still. Everything in its path tightening until—he gave that same little nip and flick combo right up the center of her lace.

"Jonah." This time his name was a plea of a different kind.

"Right here, Trouble," he chuckled, and in case she wasn't clear where *here* was, he did it again, this time pulling the panties to the side so all she got was hot skin on deliciously hot skin.

Shay lay back—she couldn't help it. What the man was able to do with just his mouth was lethal. And his hands . . . strong and oh-so capable, they skillfully tracked over every inch of her body, visiting all the good parts twice, driving her completely out of her mind and bringing her right to the point of no return.

Only he kept bringing her there, then backing off.

She lifted her hips, showing him exactly what she needed, because he was right there and she was so ready. God, so ready. All he had to do was go a little bit harder or softer and he would hit the sweet spot. But these kisses weren't sweet, which was fine with Shay, since she wasn't feeling very sweet. She was achy and worked up and in need of something that seemed to be getting farther and farther from reach with each swipe of his tongue.

"Now," she moaned, hoping that verbal communication would spur him into action.

"Soon," was his only response, followed by a chuckle.

"This isn't funny," she groaned. "Nothing about slowly being driven crazy is remotely funny to me."

"Tell me about it," he said, sounding a little crazed himself, a little out of control—and man, was it a turn-on. Jonah slowly losing control was about the sexiest thing she'd ever seen.

"This"—he whispered while slipping three fingers into her swollen, wet flesh, curling them until they hit the money spot, sending a million tingles racing through her body at once, with no exit in sight—"is how crazy I feel every time I see you."

"Then come and be crazy with me," she said.

"Soon." He gave her one final kiss, the perfect kiss, gentle and demanding and everything she needed, his fingers hitting the spot he'd been teasing around for what felt like eternity, and then she exploded. He literally drove her right out of her mind and over the edge and into the best orgasm of her life.

She cried out, his name slipping so freely from her lips it should have startled her, but her body was too busy trembling from the aftershocks of sheer pleasure for her mind to function properly. In fact, she felt so good she couldn't have made a coherent thought to save her life.

Jonah stirred and she slowly opened her eyes, realizing she was on her back, the couch beneath her and Jonah on top. And they were somehow both completely naked. A condom wrapper on the floor.

"Now?" she asked.

"Yeah, Trouble." He kissed her gently on the lips. "Now."

He entered her in one long thrust, letting her get used to the delicious pressure. After a moment, he began moving inside of her, sure and strong, and if she thought he was a master with his mouth, well, *sweet baby Jesus*, this was even better than before—and that had been the best orgasm of her life.

"I like now," she whispered, her arms sliding around his neck, pulling her to him as he slowly pumped in and out.

"Better than soon?" he asked, kissing her.

"Even better than anytime." She kissed him back and then his hands were everywhere at once.

Touching and gripping, clinging to one another until their skin became slick, hot and burning, creating a friction as they moved, so raw and electric it arced between them, back and forth until they had to fight to cling to one another. But soon the fight became easy and they began to glide in perfect unison.

As if sensing the change, the newfound ease between them, Jonah pushed up on his arms, looking down to where they were joined. Shay watched too, watched as they both found the connection they needed—and maybe more than they expected.

Then his gaze rose to Shay's, raw and fierce, and her skin flushed hotter and she felt Jonah right there with her. Seeing all of her. The parts she kept hidden and the parts she denied.

Suddenly, Shay didn't want to deny herself, she wanted to feel cherished and needed and . . . a part of something more than herself. And Jonah was more, she decided, in all the right ways.

She tightened around him, pulling him in deeper and deeper until he gave one final surge and together they both lost their minds in the most incredible way.

Several moments went by, and Shay lay motionless, relishing the heavy weight of Jonah on top of her. He nuzzled her neck before lifting his head, and Shay changed her mind.

Jonah wasn't the rock star of hot couch sex, he was the grand master. She had the fabric burns on her back to prove it.

"I'm glad we established that *soon* and *anytime* pretty much suck," she said.

"I hate *soon*. With you it's too far away," he said against her lips. "I think *now* is more us."

She liked the sound of *us* coming from his lips.

"Well, how about we try out the word *more?*" she whispered, running her hands down his chest. She couldn't seem to stop touching him, which was fine with her since he couldn't seem to keep his paws to himself either.

"More, huh? That can be arranged." He playfully snagged her lower lip with his teeth, sucking it into his mouth, getting her ready for *more* when his phone gave a distinctive ping.

He groaned, but not the kind that promised any of that *more* she was hoping for. It pinged again. With a tired huff he rested his forehead against hers. "It's work."

Shay reached down and blindly felt around for his jeans. Panties, bra, condom wrapper, denim—bingo. She rifled through his pockets, surprised to find a whole pack of condoms—confident guy—then grabbed his phone. "Here."

He looked at the screen and took in a deep breath. "It's a call-out. Nonemergency."

"Are you on call tonight?" she asked, and he gave her a pained look that said he was always on call. Even worse, she could see that he was conflicted about what to do.

Shay framed his face with her hands, drawing him closer so he knew how serious she was. "Whatever you need to do tonight, Jonah, I'll understand."

And she did. Did she want him to leave their little cocoon that was safe from the outside world? No way. In her shop they were just Jonah and Shay, no distractions, no expectations, no conflicting lives. And she wanted more of that. More talking, more kissing, more sharing.

More Jonah.

But she also didn't want him to feel like he had to change or hide who he was around her. A huge part of Jonah was his job, and she understood and supported that.

"What I need right now . . ." He smiled wickedly, then, to her surprise, powered down his phone. "Is you." He looked over her head and flapped his hand. "And maybe a little privacy, guys."

Shay craned her neck to find three sets of eyes staring back, and laughed. "I forgot to feed them."

At the mention of feeding all three pairs of ears perked up. So did her stomach.

Jonah looked down at her belly and quirked a brow.

"I forgot to feed myself too," she said, using her hands to muffle the embarrassing growling. Resigned to leaving the couch, she tried to move, an impossible task when he refused to budge. "I have to feed them or they will continue staring and then the whining will start. It's not pretty, trust me."

"Are you always on duty?" he teased but didn't let her answer, giving her a quick kiss. "Glad that's settled. Now, you stay here. I will feed the mutts. And then," his eyes roamed down her body and back up, "I will feed you."

"Dessert for dinner?" she said as he rolled off, completely at home in his gloriously naked state.

"I already had my dessert, now I want cake. Don't move."

She watched as his very fine ass stalked to the door, then he stopped and stalked back. The man was impressive from all angles. Taking her wrists, he lifted them above her, made a big deal about positioning them on the arm of the couch, then leaned down and pressed an openmouthed kiss to each of her breasts.

"Now don't move," he ordered. "I'll be back with the cake."

"I don't have any plates," she explained as he disappeared into the other room.

"Then I guess we'll have to get creative."

Shay could do creative. All night long if she was lucky.

ch🐾pter
fifteen

A light tapping woke Jonah with a start. Pulse beating out of his chest, ears dialed to alert, he took stock. He was sticky, hot as hell, and couldn't remember where he was. Then a warm ball of woman snuggled closer, her ass rubbing up against his morning wood and—ah yeah, he remembered now.

Every little detail.

He tightened his arms around her and tried to ignore that his entire left side was stuck to the couch with what he assumed was a superadhesive combination of sweat and icing. His hand immediately found her breast and he pressed a few kisses down her spine, wondering just how tired she was.

She gave a sexy little sigh and burrowed deeper into him, wiggling in a way that made going back to sleep impossible, then she was dead to the world. He wasn't surprised, since he'd checked off nearly every wish he'd had during their marathon meet-and-greet last night.

Well, every wish minus the cuffs.

Taptaptap.

A low growl vibrated on his calf. Jonah peered over to find himself, Shay, and two of the mutts snuggled on the couch. One big fucking happy family.

With a groan, he scooped Socks off his hip and set her on the floor, then shooed Boss off, who landed with a big thud. Jabba was already at the door, tapping *I gotta pee* in doggie Morse code against the glass pane.

"As much as it kills me to say this, baby, I need to get up," Jonah whispered, running a hand over her stomach and back up, maybe high enough to brush her breast. Okay, definitely high enough. She had great breasts—full, high, and just his size.

The perfect size, as far as he was concerned.

Shay stretched, giving him all the go-ahead he needed to continue his inspection, then rolled over, nuzzling even closer and pressing her face to his chest. The rest of her was doing some pretty amazing pressing too, so amazing he felt his eyes roll to the back of his head when she tossed her thigh over his.

"Baby," he groaned. "You're not making this easy."

"You smell good," she whispered, her voice so thick with sleep he wondered just how awake she was. Then her tongue ran up his chest, circling his nipple and answering that question. "Like cake. I love fig cake."

Jonah was a pretty big fan too. After last night, it was his new favorite cake, and he was considering finishing it off for breakfast. He'd just started licking the remains off Shay's shoulder when—

Taptaptap.

He groaned. "Don't move," he whispered, carefully untangling Shay's body from his. Smart-ass that she was, she raised her hands above her head and laid them across the arm of the couch.

"Assume the position. Got it, Sheriff."

She was the most beautiful woman he'd ever seen. And lucky

son of a bitch that he was, she just lay there, spread out like a feast for his eyes, letting him look his fill.

Taptaptap.

This time it was followed by a long-suffering whine that had Jonah pulling on his pants. "Be right back."

He smacked his thigh and the other two dogs followed him to the front of the shop. He clicked on the main floor lights and stopped.

Jabba wasn't trying to get out, he was trying to let someone in. Regardless, Jonah opened the door, and all three dogs bolted past Adam to the nearest maple tree to do their business.

Jonah took in the grim lines on his brother's face and the exhaustion rolling off of him. *Ah shit,* this couldn't be good.

"You're a hard man to find," Adam said, leaning against the doorframe as though it were the only thing holding him upright. His SHFD blues were streaked with dirt and his skin was damp with sweat. "Been calling you all night."

Jonah patted his back pocket and found it empty. He closed his eyes. "Turned it off."

"When I spotted your car," he motioned to Jonah's cruiser at the curb, "I figured it was either that or you were too busy to answer." He looked at Jonah's state of dress, which was more *been busy getting busy* than *fell asleep cat sitting,* and he grinned. "Guess it was both."

Yeah, yeah. "Is everything okay?"

Adam's smile died. "Giles was reported missing at lunch check-in."

Jonah looked at his watch and swore. "That was over sixteen hours ago."

The first eight to twelve hours were the most critical in situations like this. Jonah buttoned his jeans and was turning to grab his stuff when Adam stopped him. "We found him, man. He's okay. A little dehydrated and hungry, but okay."

"Where was he?"

"Asleep on Clovis's back porch," Adam explained. "I guess he went there to get his shag on or whatever it is old people do after hours and had a breathing issue. He didn't have his meds."

"Of course he didn't. Because why would a man with a breathing problem carry his meds when walking across town?"

Adam looked at Jonah's state once again and laughed. "Do you really have to ask?"

No, no he didn't. He understood perfectly.

"When he didn't show for dinner we sent a callout to all departments and Search and Rescue as far as two counties over." The callout that Jonah had ignored. He hadn't even read it, just saw that it was a nonemergency and thumbed his phone off. "Someone matching his description was seen heading into the foothills, by the Old Mill Trail."

Which explained the condition of Adam's uniform. If any team would handle the hills, it would be Adam's. "Why the hell was he hiking?"

"He wasn't. Clovis called about an hour ago, saying there was a peeper on her porch making heavy breathing sounds. The officer who responded found Giles. He was sitting on her porch swing, semiresponsive."

"Where is he now?"

"En route to St. Helena Memorial. I wouldn't be surprised if they kept him overnight for observation. I was headed there when I saw your car."

Jonah dropped his head, letting the reality of what had just transpired wash over him. If he'd answered the callout, Clovis's place would have been at the top of his list for places to check, because he knew what was going on between the two of them.

Man, he'd fucked up. Big-time. And now his uncle was in the hospital.

"Give me a few minutes to grab my stuff and check on the cat, and I'll meet you there."

It was the perfect summer morning, Shay thought, making her way toward Cork'd N Dipped, the completed permit petition in her hands. The sun was bright, and there was a light breeze teasing at the orange poppies and yellow snapdragons that filled the wine barrels lining Main Street. And every few feet she'd come across a resident who would smile her way or wish her good afternoon, as though she was part of the inner sanctum.

The best part? Hanging from every gas lamppost was a banner advertising Prance for Paws Charity Pet Walk and three celebrity judges. Shay had no idea who the judges were, only that Peggy must have been hard at work to secure them this fast.

The banners looked professional and polished and, with a different animal peeking out on each banner, impossible to resist. Harper had designed them, Ida had talked a local printer into donating them, and Emerson had gotten them hung in record time. Her friends had done an amazing job, and not just with pitching in. No, their efforts had gone way beyond that. They'd made Shay feel as if signing that lease had been the best decision of her life.

Funny since last night with Jonah had been the best night of her life. She still wasn't sure what it all meant, but she knew there was something between them that wasn't going away. It was something she would have liked to explore more this morning, but she had fallen asleep only to wake to a note.

Just thinking about Jonah had a little zing buzzing in her belly, and instead of pretending it wasn't there, Shay embraced it.

Smiling like an idiot, Shay pushed through the door to the wine bar. The sunlight reflected off of the floor-to-ceiling glass walls that housed thousands of wine bottles. Cork'd N Dipped had one of the most extensive wine menus on Main Street, and with its midnight lighting, mahogany wood floors, and deep red linens, it exuded elegance and seduction.

Today, however, it was filled with every person she'd gathered to help with the charity walk, all wearing Booty Patrol shirts. The free chocolate-dipped strawberries didn't hurt.

"Look what I have." She held up the completed permit and waved it a few times. Jonah had not only signed it, he'd put a rush order on it. "Kelly at town hall said I can pick up the official permit from Civic Services on Tuesday. But that's a formality and we should be good to go."

"Great news," Harper said from the front of the bar. She was dressed in a pair of faded overalls and glasses and had paint on her right cheek. Not that it detracted from her ability to control the room. "Now, have a seat. Peggy was just getting ready to tell the group who she secured for the Prance Prince and Princess judges panel."

"I saw the flyers," Shay said, taking a stool at the bar next to Emerson and mouthing *thank you*, since Harper was back to running the meeting.

"The pledge sheets are done and ready to be dispersed, so make sure you grab a stack on the way out. They are by the exit. And the sign-up sheets will be in next Monday. On to judges. Peggy, you have three minutes. Starting," Harper looked at her watch, "now."

"This is what happens every time the Coat Crusader hits town," Emerson grumbled, shoving a strawberry in her mouth.

Peggy stood, smoothing down her polyester slacks. "First we have our very own superstar vet, Dr. Huntington, who was more than happy to offer his services." A few hoots and whistles went out for the handsome silver fox, whose way with animals—and women—had become the topic of many a Sunday tea at Paws and

Claws. "I told him we would put a coupon for a discounted consultation or vaccine appointment on the back of each application for his services."

What a great idea, Shay thought. Not only would it encourage people to be proactive with their pets' health, but Dr. Huntington could help spread the word about the charity walk to his patients.

"Will it have his home number as well, for *other* services?" Ida wanted to know. "Because if I told the ladies in my canasta group that he was giving out his digits to anyone who entered, I bet they would all borrow a pet and sign up."

"I'll ask," Peggy said as if *that* was a legit suggestion. She perched her reading glasses higher on her nose and read her agenda. "I also have that TV pet psychic lined up."

Shay's mouth dropped. "You got Sonya Fitzpatrick?"

"Who the hell is Sonya Fitzpatrick?" Emerson asked around bits of red chunks, seeds, and chocolate.

"The lady on Animal Planet who talks to animals," Shay explained. Holy cow. Sonya Fitzpatrick was going to be here in St. Helena, at her charity walk?

"Oh, no, dear," Peggy said, taking her glasses off to hang on the studded chain around her neck. "I was talking about June Whitney. She has a channel on YouTube about how to make crocheted oven mitts and costumes."

Several *oohs* and *ahhs* went up from the over-seventy crowd.

"But she is a pet psychic?"

"Well, yes dear. She has birds. A whole aviary of them. She used to have them deliver messages, but now with everyone having cell phones and e-mail, she rents them out for weddings and such."

"She rents out pigeons," Emerson said, reaching for another strawberry. "Not doves. And the pigeons crap all over the guests. I went to a wedding last year up valley and it was like Alfred Hitchcock's *The Birds*, only instead of blood, there was poop."

Great. "But she talks to her birds?"

"No, dear, her dead lovers haunt her, scratching at her windows and hooting at all hours of the night." Peggy looked at Shay as though she were the slow one. "And who talks to birds?"

"Sonya Fitzpatrick," Shay said. "The pet psychic on Animal Planet. It sounds like June is a psychic who has pets—that's not the same thing at all. You know what? Never mind. Who is the third judge?"

Peggy smiled. "You. As the best pet stylist this town has ever seen. We all think you should be the final judge for the walk."

Well, if that didn't make her all warm inside.

"I'd love to, but I don't know if I'd be the best person. A good portion of the contestants will most likely be St. Paws' former fosters and I really want to enter Jabba and Socks, but I can't if I'm judging. It wouldn't be fair."

"They'll find homes no matter what," Ida said confidently. "And with a five-hundred-dollar St. Helena gift card for first place, we need a good judge."

"We're giving away five hundred dollars?" Shay asked, looking at the crowded bar and wondering if she was supposed to come up with the money.

"It was all donated by local shops." Ida smiled. "And that's just for first prize. We have several smaller prizes for runner-up."

Shay was stunned and completely touched that local shops had donated that kind of money to her cause. That warm feeling expanded to fill her chest.

"Great work, ladies. Moving on to the next topic on the agenda," Harper said, gaining control of the room again.

"There's an agenda?" Shay whispered. Emerson sent her best *welcome to it* smile.

"Since Clovis can't be here today," Harper started, "I told her I would bring up her boa idea."

Harper went on about boas, colors, and themes, and Shay leaned in to grab a strawberry and asked Emerson, "Where is Clovis?"

"She's at the hospital with Giles."

Shay's hand stopped midway to her mouth. "Giles is in the hospital?"

"Yeah, he went missing yesterday, but they didn't find him until early this morning. Nearly every first responder and volunteer turned out for the search." Emerson paused to study Shay with disbelief. "How have you not heard about this?"

Shay put a hand to her forehead and admitted, "I was with Jonah all night."

Emerson's expression was one of surprise and pride. "Wow, you go, cat lady." Then she stopped and her smile faded and she gave a low whistle. "Oh boy, so if Jonah was with you, then—"

"He wasn't out doing his job." And his uncle was hurt. Not that Jonah could have prevented Giles from wandering around town, but he wouldn't see it that way. Jonah was such a protector, the mere thought of what he must be feeling made her throat tighten. "I gotta go. Tell Harper thanks for everything and I'll call her later."

"You understand that you are admitting to an officer of the law to peeping on Ms. Owens?"

"Are you hard of hearing, son?" Giles asked, spooning in another mouthful of Jell-O. "I went to Clovis's place to peek over her fence. Heard she goes in her hot tub after hours."

Jonah leaned in and lowered his voice so only Giles could hear. "A Peeping Tom charge carries a thousand-dollar fine and possible jail time in this state."

"It's not a crime when everyone involved is privy to it," Giles bristled, then lowered his voice and waggled a bushy brow. "It's called foreplay, son."

Jonah looked at Clovis, who was sitting in the chair next to the bed, her hands folded in her lap, her frown so big it nearly detracted from the strapless corset she was trying to pass off as a top. He turned back to his uncle. "What about Celeste?"

Giles made billowing gestures to his chest. "They didn't move, not even when the current in the water picked up. That's not natural. And the girl thinks bocce is an island in the South Pacific, and she doesn't eat meat or sugar. What kind of woman doesn't eat sugar?"

Now things were making sense. "I take it you got Clovis's cake?"

"Lemon-iced fig, my favorite. Set it on my doorstep with a note that said, 'There's arsenic in the frosting. Enjoy.' So I enjoyed me a slice, then went off to return the favor."

"By peeping?"

Giles snapped his fingers. "Now you're catching on. After a decade of circling, I'm closing in. Maybe it's the real deal you hear about in books, or maybe she'll wind up killing me. Either way I'll die smiling. Now, watch and learn." Giles cleared his throat and raised his voice. "Heard she goes in the hot tub nekkid too. Now, write that down and see when the doctor will let me go home."

"You heard him, Deputy," Clovis said, gesturing for him to open the pad of paper in his hand, looking more titillated than terrified. "He was peeping. On me. Clovis Owens. Owner of the Boulder Holder, St. Helena's supplier of naughty and niceties. Write that down. O-W-E-N-S."

Jonah diligently opened his pad, jotted a few notes, then snapped it shut. "Ms. Owens, would you like to press charges?"

Her hand flew to her chest, as though horrified by the idea. "Of course not, Jonah Baudouin, and shame on you for saying such a thing." She checked the doorway to make sure no one was coming and leaned in, "But you make sure that it gets filed in this week's *Sentinel* police beat. I want to frame it for the shop."

And with that, Jonah gave up any pretense of trying to make sense of this mess and shoved his pad in his pocket. "I'll see what I can do." Jonah eyed the two. "No more peeping and no more ridiculous reports, understood?"

Neither answered. They were too busy glaring at each other. Even worse, Jonah thought, using all of his carefully honed control to resist arresting them both for being a pain in his ass, Giles's little stunt had landed Warren, the responding deputy, another gold star in the town's eyes. They were probably going to commission a statue in his honor.

Done, done, and so done, Jonah left the room, punched the button on the elevator, and rode it to the bottom, frustrated beyond belief.

He was relieved Giles was okay, relieved that no one had been seriously injured, yet he couldn't get past his decision to shut off his phone. He was off duty, had done nothing wrong, but for some reason he couldn't seem to let go of the possibility of what could have happened, especially when he turned his phone back on and it blew up with missed calls, texts from Adam, and even a message from Sheriff Bryant wanting to make sure he knew his uncle was missing.

If he won this election, his responsibility to the town and the people in it would increase tenfold. He knew that. Was ready for it even. What he wasn't ready for was last night.

And Shay.

"Shit." He looked at his watch. It was nearly noon and he hadn't called Shay to explain why she'd woken up next to a note instead of him. When he'd gone back to grab his things, she'd fallen back asleep, looking adorable, well-loved, and just his luck, obedient with her hands above her head.

Rather than wake her, which would have led to testing just how obedient she could be, he'd settled for leaving a hastily scribbled note.

Work calls. Last night was amazing . . . J
P.S. The wishing couch works.

On a bag of dog food.

Okay, so at the time he'd been in a hurry and a little out of his mind with worry and guilt. Then his day had gone from bad to shit real fast, and now the window to call and explain had come and gone. And she probably thought he was a complete ass.

Not all that surprising. Nearly every woman Jonah had attempted a relationship with had thought the same in the end. "Emotionally unavailable," his last girlfriend had called him, when in reality he hadn't been physically available enough to even get to the emotional part.

Being on call 24/7 didn't rank up there in the top ten things women looked for in a man. The whole man-in-uniform fantasy got old real quick once they learned what the uniform really meant, then they walked.

He wasn't ready for Shay to walk, he thought as he crossed the empty parking lot toward his cruiser. Which meant he needed to drive to town and explain.

"Hey." The sexy voice had Jonah stopping short. Shay sat on the hood of his car in cutoffs and a tank top that hugged her curves. Her bare feet were on his bumper, and she had a bag in her lap and a sexy smile on her lips that had him remembering every detail of his hands on her silky skin as she cried out his name.

Maybe the universe was throwing him a bone, giving him a chance to get that *more* they'd talked about.

"What are you doing here?" he asked.

Then again, maybe not.

Her smile died at his question and he could see a potent mixture of concern and regret forming on her face. The concern did a number on his chest, but the regret was like a nine millimeter straight to the gut.

"Waiting for you. I heard about Giles and came right over."

Right. Giles. "He's better. A little dehydrated, a major pain in my ass, and quite possibly looking at adding Peeping Tom to his dating résumé, but he's fine."

"Actually, I came over to check on you," she said, never once looking away, but the uncertainty in her eyes did him in.

"Me?" His boots clicked on the pavement as he walked toward her, not stopping until he was in her space. "It was just a search and rescue." One that happened before he'd even gotten off her couch. He was as far from the action as an officer could get. "Why would you worry about me?"

"I figured you heard about Giles and were so busy taking care of everyone else you'd need someone to take care of you." Shay held up the bag, shaking it. The grease stain at the bottom told him there was food in there. Greasy, sent-from-heaven food. "Hungry, Sheriff?"

She shook the bag again.

"Starved." The last thing he'd had to eat was icing, and even though he could go for another helping of last night, he was pretty sure that wasn't what she was offering. Taking the bag, he opened it and smiled. "It's a sandwich."

"Not just any sandwich, but a bro-wich. The triple *B*, if you please. Bacon, bread, and more bacon." She leaned back on her hands, giving him a view of a couple more inches of thigh. And that tank of hers had serious clinging action going on, which made him think of another sacred *B* that would make a nice bro-wich.

"Oh, and there is a doughnut at the bottom, raspberry filled if you're feeling healthy. And," she reached behind her and grabbed a paper cup off the hood, "coffee, black, no frills. Just how you like it."

Something in his throat caught, making it difficult to speak. He'd like to chalk it up to sleep deprivation, or an endless night of sex, but feared it was that elusive *more* sneaking up on him. "Thank you."

She shrugged. "Even Superman has to eat, right?"

He smiled his first real smile of the day. "I'm not Superman."

"Right." She snorted. "Then explain that complex you're so fond of, the one that has you rescuing cats from trees in a single bound and makes you incredibly selfless . . . don't make that face at me, I think it's one of the sexiest things about you. It goes along with that secret sweet side you work so hard to camouflage."

She tugged at his belt, weaving her fingers under the loops and pulling him closer until sweet didn't sound so bad. In fact, it sounded a whole lot like that foreplay Giles was talking about.

"Superman wouldn't have bailed without much more than a note," he said, noticing that the lot was empty and stepping between her legs to rest his hands on the hood next to her thighs. The position gave him a clear view of that summer top she had on, and what she had on beneath—orange satin.

"Jonah, you found out your uncle was missing. Of course you'd leave." She said it without an ounce of mockery in her tone. "You would have gone no matter who was missing. That it was your uncle only made it more personal. But saving people, making their world better is what you do. Who you are. Why would I be upset about that?"

Jonah stood. He was shocked and honestly impressed. "Most people would." And most women in his past had.

"Yeah, well most people suck."

And that was why Jonah couldn't seem to stay away from her. Shay wasn't most people. She might come off as impulsive and reckless, but she was one of the most observant and real women he'd ever met. She took people for who they were, the good with the bad, embracing all aspects. And she had the ability to cut through the small talk and BS and get down to what was important. What mattered.

"You are a protector, Jonah. You take your responsibility for this town and the people you love seriously. Don't ever apologize for that. Things happen, sometimes really shitty things, but that doesn't diminish all of the amazing things you *have* done. No one can be there one hundred percent of the time for one hundred percent of the people, but you can give one hundred percent of yourself when you are there, and that makes a difference in every life you touch."

Jonah hadn't gone into law enforcement because it sounded fun. He'd become a deputy because protecting and serving was who he was. At his core. Even after the tragedy that shattered his world in San Francisco, he'd never once considered quitting.

Sure, he'd come back to St. Helena a little jaded and broken, but he'd signed on as a deputy determined to make a difference, do his duty, and hopefully find some kind of peace. It was ironic the only time he felt any semblance of peace was when he was with the one person who made him forget his duty.

But as Jonah looked down at the understanding in Shay's eyes, he wasn't all that convinced that time off was a bad thing. It had been far too long since he'd allowed himself to breathe. That he was able to with this woman was going to make things hard.

But Jonah had never let hard scare him off.

"Every life counts," he whispered, running his finger over the exact words written on her St. Paws tank top. "Is this the same kind of pep talk you give your strays?"

"No, but I have given it to myself a few times over the years." She looked at him and he felt his entire chest still. "I've actually given it to myself several times since meeting you."

"Why?" he asked, stroking her leg.

"Because you're just so,"—she waved a hand—"you. And I'm not."

His eyes fell to the creamy cleavage peeking out from beneath her tank and he smiled. "I'm glad you're not."

She rolled her eyes. "No, I mean . . ." Her voice softened. "My life wasn't like yours growing up, and I've made some crazy choices. Some I'm proud of and others I question, but I own them all," she admitted, tugging on her necklace, something he noticed she did when she was nervous. "I can be spontaneous and unpredictable and understand that leaping without looking for the net doesn't always work out. But following my heart, even when my head is telling me to slow down, is who I am. It might complicate things or blow up in my face, but I'm okay with that, because it makes life fun and exciting."

And it made her irresistible. For Jonah, a guy who loved structure and a by-the-books approach to life, Shay's guns-blazing lifestyle was a complete turn-on. Not practical in his line of work, but sexy as hell on her.

"What I need to know, though, is if you're okay with that," she said quietly.

It was strange. She wasn't asking his permission or apologizing. Yet at the same time she was giving him a way out, a way to blow this popsicle stand and not be the bad guy. As though this were a breaking point for most people.

Like Shay, he too wasn't most people. In fact, around her, he was the best version of himself.

"I know exactly what I am getting into," he said, cupping her face and drawing her in. "You are the most complicated woman I have ever had the pleasure of meeting." He was close enough to see the stubborn determination flash in her eyes—but also with a deep sadness that came from somewhere else. A place of experience that prepared her for the blow of not being embraced. "Yet when I am with you, nothing seems complicated."

Her eyes became a sea of confusion and hope—he could see the hope hiding way in the back. "What does that even mean?"

"That what I told you last night hasn't changed." He brushed her lips and definitely tasted strawberries. And maybe a little chocolate, and a whole lot of trouble. "I want you."

Then, being a man of action rather than words, he decided to show her just how much.

ch🐾pter
sixteen

By the following Tuesday, the old barbershop was beginning to look like an actual shelter. The debris had been carted away, the walls of the meet-and-greet room were now a welcoming terracotta, and there was a friendly turquoise throw rug and matching pillows Shay had picked up for half price at St. Helena Hardware and Refurbish Rescue to add a pop of playful. The open-air kennels Ida and Clovis had donated had arrived yesterday and were the perfect solution to containment without the downside of confinement.

The shop was ready for the construction crew to come in next week and build out the rest.

And the good news kept coming. Harper had collected nearly one hundred checks from people who had preregistered for the charity walk. At thirty bucks a head, Shay was three thousand dollars closer to St. Paws being a legit shelter. All that was left was to pick up the official permit from town hall. Shay was just waiting on the call.

"Good thing since we only have twelve days until animal control rolls up and starts asking for papers," Shay said to the two wet black eyes blinking back at her.

With Boss now settled happily in his forever home and Jabba already outfitted in his Saints baseball uniform, complete with a bat to keep his mouth busy for the charity walk, Shay needed to make sure Socks looked—and felt—her best for the big day.

A white ball of fur with barely-there legs and haunting doe eyes, Socks was tiny, too cute for words, and terrified of just about anything that made sound. She was also the biggest love bug on the planet and would make someone a wonderful companion, as long as they whispered.

Socks was one of those dogs that, because of a rough start, was sensitive to loud noises. And Saturday she was going to be walking up Main Street in a jungle of shoes and paws clicking the asphalt, with hundreds of mouths moving. Not the best situation for a dog who jumped every time Shay so much as hiccupped.

Shay gave a little clip at the fur around her ears so they would lie flatter. Satisfied, she reached into her apron pocket and pulled out a knitted onesie and held it up for Socks to see.

"Here is what I was thinking," Shay said in her best quiet-time voice. "Saturday, you go as a sock monkey."

It turned out June Whitney didn't just crochet oven mitts on her YouTube channel—she also did specialty items on commission. And Shay had commissioned her to make Socks a couture sock monkey costume with a headpiece specifically designed to block the noise.

"It will muffle all the sound. And . . ." She pulled out the rest of the costume. "It comes with matching little booties, so you don't have to hear your paws click on the asphalt."

Nose twitching with conviction, Socks craned her neck and took a tentative sniff. When she was acquainted with her new out-fit, Shay scooped her up and put the little booties on her feet. Once back on the ground, Socks picked up one foot, then another, trying unsuccessfully to shake off the offensive trappings.

"You have to get used to them," Shay said, getting down on her knees. Carefully she slipped the onesie over Socks' head and body, making sure her booties didn't come off as she slid her munchkin legs through the leg holes.

"You make the most adorable sock monkey."

Socks wasn't sold. Not even close.

"I promise. Go look in the mirror." She set Socks on the ground. Socks took one step and fell sideways. Flat as a board, *boom*, right to the floor. Then lay there. Unmoving. Like roadkill, her little feet sticking straight out to the side.

"It isn't that bad."

It was actually awful. A herd of rabid dogs could have blown through the shop and Socks wouldn't have budged in protest. The door opened and Socks's eyes went wide. *People! People I don't know. Making sounds . . .*

"Yeah, yeah." Shay picked her up and took off the onesie. "But you have to give the booties a try."

Socks hightailed it to the back of the shop, her feet moving so high she was like a dwarfed Clydesdale.

Shay turned around and found Emerson in the doorway, her food cart parked at the curb. She was apparently headed for work—which, based on the red rubber nose and rainbow afro, was a kid's birthday party. "If a single Bozo or Ronald McDonald comment leaves your mouth, I will punch you. In the throat. Understood?"

Shay bit her lip to keep it from curling up and nodded.

"Have you checked Facebook lately?" Emerson asked.

"No, why?" But Shay was already reaching for her phone. From Emerson's tone, she suspected it was a much bigger deal than it being her turn in Words With Friends.

Shay went to the St. Helena page and felt everything inside of her catch and tighten. That terrifying sense of change, one she'd felt too many times to count, pressed in until it was hard to breathe.

Because the top post, with over two hundred comments and likes, was a link to an article Shay had hoped never to see again.

GROOMER TO THE ELITE CHARGED WITH THEFT. FORCED TO PAY BACK THOUSANDS IN STOLEN MONEY TO CLIENT.

Beside the headline was a photo of Shay from two years ago. A photo that brought back every awful memory she had worked so hard to overcome. Every fear and insecurity that Lance had drilled into her, that her childhood had confirmed, and that she'd refused to ever give in to again.

Shay pushed past the lump in her chest that was threatening to crush her whole and looked up, sure to hold her head high.

"It's not what it looks like," she said to Emerson, needing desperately for her friend to believe her. Because if not Emerson, then Shay had no hope of convincing anyone.

"I went to chichi culinary school in Paris and now live in one of the foodie meccas of the world. Yet I peddle a food cart around town and am forced to humiliate myself daily for tips. Nothing is ever what it seems."

"You believe me?"

Emerson shrugged. "Sure. Animals love you and so does Harper. That means you're good people."

"Thank you."

That small offering of faith was huge.

When the whole ordeal had gone down, not a single friend had remained by Shay's side. None had even been willing to hear her out, Lance had made sure of it. She hadn't only lost the man she'd thought of as her family, she'd had to let go of every dream that came along with making Monterey hers.

She wasn't about to let that happen here. Not when she was so close to finding home.

It was nearly five. The *St. Helena Sentinel* was about to go to press any minute, and Shay found herself staring up at Estella's front door. It looked just like all of the other doors Shay had faced down in her childhood—a big, unbreachable barrier that stood between her and what she wanted so desperately.

Acceptance.

"You've got this," she whispered, lifting her hand to ring the bell.

She stopped before making contact because she *so* didn't have this. She was nowhere close to having this. And Estella would take one look at her and know.

Shay drew in a deep breath, threw her shoulders back, and adopted her best *come out swinging* stance. But it didn't help.

All of that take-charge attitude she'd channeled on her way over here evaporated the second she saw that door. Two minutes ago, she had been ready to be the bigger person and extend that olive branch. She'd been ready to take the leap. One look at the door and every memory of just how small she was, how what she had to offer might not be enough came rushing back and she started looking for the net.

And just like when she'd been a scared kid, there wasn't one.

Shay wasn't naive enough to think that leasing a shop meant the town would suddenly embrace her wholeheartedly. She finally understood that if she wanted a home, a real place where she belonged, here in St. Helena, she had to stop waiting for someone to invite her in and just go for it.

Conviction harnessed, she rang the bell. Twice to be sure she was heard.

Nails skidding across a hard surface sounded, followed by snarling, yapping, and Foxy Cleopatra throwing herself against the door—which only made Shay smile. No matter how big the bark, there was only so much a five-pound Pomeranian could do.

Shay decided to take that to heart.

Estella opened the door, but not the screen. She was dressed for dinner with the queen, with designer shoes on her feet and Foxy in her arms. Both dog and owner shared the same bitter expression. "If you're here to ask about Bark in the Park, the answer is still no."

"Actually, I came here as a fellow dog lover to ask you to pull the article in the *Sentinel*," Shay stated.

If the woman was surprised Shay knew, she didn't show it. "I have no control over what the paper prints, as you well know."

Shay resisted rolling her eyes, barely. "No, but you are one of the most powerful women in town and I know you are the one pressuring them to print the article."

"The people have a right to know what kind of person they are entrusting their money to."

It wasn't an admission but it was enough. "That article you found only tells part of the story." A very one-sided part.

"Did you steal that man's money?"

"According to the law, yes." Shay wasn't going to apologize or make excuses for it either. It had been her money to take. Just because Lance had put it in his account didn't change that. "But I'm not a bad person. It was just a bad situation."

"Huh," the older woman said, crossing her arms and not making this any easier.

"This charity walk is going to help a lot of dogs find homes," Shay said softly. "It will also allow me to move the pets I do have to a location where their barking won't bother you. I don't understand why you wouldn't want that to happen. This is a win for everyone."

"Well, it's sure a win for you. Either you walk away with a stack of money or you walk away as the new dog lady."

And suddenly, everything made sense. She had been so busy trying to figure out why Estella didn't think Shay measured up. When in reality, Estella was lonely and scared and she relied on her animals for the same reasons Shay did, to feel love and belonging.

Shay coming in with her blog and calendar threatened the only outlet Estella had to the town as president of the Companion Brigade. It took away her usefulness. And people who had no purpose had no way to connect with others.

"I never meant to make you feel unappreciated for all of your efforts on behalf of dogs in this community," Shay said. "You are one of the leading dog experts around, and I can see now how not asking you to be on my blog or a part of the fund-raiser could have hurt your feelings. That wasn't my intent."

Shay dug into her bag and pulled out her judges' packet. "But intent doesn't matter if feelings get overlooked." She handed the papers to Estella.

"What's this? A signup sheet for the walk-a-thon? Because Foxy and I are not interested."

Of course they were. Estella wouldn't be able to pass up the chance to parade her champion down Main Street.

"No, it's the judges' packet for the Prance for Paws Charity Pet Walk." Harper had put together a list of criteria and guidelines so judges would be on the same page. "This walk is about celebrating pets and their owners, and I can't imagine a better celebrity judge than the president of the Companion Brigade and her seven-time blue-ribbon champion."

"You just want to make sure Foxy doesn't enter because she'd win that crown," Estella said, her eyes glued to the envelope.

"I imagine that she would, but I thought you weren't entering?"

"I'm not. Already told you that."

"Perfect. That means you will be free to judge." Shay extended the packet again.

Estella took it and glanced down at the first page. Her eyes sparkled with excitement that she quickly masked before offering the packet back. "Judging this doesn't mean I will retract that article or that I will lift the ban for Bark in the Park."

"I didn't imagine it would," Shay admitted, although she'd been secretly wishing it would be so easy. "Just like that article won't stop this walk from happening, and it won't stop me from opening my rescue."

And that was the truth.

"I didn't imagine it would," Estella said, then closed the door, but she had the judges' packet and that was all that mattered.

Wednesday morning a loud pinging yanked Jonah from an amazing dream starring Shay, in nothing but skin and cuffs, screaming his name.

He looked at the nightstand to find his phone blinking, then gave himself a second to let his eyes adjust and to take stock. It was eight o'clock and the warm body curled into his chest was not a woman.

It was an annoyed cat, who, grumpy over the disturbance in his world, stalked off to find a new sleeping spot, sure to use his nails in the process. Settling on Jonah's pillow, he gave a big stretch, then curled up, one eye peeled in disgust.

Right, don't disturb the sleep-disturber's sleep. Got it.

Jonah grabbed his cell off the nightstand, sitting up when he recognized Sheriff Bryant's home number. Given the fact that Jonah had ended his shift two hours ago and it was his day off, his best guess was it had to be some kind of emergency.

"Please tell me Giles isn't missing again, because if so, you have my permission to arrest him."

"Giles is at home." The sheriff paused. "As far as I know."

Relieved, Jonah lay back down, propping the phone against his shoulder. "Then what can I do for you?"

"Sorry about the hour. I considered waiting to call, but the longer this goes on the worse it might get." Well, that sounded very doom and gloom. "Are you officially heading up the team for the dog walk?"

"Pet walk, and yeah, I got a few guys from the fire station."

"You might want to reconsider and pull out."

"Why?" Jonah felt every protective instinct he owned man up.

Shay had busted her pretty butt these last few weeks to make this event possible. If he pulled his team, she wouldn't be in compliance with the permit and the event would be canceled.

"According to the morning paper, the woman heading it was arrested for theft a few years back in Monterey County," Sheriff Bryant explained through a yawn.

"Theft?" *Shay has a file?*

Jonah sat back up and turned on the light. The cat quickly flicked his tail around and burrowed his face beneath it. "What does the article say?"

With Shay, theft could have been as simple as liberating animals from a puppy mill or dog-fighting ring. Theft, yes, but enough to cancel the charity walk?

Jonah stopped. When had he become the guy who quantified just how illegal something was? Illegal was illegal, no matter how sexy the perpetrator was.

"I don't know the whole story, to be honest—I'm still in my trunks—but according to the paper, she stole money from one of her customers' bank accounts," the sheriff went on, and Jonah let him because he was too busy trying to wrap his head around the situation to speak. "And yes, I asked. The reporter clarified the facts with someone from our department."

"Someone, huh?" Jonah said, because this had Warren written all over it.

"They wouldn't reveal their source, but if you ask me the timing is weird. Problem is, police records don't lie, and now we have you tied to her charity event two months before the election. It's not going to look good."

Jonah didn't care how it looked. All he cared about was what this would mean to Shay's charity walk. He didn't know a lot about her life before coming to St. Helena, but he knew enough to understand that she'd had it hard. Hosting this event and leasing that space were huge leaps of faith for her.

It was also a great event for the town. So many people had donated their time. He didn't want to cancel it before he had the facts. All the facts. And that meant talking to Shay.

"Give me a day to figure this out," Jonah said, climbing out of bed and heading toward the bathroom.

The sheriff considered that long and hard, giving a heavy exhale. "I can give you until five. But I need your decision by end of the day. I already have Kelly from Civic Services calling to see if she should retract the event permit, and the mayor is breathing down my neck to protect the town from corruption."

Warren probably fed his dad an earful, and even though the mayor was, for the most part, a decent guy, officiating a charity event that Warren tried to sink might come off as disloyal. Even worse, it might appear as though dear old Dad didn't think his son had good judgment. Easier for the man to just eliminate the event altogether.

"You'll hear from me by five," Jonah agreed. He could work with that. It would give him enough time to talk to Shay, read the report, and figure out what was going on. Making a decision based on hearsay and speculation never ended well.

"Just remember, son. This one is on you. No matter which way it swings, it will all fall to you."

Which was what Warren had most likely been planning on.

Jonah ended the call and immediately dialed Shay. Sent to voice mail, he strode to the window and looked out. Her car was gone, but the porch light was still on and—

What the hell?

Lining his street, in nearly every yard, were BE THE BOOTY: VOTE WARREN FOR SHERIFF signs. And in case there was any lingering doubt as to exactly who had decorated the neighborhood, on Estella's lawn stood a larger-than-life cutout of Warren dressed like a smarmy Uncle Sam and pointing. The caption read, WARREN WANTS YOU.

Twenty minutes and sixteen unanswered calls to Shay later, Jonah pulled up to the station. On his way in he grabbed a copy of the *Sentinel* off his desk and headed straight for the locker room. Warren should have started his shift fifteen minutes ago, but since his cruiser was still in the lot, Jonah figured the mayor's son was taking his time primping for his adoring public.

"You want to explain this?" Jonah said, crossing the room and tossing the morning paper on the locker room bench, working hard to keep his anger in check.

"Yeah, I saw that this morning. Tough break," Warren said, not even sparing the front page a glance.

"Are you going to man up and tell Sheriff Bryant you leaked Shay's police records or do I need to?" Because someone sure as hell was going to fess up, and if Warren was too much of a pussy, then Jonah didn't mind setting the record straight.

He had no idea what Shay was feeling right now. Or even if she knew. Which left him fighting a fight where he didn't know the rules.

This kind of story was bad news all around. That it was released a few days before the walk wasn't a coincidence, it was a strategic shot, pure and simple. What Jonah couldn't figure out was the target. Him or Shay.

A few calls around town and he knew Estella had brought the original article to Nora's attention, which prompted the Facebook post. A post he should have known about before this morning.

"Last I heard, police records, for the most part, are public. So nothing to leak." Warren slipped on his duty belt, seemingly unconcerned that in his attempt to get back at Jonah for . . . whatever . . . he'd crushed Shay's chances of opening her rescue. "Just goes to show first impressions can be misleading. I mean, who would have expected your cat-lady girlfriend was a thief?"

First impressions were misleading, but not how Warren was implying. A few weeks ago, Jonah wouldn't have even blinked at the accusation against Shay, but after getting to know her, he knew there had to be more to the story.

"What's your end goal, Warren?" Jonah asked, getting more than a little up close and personal. "To discredit Shay and discredit me in the process?"

"I don't have an end goal, *Deputy*," Warren said, buttoning his shirt. He was lucky Jonah thrived on control. Otherwise Jonah would knock the prick out and be done with it. "Other than to be sheriff. And while you're off getting your fix with the girl next door, I'm out fixing this town's problems."

"That's just it. You're so busy trying to win votes you don't really see what this town needs."

Warren slammed his locker door and spun to face Jonah, getting so close Jonah felt his fist clench. "Ever since you came back to town, you walk around like you're some kind of fucking god. So noble and self-sacrificing. You've convinced people that your shit doesn't stink. Well, that shit you stepped in, it stinks, man, and this time there is no getting past it."

"The difference between you and me is that I'm trying to do what's right for this town and you're only trying to do what's right for you."

"Last I heard, a sheriff hopeful backing a charity event where the benefactor has been convicted of grand theft charges isn't the best thing for this town." Jonah's silence must have set off an alarm with Warren because he laughed like he'd just won this battle. "You're even stupider than I thought. You haven't even taken the time to read her file, have you?"

He should have. The information was available through the police database. All Jonah had to do was pull it up. But something had held him back. He knew there was more to Shay than what was on those pages. Sure, he wanted to know the truth—who wouldn't?—but his gut kept telling him to hold off, that asking Shay was the right thing.

Only his gut had been wrong before, and no matter how much he didn't want it to be wrong this time, facts were facts. And after reading the article, he wasn't sure what the right thing was. Shay wasn't returning his calls, Warren looked way too cocky for this to be some simple explanation, and he had a note waiting on his desk telling him to get his ass in the mayor's office ASAP.

"Yeah, that screams *sheriff* to me." Warren clapped Jonah on the shoulder. "Didn't they teach you at the academy? The first rule in hooking up: always do a background check so you don't get fucked when you're getting fucked."

ch🐾pter
seventeen

Warren was right.

Jonah sat in his recliner, sipping a beer and staring down at the still-closed file in his hands, wondering when his life had spun so far from center. A few months ago, he'd been sharing his bed with a cute EMT from Sonoma, riding the high that he was the frontrunner for sheriff, and running his life much like he did his career—by the books.

Now he slept with a cat that hogged the pillow, he was going to lose the election to a guy who had to go through the academy three times before barely graduating, and he was throwing the whole fucking book out the window for a woman who drove him crazy. And the worst part was, no matter how he handled things now, he was fucked.

No doubt about it.

Which was why, instead of picking up the file and reading about Shay's transgressions, he'd spent the last hour of the workday staring at it. There was no point now. He'd already delivered his answer hours ago—to a shocked mayor and amused sheriff.

It was official, the first annual Prance for Paws Charity Pet Walk was a go. And Jonah was no longer pulling a side job. He was on the books—and the record—representing the sheriff's department as an on-duty deputy. He was also to kick off the event on behalf of the city, since the mayor had a "previous engagement." If anything went wrong during his watch, the mayor had been more than clear the blame would lie solely on Jonah's shoulders.

Meaning if this went south, he'd lose a whole lot more than the election.

Yet every time he looked at the file, all he could think about was the look on Shay's face the other day at the hospital when she'd given him the out. She was certain he was going to take it. And he could have. But he didn't.

He'd meant what he said. Jonah knew exactly what he was getting into with Shay. Which was why he'd gone down to pick up the permit himself. Oddly, it was delayed, he'd been told, because of a hold placed on it from Judge Pricket's office. Something that only cemented his decision to stand behind her. He wasn't sure exactly what had happened two years ago in Monterey, but he sure as hell wasn't going to stand by and watch Shay get shafted because an old lady formed a grudge.

Tossing the file on the table, he glanced at his phone, checking to make sure he hadn't somehow missed a call in the past thirty seconds. Nope. It was after seven and still no word from Shay. She hadn't come home yet either. In fact, he'd called around town looking for her and she was MIA.

What that meant he had no clue, only that his head ached from trying to figure it out. He was equal parts concerned and irritated over her lack of communication.

"Jesus, let it go," he mumbled, leaning back and taking a long pull of beer. One night. They'd had one insanely hot night and he was waiting by the phone and whining that she hadn't called him back. Granted, he had something really important to discuss with her, like why she'd been convicted of grand theft, but he didn't sit around whining about his other cases not calling him back.

If Adam saw him like this, he'd bust his balls.

Mew.

Speaking of busting balls. His ungrateful roommate hopped up on the arm of the chair and started kneading the crap out of the leather. Too tired to reach for the water bottle, Jonah petted him instead. The clawing halted and a low motor started in the cat's belly, which seemed to piss the guy off. He even lay completely flat, not happy about it in the slightest, his eyes somewhere between *I'm going to pee on you when you're asleep* and *don't ever stop.*

The motor revved and the cat flopped onto his side, his eyes sliding shut as he rolled off the chair and onto Jonah's lap with his legs in the bicycle position, making air muffins, which was better than the alternative.

Jonah kept up the attention, noticing that with every scratch *he* was getting closer and closer to feeling relaxed. Kitty Fantastic was getting closer and closer to the drooling level of ecstasy. Jonah felt his breathing become lighter and let his eyes slide shut.

Sometime later a soft knock sounded and he opened his eyes. The chair was tipped all the way back, Jonah's eyes were gritty, and the cat was passed out flat on his back—still in Jonah's lap. Another knock sounded.

"Hey," Jonah said, tapping the cat. "Wake up."

The cat ignored him, dropping his legs to the side to give Jonah full belly access.

Jonah flicked his hands in the universal gesture for *move your ass.* "I've got to move, which means you've got to move."

Like talking to a wall. He gave a little push.

Nothing but purrs.

"Fine." Jonah lifted the cat and placed him on the floor. The second he stood the cat was back on the recliner, curled up and feigning sleep in Jonah's spot.

"When I get back you better be gone."

Not concerned in the slightest, the cat's tail swished up and back and landed securely over his face.

Jonah padded to the door and opened it, letting out a tired breath. He couldn't explain it—the woman he'd spent his entire day chasing was right there on his porch and he didn't know whether to pull her into his arms or strangle her. Both would go a long way toward making him feel better after the day he'd had.

He stepped out onto the porch, and even though the sun had set and night had moved in, the boards were still warm under his bare feet. One look at Shay leaning against the rail, looking out over the street as the breeze teased her hair and the moonlight played off her smooth skin, and Jonah did something he never did.

He hesitated.

First, because her dress, a flowy soft cream that secured behind her neck with a simple bow, exposed the entirety of her back— which meant she most likely wasn't wearing a bra—and showed off those amazing legs. But mainly he hesitated at the vulnerable way she held herself, as though waiting for the porch to crumble right out from under her. And suddenly Jonah understood what Giles had been talking about.

Being with Shay either made him the luckiest SOB on the planet or would eventually kill him. Slowly and without apology.

"So I take it you're still hiding, but no longer from me," he said, walking until he was directly behind her.

"I'm not hiding," she said, continuing to stare out, then she looked over her shoulder. "I never hide."

No, she didn't. Shay might be a lot of things, many amazing and a few irritating beyond belief, but she didn't have a cowardly bone in her.

"I took the day off to drive to Monterey and get proof," she said.

"Proof of what?" Although he knew what she was trying to prove. He just wasn't sure who she cared about convincing. Him or the town.

She snorted. "I'm sure you have a file on me and think you already know the whole story."

"I know what people think happened," he admitted. "As for your report, I haven't read it yet."

She turned around, those big brown eyes zeroing in on him. "You haven't?"

"No, I was waiting to talk to you, to hear what the report wouldn't tell me," he admitted. "Only you wouldn't return my calls."

She closed her eyes and grimaced. "I was so flustered when I left last night, I forgot to charge my phone and it died halfway there." She looked up at him through her lashes. "I wasn't avoiding you, Jonah. I was getting this."

She pressed a file, which looked suspiciously like the one he had on his coffee table, into his chest. He didn't move his hands off the railing.

"You're going to make me tell you, huh?"

Yup. He'd gone this long without peeking inside that file and had faced down his superiors on her behalf. Damn straight, he wanted to hear the story from her lips. Not the black and white that he'd built his career on, but the full-color version that gave him the context of the situation, the texture of her life in Monterey.

So he remained quiet, patiently giving her the time she needed, but not moving an inch.

"One thing about me is that I hate being played." She also hated being wrong, but he kept that to himself. "And I got played and it was embarrassing and it broke my heart and instead of going through the proper channels I reacted."

"Throwing a drink in some guy's face and grand theft are two different things."

"I thought you didn't read the file."

"I didn't. I read the morning paper."

"Oh," she said quietly, looking at her feet. "I was somehow hoping Estella would realize she's hurting more than me and convince them not to print it."

He didn't have the heart to tell her that this now went way beyond Estella.

"You reacted, go on."

"After I turned eighteen I kind of bounced around for a while and somehow found myself in Monterey. It was a big enough city to get lost and small enough to feel safe. I was starting to feel like maybe it was a fit. I had a few friends, a studio by the beach, and a job as a trainer for difficult animals. Then Bruno walked in and stole my heart."

"You dated a guy named Bruno?"

That pulled a small smile from her. "No, Bruno was a pit-rottie mix and former dog fighter with more scars on his beautiful face than anyone should ever have to suffer through. A lost cause in the rescue world. But Lance had seen something in him and adopted him on the spot.

"The only way the rescue shelter would agree to the adoption was if he got professional help dealing with Bruno's aggressive behavior. Bruno was stubborn and scared and most people would have given up the first week, but Lance was determined to make it work."

Which would have made this Lance guy seem like a knight compared to the other people in Shay's past.

"When the last session was over and Bruno graduated, Lance asked me out for drinks to celebrate. He was everything I had dreamed of—nice guy, attentive, loved his dog. He also had a big family and lots of friends, and I fell. A few months later he lost his job and moved in with me. A few months after that he found a new job. In Portland."

Ah, Jesus. Jonah could tell from the look on her face exactly where this was going.

"I guess I wasn't a part of the relocation package, but all my stuff was." She looked at the floor again and Jonah could tell she was working hard to hold it together. "I came home from work and my apartment was empty. I called the cops, thinking that someone had broken in. When Lance didn't return my calls or come home that night, I thought he was hurt. I called every hospital, his family, everyone. Either they hadn't seen him or they wouldn't return my calls. Imagine my surprise when I found a slip from the pawn shop in the garbage for this."

She held up the ring that was always on a chain around her neck. It looked like an antique, with dozens of little diamonds surrounding a deep blue sapphire. Jonah took it in his hands, surprised at how ornate the band was.

She twirled it in her hand, then pressed it to her chest. Finally her eyes met his and the charity walk, the election, none of it mattered. Everything he'd been stressing about all day was obliterated. Because being a protector didn't even begin to explain what he became in that moment. What he felt when he looked into her eyes, seeing the pain and betrayal and heartache that she kept so well hidden, changed everything for him.

It changed him.

"It's beautiful."

"It was my mom's," she said, a sad smile on her lips. "She got it from her mother and passed it on to me, and I wanted to pass it on to my daughter." He hated how she worded it past tense, as though having a family wasn't in store for her. Because she'd make one hell of a mother and a wife. "The man at the pawn shop wanted three thousand dollars for it."

"What did you do?" he asked, although he already knew how this story ended and it broke his heart.

"I found one of Lance's checkbooks in my purse, wrote out a check for three grand, and got my mom's ring back." The look she gave him was pure Shay—raw and defiant and 100 percent unapologetic. And Jonah might have fallen a little more in love with her because of it. "It turns out that even though the money was mine, it's considered grand theft and bank fraud because it was in his account."

There were so many things he wanted say about the situation and that fucker, Lance, but none of them would make it better. Nothing Jonah did could undo what had happened or erase the pain of the fallout. So he pulled her into his arms and held her.

At first she was stiff, not sure if she wanted to give in, but then her body gave up trying to carry the weight and sank into his. He ran a hand up her spine, slow soothing strokes to reassure her that he was here for her. No one had been there for her when it had all gone down, and that pissed him off, but he could be here for her now.

Little tremors shook her body, so he tightened his hold. To his surprise she didn't cry or even speak, just slid her arms around his waist and absorbed his hug like it was her lifeline. And he admitted, silently to himself, that he was pretty sure she was his lifeline too.

The silence stretched on as the gentle summer night surrounded them, the breeze brushing across their bodies and pressing the skirt of her dress against his thighs. The silence drifted past comfortable and into something charged, simmering with growing sexual heat. Jonah noticed that goose bumps dotted her back everywhere his hands moved, and that her arms were no longer around his waist but resting on his hips, her fingers dangling off his back belt loops.

Lifting her head, those eyes of her slaying him, she rose up on her toes, pressing all of her curves against him, making him question yet again if she was wearing a bra. She didn't look away, instead holding his gaze so steady he felt it all the way to his bones. Then she dropped it to his mouth and he felt it somewhere else a whole lot more interesting.

"You could invite me in," she said against his mouth. "If you want."

Oh, he wanted to all right. He wanted to badly.

He wanted to bring her to his bedroom. And it wasn't just to see if her dress would hit the floor with one calculated tug of that bow. Although he wanted that too. Desperately. But he wanted more. And he wanted it with Shay.

Only when he forced his focus off of that bow and back to her eyes he was confused as to how to get there. By the looks of things, so was she.

"Invite me in, Jonah," she whispered, all of that earlier playfulness gone.

She pressed her mouth to his, light and tentative, as though asking permission, and Jonah knew they weren't talking about his house anymore.

"Only if you'll stay," he whispered.

"Even if you have to leave for work?" she asked, her eyes so big and wary his chest tightened.

Shay had spent most of her childhood being shuffled from one home to the next without ever finding a family, and her adulthood giving away animals she loved in hopes that they'd find what she was afraid she'd never have. It was easier for her to grant other people's wishes than to wish for someone who might wish for her back.

"Especially then."

She wrapped her arms around his neck and kissed him. And just like that, everything felt like it fell into place. With a sexy little sigh, she deepened the kiss and all of the weight from the day, from the past few weeks, even the past few years collided in his chest, and he knew that she was so deep under his skin he wasn't sure how much farther he could invite her in. Wasn't sure that he could breathe without her.

One minute his hands were right there, next to that damn bow, and the next they were lifting her. He carried her into the house, kicking the door closed with his foot, his mouth never leaving hers as he walked her down the hallway and into his bedroom.

Once there he didn't waste any time, setting her on her feet and breaking away long enough to find the bow. With an easy tug, the dress fell off her shoulders and to the floor in one amazing swoop, leaving Shay in mile-high heels, cream-colored panties that had her cheeks playing a game of peekaboo, silky skin—and no fucking bra.

"Christ, Shay." She was beautiful. His mind was telling him that she was his.

"My turn," she said, walking toward him, her heels clicking on the hardwood floor. Again she held his gaze while her clever fingers went to work on his shirt, his belt, his pants, then—*hello.*

Her hand wrapped around the length of him, gentle but sure. The heat from her touch shot through his body as she slowly stroked him, base to tip, base to tip, base to fucking tip until he was sure he was going to pass out. His breathing was already nonexistent, then she dipped even lower on the return, delivering a gentle squeeze. Then a not-so-gentle squeeze.

"Christ, Shay," he groaned, his head falling back.

"You already said that, Sheriff," she teased. "Let's try for something more original."

He was down for original. He was down for anything that included Shay's hands on him. And he was especially down with what happened next.

Shay sat on the edge of the bed. He stood between her legs, although he had no recollection of moving, and her mouth—*God, that mouth*—took him in. And he bucked into her, he couldn't help it. She was looking up at him, pulling him deep into her mouth, and his hips went for it and she didn't even flinch, seemed turned on actually, and then before he knew it his hands were fisted in her hair and he couldn't seem to look away or stop moving.

"Fuck." He didn't want to stop moving. He didn't want to stop her. What man would? But he wanted this to be about them and he knew that if he didn't pull back, this would be over before they got to more.

And he wanted more.

"Fuck," he said again, forcing himself to step back.

She released him with a smile. "Is that an order, Sheriff, or your way of making small talk? Because the first time I thought it was conversational in nature, but now I'm not so sure."

"The name is Jonah," he said. "And that was me telling you just how crazy you make me."

Her smile faded. "In a good way?"

"In the best way." With his hand still in her hair, he crushed his mouth to hers. Reaching down, he palmed the globes of her ass, which were straining to be free of the lace confinement. Being a gentleman and always willing to do his part, he divested her of them quickly.

She groaned, locking her arms around his neck and her legs around his waist, then leaned back. All the way back. So that she was lying on the bed and he had no choice but to follow. Crazy thing was—he was pretty sure he'd follow her anywhere.

No questions asked.

He settled over her, a hand sliding up to the small of her back so she was arched off the bed. Taking a moment to enjoy the view, a long, appreciative moment, he dropped an openmouthed kiss to the valley between her breasts and, to cover all bases, he explored the entire region, teasing her until she was panting his name.

Her legs tightened around his middle, pressing his erection against her core. Using their position for leverage, she lifted her hips and rubbed herself deliciously down his length, then back up. Her breathing picked up and he could feel her body straining to create the right friction, friction that had his lungs struggling to take in air.

"More," she moaned. "I need more."

No further explanation needed, Jonah blindly reached for a condom out of his nightstand drawer. He had it located, unwrapped, and in place in record time and finally slid home. That was what it felt like, what she felt like. Coming home.

Being here with Shay, with her looking up at him as if he was everything she could hope for and more, he felt his whole world come into focus. Like he was on the edge of the biggest moment of his life and with the next breath everything would be forgiven, everything would be right.

Jonah slowly started moving as he took a breath. Then another, and by the third he felt like he was floating, but not freely. It was like spiraling out of control.

"Jonah," Shay whispered, framing his face with her hands. That was all it took, that one simple reminder that she was there, and he exhaled. Long and hard, it came from his soul. "I've got you."

"I know," was all he said, and then he was kissing her, touching her, holding on with everything he was because she had him. In the most unexpected way, Shay had him. In every sense of the word.

Jonah moved faster, feeling her body clench around his, but no matter how fast he moved everything seemed to slow and fall into place. Even when Shay's body coiled and they both let go together, she never once looked away, and Jonah realized he was finally breathing and she was his oxygen. He also realized he didn't just want more.

With Shay, he wanted everything.

chapter
eighteen

So you're not even going to read what I drove all that way for?"
Shay asked, looking up at Jonah through her lashes. She was
lying on top of him, her arms folded on his chest, and he was making amazing circles down her spine with his fingers.

"Nope," he said with a grin. "And batting your lashes doesn't
work. Ask the cat."

The cat Jonah referred to was curled on the pillow between the
file and them. Staring.

"What if I make it worth your while?" she purred, giving his
chest a bite.

"Not even then. And before you start sinking your teeth in—
ow!" He smacked her butt. "Are you listening?"

"Yes." Although now he was rubbing where he smacked, and
focusing on much else was difficult.

"I don't need to read it because I already know everything I
need to," he said, tucking a strand of hair behind her ear. And with
an answer like that, how could she be mad? But she was. She'd gone
through a lot to get that file and she wanted him to read it.

The truth was she wanted to make sure he believed her. And that file validated her story. Shay wanted to believe she had overcome her childhood need to be validated, but she had the overwhelming urge to prove to Jonah that she wasn't what her police report said. That she was more than a difficult and temperamental transient thief who bucked the system. Yes, she wrote that check, and yes she knew it was wrong, but her mother's ring was all she had left of her family. Lance had taken everything else. She wouldn't let him take her ring.

"You're not going to let this go," he said, letting out a long-suffering sigh, then craned his neck to kiss the tip of her nose. "All right, if it will stop you from frowning, you can give me the high points."

"I'm not frowning." But she was. Relaxing her face, she said, "It's a copy of the transcript from my trial. At the end, the Honorable Judge Lipmann only fined me one dollar."

She saw the surprise in Jonah's face. "One buck?"

"Yup." She smiled. "He said he would like to throw the whole case out because Lance is a dickwad of the most extreme kind."

"He said *dickwad* in a court hearing?" Jonah reached for the file. "Let me see."

"I'm paraphrasing. Creative license applies." Shay yanked it out of his hands and put it behind her back, which had all of her weight resting down on him—and the man was ready to go again. "Can I continue?"

He ran his palms to her butt and pulled her against him. "Make it fast."

"The dollar part was real. He also let me keep the ring, I just had to pay Lance back for the amount of the check, unless I chose to press countercharges, which I did not." She'd just wanted the whole thing to be over so she could move to a new town—and move on.

"He said he wished he could throw the whole case out, but I did write a hot check and tried to pass it off as mine. So he was stuck."

"And Lance?"

"Off living his life, I guess."

"I'm sorry, Shay," he whispered with so much sincerity she felt her heart sigh.

"It's okay." Holding on to bad things made it impossible to find happiness, so in order to move on Shay had learned to let go. And now she was here. In a town that might just be home with a man she was pretty sure she had fallen in love with.

Mew. Kitty Fantastic stretched out a paw so that it barely touched Jonah's biceps.

"Is it always like this?" he asked and Shay wanted to say no, that she'd never felt like this before. Ever. But she knew he was talking about their audience.

"I find it odd that a man who claims to dislike cats as much as you do owns a cat tower."

"Yeah, I'd been hoping you'd miss that," he said and she laughed.

No one could miss the Towering Tree Bungalow next to his dresser, with all seven feet of carpeted kitty hideouts, a trapeze, and spinning play circle. The only one who seemed to have looked right past it was Kitty Fantastic, who seemed to prefer Jonah's bed to the Harmony Hammock.

"It was either that or accept my recliner is nothing more than a glorified scratching post, and I'm not ready for that yet."

"That's so—"

"If you say sweet," he warned, smacking her butt again, this time a little harder, "I will pull out the cuffs."

A zing of heat shot through her body at the threat. Who knew bossy Jonah could be such a turn-on?

Flashing a wicked smile, Shay leaned up to kiss him, making damn sure that her breasts were grazing his chest, and their other parts were properly aligned. "You, Jonah Baudouin, are a closeted cat lover." She kissed his nose. Then his jaw. "And I think that is about the sweetest thing ever."

Then before he could move, she rolled off of him onto her back. Lifting her hands to the headboard, she crossed them at the wrists. "Is this the position you wanted me to assume, Sheriff? Or did you have something else in mind?"

The sun was high and a cool breeze kicked down Main Street, rustling the leaves of the maple trees and the big GET GLAM AND GET WALKING sign that hung between the marble columns of town hall. Shay sat behind a table, wearing her favorite mossy-green sundress and a neon-orange boa—compliments of the Boulder Holder—and watched as, one by one, pets and their owners lined the sidewalk. They were decked out in their finest attire. It was a sea of studded leashes, faux-fur collars, and critter couture as far as the eye could see.

Registration for the first annual Prance for Paws Charity Pet Walk was officially open and Shay felt like throwing up. She had her permit, everyone around town had been cordial the past few days, and most people even kept their grooming appointments.

But as she sat there, a stack of racing numbers ready to go and a smile so big on her face she feared it might crack, not a single person came over to actually pick up their number.

"Don't everyone rush all at once," she said with a laugh.

No one laughed back. Even worse, no one moved, except Socks, who burrowed deeper into her lap. Shay wished she had someone to burrow into. Sitting there, all alone, it was like she was twelve again, everyone curious about the new girl but no one willing to be the first to welcome her, in case she was deemed uncool.

The Booty Patrol was at the other end of the street, prepping the starting line for everyone's big prance down Main Street, so it wasn't as if she could form a fake line to let the others know that, hey, she had friends. She was cool.

Her eyes scanned Main Street, looking past the swelling crowd, past the Pita Peddler cart stationed on the corner, and past the sheriff's department roadblock, which was keeping cars off the street in downtown, and toward the long red carpet that led from the finish line to the stage. Seated there were two of the judges already in their places and talking to Harper.

The third seat was ominously vacant.

Estella hadn't actually committed to judging, but Shay had been relying on the fact that the older woman wouldn't be able to stay away. Her absence wasn't the end of the world—Shay could always judge if need be. Nope, the end of the world would be if Estella's absence set the tone for the day and sank her charity walk.

Because if nobody came over to get their numbers, Shay would have a charity walk of herself, three old ladies, two dogs, and a duck, and then she'd have to refund all of the preregistration money they'd collected. Money that she'd already given to the contractors who'd been hard at work all week.

"They're waiting for me," a low and gritty voice said from beside her.

Shay turned and the jitters in her stomach kicked up a notch. Because there, coming in at six feet two of department-certified alpha swagger and armed to the teeth with enough yummy male to make a grown girl sigh, stood Deputy Baudouin. He wore mirrored aviator glasses, combat boots, and a smile that told her beneath the Kevlar and ammo was just Jonah. Her Jonah. The guy who caused those silly little zings.

Zings that did double time when she saw what he had strapped to his hip. In his holster, also looking locked and loaded, sat Kitty Fantastic in a black tee that said BACKUP.

Following her gaze to his hip, he shrugged. "Wouldn't let me near him with a leash, acted like it was an insult to his entire species, so I told him he could ride sidearm, as long as he promised not to scratch my recliner."

She fought hard to hide her grin. "How is that going?"

He looked at Kitty Fantastic, who had his little paws on the rim of Jonah's holster, and gave his ears a ruffle. "Don't know. We haven't really figured out the whole 'no litter box' thing today, but we're working on it."

"Are you allowed to have him when you're on duty?" Shay asked.

"After we finish the walk, he'll go back in his cage at the station."

Shay found it hard to talk past the lump in her throat. "You're walking?"

"Yes, ma'am." He smiled. "That's what I was saying. Everyone here is waiting for me so they can pick up their numbered bib."

Shay looked around and noticed that people were starting to meander a little closer to the table now that Jonah was there. Was he her ticket to acceptance? Not that she wouldn't accept the one degree of separation, but she had hoped that she could win the town over on her own. Not on who she was sleeping with. She'd been there with Lance—and look how that ended.

Shay swallowed. "I don't understand."

But even as she asked the question, it started to make sense. Mrs. Moberly was standing just a few feet away with Boss, who was decked out in enough gold chains to pass for a mob don. She raised her hand and waved, big and open and all smiles.

Beside her, parked next to the curb in her scooter, was Ms. Abernathy with Yodel riding shotgun, a silver helmet on his head, a black leather vest on his back, his paws resting on the handlebars. Even Mr. Barnwell was there with Domino.

"Trouble, in this town every parade is kicked off by someone in the mayor's office. Usually it is the mayor, but he put this event in my hands, so today that honor goes to me."

Shay wondered if the mayor's absence was due to the article or his son's ridiculous campaign, then decided not to focus on who wasn't there and instead on who was.

"And since there is some kind of numbered bib rumor flying around, people were waiting for me to sign up before they got in line." Then he pulled an application from his front pocket, making sure to flap it around to draw as much attention as possible, before setting it on the table. Not that he needed the theatrics. Pretty much every eye on Main Street had zeroed in on her table the second Jonah strode up. "I'd like to enter Kitty Fantastic in the charity walk."

Adam came to stand beside Jonah and cleared his throat. When Jonah let out a big, irritated sigh, Adam waved his hand impatiently as if to say *Please, go on.*

Jonah glared but pulled out a deputy's ball cap that was hanging from the back of his utility belt. "And I have over a dozen sponsors, mostly guys from the department and family members, each pledging a hundred bucks if I wear the hat."

He shook out the hat, placed it on his head, and frowned. Across the front of the cap, and under the department title of deputy, in the space that was usually blank, was an additional word. It looked a part of the hat, as if it were officially department issued.

"Deputy Pussycat?" Shay put a hand to her mouth to keep from laughing. "You'd really wear that?"

He quirked a brow.

Of course he would, she thought. Jonah would do just about anything for the people he cared about. At the thought a zing ricocheted through her entire body and that bead of hope that had started a few days ago began to grow and take form.

"I offered him a grand to scratch out the cat part, but he wasn't game," Warren said, walking up to the table, his hand resting on his sidearm. "Guess he wasn't man enough."

"Oh, I guarantee you that isn't the case," Shay said with a knowing smile. Then she turned her attention to Warren. "Jonah could walk down Main Street in nothing but those pink fuzzy cuffs of yours and this town would only see a hero."

Shay plucked a button from the box on the table, one of the hundreds she'd had made up especially for today, and pinned it on her shirt. It was blue and simply said, BAUDOUIN FOR SHERIFF.

"Jonah doesn't need frills or cute gimmicks to win. He's already sheriff. He just doesn't have the title yet."

"I like you," Jonah's sister, Frankie, said, shoving Warren aside. She was tall, toned, and looked like she could do some serious damage if she chose to. Thankfully, she pulled out two buttons from the box and pinned one on herself, the other on Warren, then smiled, daring him to take it off.

"Whatever," Warren said, storming off and, Shay noticed with amusement, not tossing the button in the garbage can until he was safely across the street.

"Good to see you too, Deputy Asshat." Frankie waved good-bye to Warren—with her middle finger—then turned back to Shay. "I want to register my alpacas."

Fingers between her lips, Frankie let out an ear-bleeding whistle that had Socks up, off Shay's lap, and hiding in the bottom of her purse before the three alpacas clopped their way across Main Street.

When they arrived they head butted their mama and started humming. Frankie snapped her fingers and, with a sigh that Shay had heard other big brothers give, Jonah produced another application and check.

"He's paying for my admission. Part of Blanket's birthday present." She rubbed the smallest alpaca's head and delivered a kiss right to his nose. Then she eyed Jonah and smiled, a bit smug. "He's a good uncle. Always knows just what to pick out for his nephew."

Shay focused on processing Frankie's paperwork, because really, the man had just done the sweetest thing ever, and laughing at him over his sister handing him his ass in one look wasn't nice. She handed Frankie a participant bib for each of her alpacas. Frankie ripped off the sticky paper, slapped the number two on Blanket's chest, then turned around and said, "Who's next?"

Once Jonah's family had cleared out, Shay handed him Kitty Fantastic's participant bib, number one for the leader of the parade. Their fingers brushed and her breath caught. Her heart . . . well that was doing some pretty serious pounding. Shay found that she couldn't look away, no matter how hard she tried. She was drawn to him. Mesmerized by the mystery of a man who was so private and serious yet scared of his sister and carried a kitten around in his holster.

"I really want to kiss you right now," she whispered because people were starting to line up by the masses.

"Trouble," he said and, even though she couldn't see through the mirrored lenses, she knew the look he was giving her. Her cheeks heated. "I traded in my gun for a cat named Kitty Fantastic and I am about to walk down the middle of town and pronounce I am a cat lover. We're going to be doing a whole lot more than kissing tonight."

Shay could deal with that. Her eyes fell to his cuffs, which hadn't come into play because Jonah had been more interested in a different position, and she licked her lips.

"Damn straight," he said, then grinned. And man, when he showed those teeth he was devastatingly handsome. "Oh, and Shay, there is something for you and Socks at Paws and Claws."

He turned to walk away, to let the next person register, and she grabbed his hand. "Thank you. For everything."

"Anytime," was all he said, but somehow it sounded a lot like forever.

Forty minutes and over three hundred entries later, Shay hustled down to the end of Main Street. The turnout was larger than she had expected, and even when she ran out of participant bibs, the people kept coming. Harper stationed two of her best art students at the table to hand-make numbers for the rest so Shay could take her place at the judges' table.

The walk was about to begin and Estella was still a no-show, which meant Shay needed to be in her seat to judge the contestants. Peggy had volunteered to walk Jabba and Socks—not that they could win the crown, but she still wanted them to participate to get the exposure. That was if Peggy could convince Socks to leave the safety of the spa's front desk, where the poor thing had taken cover the second Shay had walked into Paws and Claws.

Shay hadn't even had the chance to see what Jonah had left them. Harper had frantically come in, telling Shay she needed to get to the judges' table immediately, that they couldn't start without her there, and that the entrants were getting restless—and loud.

Shay had left her pups to the care of Peggy and was about to take her seat.

"I can't believe how many people came," Harper said, ushering her toward the stage. "I mean, even the St. Helena's Mommy Club is here with their strollers and toddlers glammed out. I explained that the winner must be an animal, and a few said they could make their case in the event they were chosen. And look over there"—she pointed—"the Stable Swingers."

Sure enough, at the back of the pack was a handful of gray-haired cowboys, swinging their lassos from atop their beautiful horses.

Still ushering, Harper went on to list every person she'd ever met who had turned out, and nearly every St. Helenian was there. Then she went on to point out the nonlocal animal groups that had come to St. Helena just to celebrate the day. It was overwhelming.

"Okay, now be sure to thank everyone for coming, then give a special thanks to all the stores and people who helped," Harper explained, handing Shay a list. "To make it easier."

"What? I have to talk?" Shay stopped and looked down at the list and felt her palms sweat. She didn't even recognize half the names there. Not to mention the sidewalks were overflowing with spectators and behind the starting line was a small army of entrants and their owners all expecting a good time.

It looked like Noah's ark had capsized in the middle of town and now the animals were waiting for Noah to lead the way.

How Shay had become Noah, she had no clue.

"Usually the mayor officiates the event, but since he is a no-show and Jonah is at the other end walking, it's all you, girl." Harper gave her a hug, then pushed her toward the mic. Hard.

Shay took a hesitant step, then tapped the mic. It echoed through town, silencing the crowd.

And there she was again, standing in the front of her new homeroom, introducing herself to a sea of strangers who, at the end of the day, may or may not accept her. "Hi. I'm Shay Michaels, and I wanted to thank you all for coming to the first annual Prance for Paws Charity Pet Walk."

A round of applause erupted and Shay even heard a few whistles. She looked down at the front row and found Harper giving her a thumbs-up and a bright smile. Clovis stood beside her, holding a YOU'VE GOT TAIL sign. And behind them, in a Hello Kitty T-shirt was Goldilocks, looking at Shay as though Shay were a true saint.

And despite all of her nerves, all of her fears that she wouldn't fit in, Shay felt a genuine smile form on her lips. This wasn't one in a long line of new classes she'd have to confront. This was St. Helena. A place she was going to spend the rest of her life getting to know. And it seemed as though they were willing to get to know her back. Some people would tolerate her, some people would like her, and if she was really lucky, some people might even grow to love her, like she had grown to love this town.

Liar, her heart whispered, because there was a whole lot more here that she loved.

"So without further delay—"

"We'd like to introduce the official for the afternoon," Estella cut in, knocking Shay aside with one swish of her meaty hip. "Please welcome one of the most influential and respected men in this county as well as a staunch supporter of animal rights, my husband, the honorable Judge Pricket.

"Well, move, dear," Estella snapped, swatting her hands at Shay. "Escort me to my seat and let the man officiate."

When Shay still didn't move, Estella took her by the arm with a tut and led her back to the judges' table, where Foxy Cleopatra, dressed in Dior and surrounded by all nine blue ribbons, was already holding court.

"You came," Shay said as Judge Pricket told a few jokes and got the crowd going.

"You couldn't have an event this close to Bark in the Park and expect Foxy and me not to show. That would be,"—the woman grimaced—"unnatural. Now, pull out my chair and make a big deal of welcoming me to the panel."

"To show how united we are?" Shay pulled back the chair.

"No, child, to show everyone that I am the official dog lady of St. Helena." Estella stopped, looked at the chair being pulled out, placed a humble hand to her chest, waved Shay off with the other, then turned to the crowd and gave a big welcoming wave.

Shay rolled her eyes but played along. She didn't care about perception, she just cared that Estella was taking the olive branch and—Shay paused to take in the sight—maybe even extending one of her own. Because walking down the street to join the others behind the start line was the entire Companion Brigade. Dressed in their dog show best, they positioned themselves, not in front of the pack as Shay expected, but interspersing themselves among the other entrants as equals.

"That's just for today, child. Come Bark in the Park, we will resume our standing," Estella said loud enough that only Shay could hear, then handed Shay an envelope. "That is the registration and payment for the entire brigade and some additional pledges we raised."

Shay felt her eyes burn. It wasn't just some additional pledges, there was over three thousand dollars in the envelope. Three thousand dollars that, because of Estella, meant Shay would meet her goal.

"Oh my God." St. Paws Rescue would be an actualized shelter. She wouldn't have to give up her pets and she wouldn't have to move. More importantly, she would be able to call St. Helena her home and really mean it.

"Thank you," Shay whispered, pressing the money to her chest.

Estella clicked her tongue. "Don't get sappy. This is because I can't stand another day of the incessant yapping and morning poops on my lawn." She patted Shay's hand and then smiled—at the crowd. "Now pay attention, here comes that man of yours."

Shay looked up, surprised to find that the walk had started. And at the front of the group, looking bigger than life and sexy as ever, was Jonah. The sun gleamed off his badge and his smile went straight through to Shay's heart.

She loved him. The most uptight, irritating, and adorable man in all the land, and she loved him with everything that she was.

"Who's that, the snow princess?" Estella asked, pointing to—*no way*—Socks leading the pack. Shay had to blink. This must have been Jonah's surprise. He wasn't just walking Kitty Fantastic—he also had Jabba, who looked sporty in his Saints baseball uniform, head high, holding that red plastic baseball bat in his mouth like it was prey that he'd hunted, captured, and was bringing home, and Socks. Little, shy Socks, who was a snow princess indeed in ice-blue booties, a matching scarf, and miniature earmuffs with snowflakes sticking up from the headband like an ice crown. She looked adorable, noble—and like a loveable, confident companion.

Her little feet picked up and down in the perfect prance, her head not moving an inch as she strutted up Main Street as though this was hers to win.

Shay found it difficult to speak through the emotion clogging her throat. "That's Socks. She's a teacup Maltipoo."

"She is a contender," Estella said, and if Shay didn't know any better she'd think the older woman sounded impressed.

Shay opened her mouth to say that Socks wasn't eligible for the prize, then closed it. She wasn't a judge, so there was no reason her dogs had to be excluded in the running.

"I don't know," Dr. Huntington said, leaning over. "The Scottish fold in the deputy's holster looks to have caught the eyes of the crowd."

Shay would have to take the vet's word for it, because it was someone else entirely who had caught her eye. As he got closer he took off his glasses, and the look he sent her said that he wanted to be caught.

By her.

ch🐾pter
nineteen

An hour later, Kitty Fantastic was back in his cage and Jonah was officially a deputy again, which meant he was supposed to be covering the corner of Main and Adams Street, not standing behind the stage watching the judges tally their scores. But he needed to speak with Shay. It was urgent. So he'd agreed to wear his new Deputy Pussycat hat to the next fire-police softball game if Adam would stand in for him.

"Excuse me, Miss Michaels," Jonah said in his most deputy-like tone. "We have a situation that needs your attention."

"Is it Jabba? Did he steal someone's baton again?" Shay asked, her eyes wide.

Her lips, however, were glossy and lush and he wondered what would happen if he leaned down, right there in front of the town, and kissed her. Then he wondered if the rumors on Nora's Facebook page were true that Shay was wearing something from the Boulder Holder, and if so what color it was. And what it covered—if anything.

Then he realized it was poor form to walk around with a hard-on in uniform and said, "No, ma'am. But if you could just come with me."

"I'll be right back," Shay said to the judges, but Estella waved her off as though she had everything handled.

"Is everything okay?" she asked once they had cleared the stage area.

"Just come with me," he said, then rested his hand on her lower back in the most deputy-like way possible.

He wove them through the sea of people, past the blockade, and into the alley next to the soon-to-be St. Paws. Once they were out of sight, he took her hand and led her around the corner. Without another word he pressed her up against the wall and took her mouth.

Shay was surprised at first, which he took advantage of, then she fisted her hands into his shirt and yanked him close. And God she tasted good. She felt even better rubbing up against him like a cat with an itch. And he wanted to scratch it, he really did, but she had a prince and princess to crown and he had to get back to his post pronto.

But he'd spent all afternoon watching her flit around town, charming the locals and tourists alike, determined to make her dream a reality, and he wanted to take a moment to tell her how proud of her he was.

He also wanted her all to himself before the winners were announced and she went back to being the rescue lady of St. Helena. He needed some serious rescuing too, and she was the only person who could help.

She pulled back enough to look up at him, her face flushed and her eyes blazing. "That is a pretty big problem you have there, Sheriff."

"It's been pressing all afternoon." To show her, he flattened her against the wall with his body and dropped his head to nip at her neck.

"Seems to be growing by the minute." With mock concern, she took his hand and placed it on her bare thigh, slowly sliding it up her silky skin, under that dress he'd been thinking about and—*look at that*—a tiny scrap of lace barely covering her. "How is it looking now?"

He ran a finger around the lace edging at the bottom. "I can't see."

"Oh." She shifted her leg, giving him better access. "Well, they match your eyes."

"Blue?" He took that access and upped the ante by sliding his finger around the back to find that there wasn't much more than a string back there.

"Lethal," she whispered.

He was toast. One touch and he could feel the dampness beneath the silk, the need pouring off of her. He ran his thumb up the center, loving it when she released a sexy little purr. So he did it again, and she pressed against his hand as though she'd been fantasizing about him touching her as much as he had her. And he'd fantasized all right.

All. Damn. Day.

"So, what do you think?" she asked.

That even though he hadn't seen them yet, he'd found his new favorite color.

"Definitely lethal," he murmured against her mouth.

Everything about her was lethal. Shay was sexy and driven and so damn beautiful it hurt to look at her. But it was this playful side, the one that made him smile and forget about all the drama, that reached out and pulled him in. All the way in.

No one had ever gotten to him like this. The truth was, no one had ever gotten him like she did.

"Ladies and gentlemen, we, the judges, have narrowed down our decision to five outstanding critters," Estella's voice boomed down the alley.

"They are about to announce the finalists," Shay said, pushing him a step back and smoothing down her dress.

It didn't help. Not one bit. The fabric was bunched and wrinkled, her lips were wet, and her eyes were heated. She looked thoroughly turned on.

She took a step forward, but Jonah didn't budge. Shay's breath caught—he could see it in the base of her neck. Pulsing. Her eyes fell to his hands, which were back on her hips.

"You have to let me go," she whispered.

It was as though he heard the words but his body refused to listen. He told his hands to let go, but they didn't. In fact, they gripped her hips tighter, pulling her closer because anything else felt wrong.

She must have felt the same because her hands were gripping the front of his pants. With a smile she gave him a quick kiss and said, "I have a charity event to host and you are supposed to be tending to the crowd and handling sheriffy business."

He wanted to be handling something else entirely but knew she was right. With a reluctant groan, he let go. "Tonight, when I get home, I expect to find you in my bed so we can finish up this issue."

"Unlawful entry isn't my thing," she teased.

"Which is why I am giving you this." He reached into his pocket and pulled out his key ring. Taking the house key off, he placed it in her hand, then brought her fingers to his mouth to kiss them. "And Shay, be waiting in nothing but the panties."

"Thank you, everyone, for coming out and supporting St. Paws," Shay said into the mic, but her eyes were squarely on Jonah, who was standing to her side with Kitty Fantastic, looking decidedly fine.

Her mind, however, was still back in that alley, contemplating the key in her pocket. The key to his house. Which he gave her.

Dear God, if she hadn't been all-in before, she was now.

Shay had never been given a key to someone else's house before. Even when she'd been in foster care she'd been forced to knock on the front door if it had been locked when she'd gotten home from school. So she couldn't help but wonder if this key was Jonah's way of inviting her into his house. Or into his life.

"Because of each and every one of you," Harper said from beside Shay. She was holding the Coat Crusader chart and it was all the way filled in, even spilling over the top. "We have raised enough money to open St. Paws Rescue and create a fund to spay and neuter over a hundred strays next year."

A loud applause filled the streets along with barking. Lots of barking.

Shay let that settle—the *we* and the money—and gave her friend a hug. "As a token of how much this means to us at St. Paws, we'd like to invite all of you to the shelter's grand opening next Thursday. We will have wine and appetizers, pet friendly of course."

"And the Cuties with Booties," Ida hollered from the front row. "Don't forget to tell them about the cuties."

"There will also be some of your favorite men and dogs from the Cuties with Booties blog on hand for a meet and greet."

At that, a slew of hoots went up.

"And now, if you will all get on your feet and give another round of applause for today's Prance Court, we will crown the winners and ask them to make their final prance down Main Street." Shay took the mic off the stand and handed it to Judge Pricket, then went to the podium to get the ribbons ready.

"The winner of the very first Prance Princess"—Judge Pricket looked down at the winner sheet—"comes straight from St. Paws rescue herself, and is available for adoption. Ladies and gents, let's hear it for Socks!"

Shay's eyes misted over a little at the announcement. She knew she was supposed to be impartial to who won, that it was all done in fun and support of all the animals, but her Socks had won.

She couldn't believe it. A pair of booties and custom earmuffs and the skittish Maltipoo had become a phoenix, rising above her fears to steal the show. Shay had already received over a dozen inquiries about adoption applications since they'd first announced the finalists twenty minutes ago. She was sure to have another dozen by the end of the event now that Socks was the crowned princess. But best of all, Socks was going to go to a nice family.

"Did you hear that?" Peggy squealed and set Socks on the ground.

Since Jonah was standing behind her holding Kitty Fantastic, who had also finaled, Peggy led Socks to the winner's circle, where Shay got down to pin a ribbon to Socks's scarf and kiss her nose. Socks let out a big *yip*, then took the steps two at a time to prance the red carpet like she owned it.

"And the Prance Prince," the judge went on, "is another local-grown pet who spends his days eating everything in sight. Congratulations, Blanket."

"Damn straight," Frankie shouted, shooting a single fist in the air. She made some kind of victory circle around Jonah and Kitty Fantastic, thrusting her hips and looking as if she'd just spiked a ball, then led her alpaca down the red carpet—Blanket humming the entire way.

"And for our three runners-up, who all receive a two-hundred-and-fifty-dollar gift card, let's hear it for Shasta, Awesome Bob, and Kitty Fantastic."

One by one they came to the winner's circle to collect their ribbons, but Jonah waited until last.

"I'm sorry your sister beat you," Shay said, taking her time to secure the button on the holster, not feeling guilty that her fingers kept slipping. Kitty Fantastic was fast asleep.

"The alternate is I win and she never forgives me." He smiled. "Trust me, this is better for everyone involved. Wait, why do I get two ribbons?"

"This one," she touched his holster, "is for Kitty Fantastic. And this one," she touched the back side of his utility belt, "is a first-place ribbon for best tail in wine country. I have finished my investigation, Sheriff, and have decided that yours is definitely worth perusing."

He grinned in a way that had her heart singing.

"Stop smiling," she scolded and he smiled bigger. "You're distracting me from my job. Go walk the carpet."

"As long as I get to distract you later." And with a wink he strode away, Shay watching him as he went. And yes, definitely best tail in all of wine country. Maybe even the whole planet.

And it was hers. She had the key to prove it.

"When you're done checking out my brother's ass," Adam said from behind her, "we need to talk."

Shay turned and froze.

Oh boy, Adam did not look happy. He didn't look mad either. He looked concerned, which didn't seem right for a man who had two speeds: easygoing and balls-to-the-wall.

"Tell me again where you got the kittens," Adam said and Shay's pulse skidded to a stop.

"I never told you where I got them." It wasn't a lie. Besides Peggy, she hadn't told anyone of their origin. In fact, she really didn't know much beyond they came to her in a box. She hadn't wanted to figure it out. She'd posted a small Found ad in the back of the paper, between the obituaries and June Whitney's ad for seasonal oven mitts, when all she had to do was ask Goldilocks. But asking Goldie would mean knowing, and knowing would mean having to go through the proper channels, and she knew that those kittens wouldn't make it.

"Good, then let's start there," Adam said, taking her by the arm and leading her offstage. "How did you happen to come across this particular litter of kittens? More importantly, how did one end up at my brother's place?"

"The owner was unable to care for them so I promised to find owners who could. I asked Jonah if he could watch—"

"Cut the shit, Shay. You're BS-ing a guy who knows how to sweet-talk his way out of any situation, including sleeping with my ex's sister, calling a woman by the wrong name, and being caught with my pants down by my battalion chief . . . when I was with his goddaughter. So get to the truth and get there quick, because I am trying to figure out if you are just too stupid for your own good or if you're trying to fuck with my brother's life."

"What?" Shay yanked her arm away as though Adam's words had burned her. "The last thing I would ever want is to make Jonah's life harder." And she wasn't stupid. Big-hearted maybe, but not stupid.

Adam turned his ball cap to the back of his head, but she could see some of his fury fade. "Okay, that's good, because telling Jonah he's screwed is one thing. Telling him that you screwed him over would suck, because I think he really likes you."

Shay wanted to ask more about this "he really likes you" comment but figured it was best to stick to the problem. "I found a box with my name on it." She went on to tell him the story, leaving out that she was pretty sure Goldilocks was the delivery person. "I asked Jonah to watch one of them. They are both stubborn and way too grumpy for their own good, so I thought they might bring each other a little companionship."

Adam let out a breath. "I just overheard Mr. Gillis talking to the sheriff about how Kitty Fantastic—thanks for naming him that by the way—was one of the stolen kittens he reported missing a few weeks ago. He saw him in the parade and wanted to have Jonah arrested for stealing the litter."

"Oh no," Shay said, feeling as if she might be sick.

"It gets worse. The guy is claiming that maybe it was a cover-up since he called the station and no one responded or followed up," Adam said. "He wants the cats back and he wants someone to be held accountable. I think he is just after the prize money but this whole thing could ruin Jonah's chances of sheriff."

Oh God. What had she done?

"I never meant for Jonah to be caught up in this and I promise I will fix it," she said, then took off running for the sheriff's department.

She needed to tell the sheriff exactly what had happened. Set the record straight. She'd taken one look at those cats and knew she'd do anything to save them, but right then Shay wasn't thinking about the kittens. She wasn't thinking about her shelter or herself.

She was thinking about Jonah, and how she had to make this right so that he wasn't obliterated by the tornado that was Shay's life. He was by-the-book and she was take-it-as-it-came, and yet he'd known that and had gone out on a limb for her anyway. He'd taken on Warren, the mayor, even the sheriff to give her the chance to prove herself to this town.

And how had she repaid him? By having him walk down Main Street with a hot kitten in his holster.

Shay hit Adams Street and shoved through the front doors of the station, only to come to a stop. Because there, looking confused and taking the heat from not one, but two people he answered to, was Jonah. And beside him was Warren, soaking it all in.

Jonah looked at her and her heart thudded hard in her chest once, and then stopped.

She was too late. And she might of have just blown the best thing in her life.

"Is it true?" Jonah asked, his voice so remote, so distant, she knew in that moment that everything between them had changed. "Did you steal the cats?"

"No," she said, then thought better of it. "Technically yes, because I didn't follow the proper channels, but a box of clearly neglected kittens showed up with my name on it and a note saying that the kittens needed a good home."

"Did you check to make sure that the person who gave you the kittens had the right to release them to you?" the mayor asked, and Shay shook her head.

She knew that was the first rule in animal rescue but had chosen to overlook it anyway. "I took one look at their condition and knew they had been mistreated."

"Why didn't you come to me?" Jonah asked and Shay felt her heart break.

Because I was scared. Because I knew you'd tell me to take them back and I couldn't give up on them. Because I think I was already in love with you and I didn't want to have to choose. "Because I didn't think that the sheriff's department would have taken my concern with the same level of seriousness. Pets get neglected every day and no one does anything."

"Got it," was all Jonah said, but his face told so much more. He was frustrated and hurt and, worse, disappointed. In her. In his decision to trust her.

It was the kind of look that Shay knew well, the kind that breaks the skin first and hurts a little worse with time. It was a look that she had finally started to believe she'd never see again. Only this one, coming from Jonah, didn't just hurt. It burned through.

"Well, I can look into these accusations," Sheriff Bryant said, his tone gentle. "But what concerns me is that you are admitting keeping property, which you believed might have been stolen, for the purpose of selling it to someone else."

"Them," Shay said and swallowed. "Not 'it' but '*them.*'"

The sheriff's expression told her the pronoun she chose to use didn't change the fact that she had stolen property in her house.

Which felt weird even thinking because Shay had never thought of her animals as property or the fees as selling. They were little lives that she got to help on their journey, and the adoption fees were there to make sure that people who applied for the animals would value them, and to help offset the medical costs.

"I don't make any profit off of my animals, sir. I just wanted to find them a safe, loving home," she explained. Then, determined not to make any excuses for her behavior, she added, "But I can see how it would look that way."

"The problem I'm having," the sheriff began, "is how it looks when one of my deputies, who put his neck out on the line for you, walks down the middle of town with stolen property on his person, while in uniform. That's a big problem. Not just for him, but for this entire department."

"I know and I am so sorry." She looked at Jonah, wanting him to see the truth in her eyes, but he wasn't looking back. "I know what I did was wrong and I would like to make a statement that Jonah knew nothing about the cats. When he came to my house in regard to the noise violation, he asked about the kittens and I was not forthcoming."

"Are you saying you lied?" Warren asked like it was Christmas morning and Santa had come.

"No." Shay turned to face Jonah, because he was the only person who mattered. "But I wasn't truthful either, and I am so sorry."

"Me too," Jonah said quietly and then looked up and, *bam*, the hurt and disappointment swimming in those blue pools shot her dead. Knocked the foundation right out from under her, with little to no chance of recovering. Her fault.

Shay had been too scared to put her faith in one of the best guys she'd ever met for fear that he'd hurt her. And in the end she'd hurt him and destroyed any chance they had at becoming more. Too bad she'd lost her heart in the process, because even though her head had a hard time trusting, her heart had become his a long time ago.

"Deputy, we'll give you a minute to figure out how you want to handle this, but know that this goes higher than me now," the sheriff said and pulled Warren and the mayor away, leaving Shay and Jonah alone.

Jonah didn't move or speak, just kept staring at her as if trying to figure out how he'd been so wrong. The longer the silence stretched on, the closer she came to tears. But she'd made this mess on her own, so she'd cry about it alone.

Jonah looked over at Warren, who looked like he was already filling out the paperwork, then shook his head. "You could have come to me and this would have all been avoided."

"I know," Shay said, her voice shaky. "I wish I would have, but that was me trying to do the right thing. I'm not sorry for saving the kittens—they would have died—but I am sorry you got caught in the middle."

"I'm not caught in the middle, Shay. I'm fucked." His voice was shaking too and that made the tears come closer to the surface. Jonah was the strongest, most sure man she'd ever met, and she'd rocked his belief in her—and himself. "You broke the law and made me an accessory. If I arrest you, you will go to jail while the fine is being set and you'll probably lose the rescue. If I don't, I'm not doing my job."

A job that meant the world to him.

The shelter meant the world to her too, but he meant more. Once word got out that she was dealing in stolen animals, the fallout would be bad, but she would recover. It would be devastating and heartbreaking, but she'd handle it and move on. She'd done it a million times before and she could do it again.

What she couldn't handle was Jonah going against who he was for her. Personal experience told her there was no coming back from that.

"I know," she said quietly, then held her hands out to Jonah, angry that they were trembling. "I guess I finally get to see your cuffs.

It wasn't how I imagined it happening, but I guess that's the problem with imagining. In the end it's kind of like wishing—nothing ever turns out the way we want."

He didn't reach for his cuffs. "Why are you doing this?"

That was easy. "Because I protect what I love."

"That's just it, Shay," he said quietly. "I don't think you know what love is."

She looked at him for a long time, playing over and over what he'd said, praying she'd misunderstood, then the tears finally spilled over.

"This time I thought for sure I had figured it out." Thought that she'd finally experienced what was so easy for her to give, yet so impossible for her to receive. "I guess I was wrong."

ch🐾pter
twenty

Jonah rolled up into his drive an hour shy of midnight, beyond exhausted, and trying to shake off the gnawing in his gut. Just like he had every night that week. A few steps up his driveway he froze and knew shaking it off wasn't an option tonight.

Sticking out of his mailbox—like a big fucking neon sign telling him that the *ignore what you can't fix* method he'd adopted as of late was leading to a dead end—was an envelope with very familiar writing.

Shay's.

The envelope was light, but it was clear there was something solid and absolute inside. And the six simple words scrawled on the outside . . . those made it clear that everything he'd been avoiding was about to take him by the throat and drag him under.

In case you changed your mind . . .

That was it, no signature, no demand, no blame, nothing else inside except his house key—and a shit ton of emotions he wasn't sure he had the capacity to handle.

Two days ago, Shay had pled guilty to unintentional theft, was booked then released the same night on her own recognizance. Until now, they hadn't spoken. Mostly because he'd done his best to avoid her. He should have been relieved that she'd given him an out, only relief was so far from what he felt.

Jonah was already so far in, he wasn't sure he'd ever get out—no matter how hard he tried to convince himself otherwise.

Every time he found a moment of quiet or closed his eyes, he saw the look on her face, and it was like he was back in the station, reliving the whole thing.

The regret and genuine sorrow in her apology had broken his heart, because he knew that Shay was just being Shay, acting first and thinking later. But the absolute despair that had filled her eyes at the end . . . that he'd never forget.

Angry and hurt, Jonah had said the one thing that could have shattered her world. And he'd said it on purpose, which made him all kinds of fucked up. The worst part was, it was a lie. Shay absolutely knew what love was. She showed it every day, in her life and in her work. She also showed it in the way she cared so selflessly for others.

But Jonah knew that some people's caring wound up hurting the exact people they were supposed to love. He'd seen it enough with his dad and stepmom to understand that sometimes two people were just too different to make it work.

So he did the best thing he could do—for the both of them. He took one last look at the darkened windows across the street and, fighting the urge to go over there and tell her that he hadn't changed his mind, that he still wanted her, he pocketed the key and headed toward his front door.

He stumbled into the house and considered turning on the lights, but his eyes were too sensitive to focus, so he walked blindly to his bedroom. He hadn't slept since the arrest. Hadn't really breathed either. So he locked his gun in the safe and shrugged out of his uniform, hoping that would help, because what used to be a part of him now felt constricting.

Suffocating.

He pulled on jeans and a T-shirt and sat on the edge of the bed, waiting for the calm to come, but it didn't. Shay was his calm and she was gone.

Feeling more restless than ever, he stood and made his way to the kitchen, desperate for a beer.

He entered the kitchen, letting out a resigned huff when he saw Adam sitting at the table, kicked back, legs propped up on the chair opposite him, eating Jonah's dinner.

"Remind me to change the locks," Jonah said, not pausing on his way to the fridge. He grabbed a beer, then, looking at the way Adam's nosy ass was rooted to Jonah's chair, grabbed another.

"Then who would feed Kitty Fantastic when you work three twelve-hour shifts in a row?"

Although Mr. Gillis was demanding his cats back, the sheriff was still looking into Shay's claim, which meant the kittens stayed where they were—for now. He'd asked Jonah if he wanted to take on the case, but Jonah had recused himself—then submersed himself in paperwork.

Adam cracked open the beer and took a long pull. He smacked his lips, then grimaced. "I liked the other kind better."

So did Jonah. Only he was out of it and Shay wasn't likely to buy him any more.

Mew, the cat said, jumping up on the table. Adam tore off a piece of Jonah's pesto chicken dinner and let the furball eat it, right out of his hand.

"Not on the table." Jonah lifted the cat and placed it in his lap. "And the sauce isn't good for his digestion." And Adam feeding Kitty by hand wasn't good for Jonah's state of mind. If anyone was going to feed the damn cat, it was him.

Adam stopped, beer midway to his mouth, and laughed. "My bad, bro. No more pesto for the cat."

Jonah ignored him and grabbed Kitty Fantastic a piece of cheese from the fridge and slipped his antibiotics inside. The cat inhaled it without chewing, then curled up on Jonah's lap.

Jonah had never wanted the damn cat, but now that he'd become used to the pest, he couldn't imagine losing him too. Only he might.

"Why are you here?" Jonah asked, suddenly ready to find some paperwork.

"You never call, you never text, I'm starting to get a complex." Adam placed his dirty knife on the table, in the same spot the cat's paws had been. "You haven't even commented on a single cat picture I've posted on your wall. That hurts, man."

He hadn't been on Facebook since everything went down. He hadn't wanted to see Shay's picture and couldn't stomach seeing what the fallout was for her. "Maybe you should just un-like me."

Adam put a hand to his forehead. "Unfriend. It's called unfriending. And I just might. I'm not big on martyrs having access to my page. They always end up posting those snarky e-cards with the 1950s couples that are worse than cat pictures."

Martyr? "What the hell is that supposed to mean?"

"That ever since San Francisco you've been walking around as if you don't think you deserve to move on. You chase away every great thing that comes your way, afraid you might actually find peace," Adam said. "I get that what happened was rough, but it's what we sign up for. It's a part of the job."

"A kid dying is part of the job?"

"Yeah," Adam said. "A shitty part, but a part that we can't escape. It doesn't mean that you don't deserve to be happy."

"I'm happy."

Adam wasn't buying it. Neither was Jonah anymore. He had

been happy. Shay made him happy, but she also drove him crazy. And she'd lied to him.

"I don't know what's going on with you and the cute neighbor, but you'd be an idiot to chase her away."

"I didn't chase. She walked on her own." Right over his trust, his faith in people, and his heart. Adam looked at Jonah as though he thought he was an idiot—and an asshole. He probably was. "And why would I take advice from a guy whose longest relationship was staying the night?"

"Because you're not me," Adam said, slamming his beer down. "You are the real deal, Jonah. The kind of guy who puts everyone else first, the kind of guy who does what's right, all the time, no matter how hard it is. The kind of guy who never gives up on people no matter how bad they fuck up."

Adam lowered his voice and closed his eyes. "Jesus, you watched me tell Dad that I would never want to be anything like him and then he dropped dead, right in front of us."

Jonah closed his eyes and slowly exhaled. He'd tried to avoid thinking about that day his whole life. There were always too many what-ifs that followed. They'd all dealt with a huge blow when they lost their father. Jonah had become the man of the family, Dax had withdrawn more into himself, Frankie had been more lost than ever, and Adam . . . Adam had taken it the hardest.

"You were a kid," Jonah said. "And Dad could be a self-righteous ass when he wanted to be. Loving him wasn't easy, for any of us, but in the end he knew you loved him."

"I don't know that and I'll never get the chance to know the truth." Adam pounded his chest with his fist. "I carry that with me every fucking day. And that kind of weight is paralyzing." Adam shook his head. "Don't be a self-righteous ass, Jonah. Don't make Shay live like that."

It was like a bullet straight through his chest, because that was exactly what he was doing. He'd watched his dad, filled with grief and anger at losing his soul mate and realizing she wasn't replaceable, strip away everything that made his stepmom special. Little by little, until she left him, and then he'd died—lonely and still angry.

"She drives me crazy," he admitted.

"Love can do that."

"I don't love her." He loved a lot of things *about* her. Okay, he loved pretty much everything, but he wasn't *in* love with her. Not like for keeps. He couldn't be. Love was supposed to be easy and uncomplicated and absolute. But nothing about Shay was easy and she was so complicated she made him smile, and his feelings were so absolute they scared him.

Holy shit. Jonah felt his heart fire and miss, only to reload and fire again.

Adam pulled out his phone, snapped a picture, and laughed. "The look on your face is priceless." He flipped the phone around and Jonah wanted to punch him. "Look, right there, it's that constipated look you get when you're trying to make everything fit into some neat and tight list that makes sense."

Adam dropped the phone and smiled, leaning in close enough for Jonah to deliver that fist to the throat. "Stop thinking and look around. The only proof you need, bro, is right there." He took a picture of the cat pawing Jonah's leg. "You own a kitty dream house and share your bed with a cat named Kitty Fucking Fantastic."

Jonah looked down and *holy shit* indeed . . . "I'm sharing my bed with Kitty Fucking Fantastic."

Mew, Kitty Fantastic said, looking up at him with those big blue eyes. Jonah laughed until it hurt. Everywhere. The hurt was so raw and deep he couldn't escape it, because that was all there was to say. That one meow confirmed everything.

He loved Shay. Every bit of her. And rather than celebrate who she was, he'd been like every other person in her life, turning her away merely for being true to herself and standing up for what she believed in.

"Did you know that the sheriff did some digging?" Adam asked and Jonah shook his head. "Turns out that Warren took the initial call from Mr. Gillis and didn't log it."

"Not surprised." At this point, nothing about Warren surprised him.

"I also talked to a hot number with a great rack who works at animal control. Our Mr. Gillis is flagged in their system as a persona non grata. I guess adopting multiple kittens a month from multiple shelters is frowned upon in the rescue world," Adam said. "Especially since he's been cited in the past for possession of illegal snakes."

Jonah looked at the cat curled up in his lap and felt his stomach turn. Kitty wasn't a pet, just like Shay had claimed. He was bought to be something's dinner.

"The sheriff knows that all Warren had to do was follow procedure and this whole clusterfuck could have been avoided. That's what he told the mayor, anyway."

"He called the mayor?"

"Yeah, Bryant told the mayor that he was done being quiet, that giving you his backing was the right thing to do, and that the mayor would be a moron to back someone who doesn't have the chops to handle the job, even if it was his own son. I guess Warren's daddy is making him withdraw from the race."

Jesus. Even after everything that had happened, the sheriff had faith in him. Which led Jonah to a verbal, "Jesus," followed by, "That means I'm sheriff."

A thought that was as humbling as it was terrifying. That kind of endorsement was a lot to live up to and Jonah didn't want to let anyone down.

You already have.

He'd let down Shay and himself. Instead of following up on her complaint and seeing just what kind of home Kitty Fantastic would have gone back to, he'd spent the past few days sulking while his brother stepped up to make things right.

"Thanks, for looking into it, and for . . ." Jonah ran a shaky hand over his face. "Just thanks."

"Are you kidding? If I am ever lucky enough to have a woman look at me the way Shay looks at you, there isn't much I wouldn't do to make her happy." Adam grinned. "And did I mention the rack on the animal control girl?"

Jonah slipped a hand under Kitty Fantastic's now-full belly and held him nose to nose. His little arms and legs hung limp, so much trust it floored Jonah. "I'm an idiot."

Mew. A rough tongue peeked out and licked his nose and suddenly he got it.

He got why Shay did what she did. She'd followed her gut, even when in the eyes of the law taking the kittens had been illegal, and she'd never backed down. She was making friends and saving lives.

And she'd saved his. No doubt. Now it was time to prove that he was worth saving.

Shay had thought nothing could hurt as much as losing her mother.

She'd been wrong.

It wasn't just losing Jonah that hurt. It was how she'd lost him that would haunt her. She'd trusted him in all the ways except the one that mattered. And he'd walked away because of it.

She'd spent the first half of the week trying to convince herself that he was mad, that he didn't mean it, because even the best people say things they regret in the heat of the moment. That moment had been so intense it burned. But then he didn't respond to her letter, didn't let her know that he hadn't changed his mind, which was as good as saying that he had, and so rather than give in to another round of tears, she'd spent the rest of the week focusing on getting St. Paws ready for its grand opening.

But as the week went on, as well as the tears, she finally got tired of crying over something that she couldn't fix and decided that Jonah was wrong.

Shay might be difficult and haphazard and a little flighty, but she knew what love was. Her mother's life and death had taught her everything she needed to know about love. It was warm and safe and risky and freeing and fierce and with complete abandon.

That was how her mother loved. That was how Shay loved. And that was how she wanted to be loved in return.

She just needed to find someone who felt the same way. Even though her gut kept telling her that she already had. It was also telling her that she got too close and he got scared. The kittens were just an excuse to gain some of that distance he was so fond of.

Well, he got his distance and in the process broke her heart. And she wasn't willing to take all the blame. She'd made a mistake, a big one, but so had he.

"You ready to get this grand opening party rolling?" Clovis asked, stepping out onto the patio.

She was with Harper and Emerson, and they were all holding giant party-bowl glasses filled to the brim with a bright pink-and-orange concoction. Emerson held two.

"I don't know," Shay admitted, but reached for the glass, waiting for her friends to hand it over. Her friends, who had hugged her when she cried, called Jonah an asshat even though they didn't believe it, and stood by her side throughout the whole scandal. "But a drink sounds nice."

"Sorry," Emerson said, taking a sip from the swizzle straw. "My Hound Dogs are too good to be served at the pity party you've got going on."

Shay eyed the glass but dropped her hand. News of her arrest was on Facebook before she'd even been processed. Although Nora swore she didn't post it—Warren claimed that deed—there were still over five hundred likes and comments. Shay hadn't had the heart to read any of them. She hadn't wanted to know what the town really thought about her.

"Sitting here, I can still hope that there will be a big turnout," she admitted. "That the town will see why I stole the kittens and forgive me. But once I open that door I will know, without a doubt, if St. Helena could ever be my home."

"This town has always been here for me," Emerson said, sucking down another long slurp. "And I've done some pretty stupid things."

"She's done a lot of stupid things," Harper said, and Emerson toasted to that.

"But you guys are one of them," Shay said, knowing they couldn't understand. They'd been raised here, had a history with the town, and that meant something. Shay had blown in and blown up the life of the town's favorite hero. That was a lot to get past.

Harper's face softened and she sat next to her. "Maybe you are too."

Shay felt some of the panic biting at her stomach drain away, and she nodded. But she didn't really feel any better. Because under the panic was an unbearable sense of loss and sadness. Even if the town could get past her action, and that was a big if, she wasn't so sure the one person who mattered the most could.

"Or maybe not," Shay mumbled.

"Well, sitting back here wondering is a total pussy move," Emerson said.

"Young people," Clovis grumbled and sank to the patio chair. "Tell me, what is the worst that can happen?"

"Um, no one shows, I end up the big loser no one wants to be friends with, and Jonah hates me forever." Wow, that last part hurt even to say.

"First off, who cares? I brought booze." Emerson ticked off on her fingers, a difficult maneuver since she was double fisting Hound Dogs, but she managed. "I'm not friends with losers,"—another finger went up—"and his loss."

This time Emerson held up one finger and Shay laughed past the lump in her throat.

"He'll come around," Harper said gently, then gave a pointed glare Emerson's way. With a dramatic sigh, Emerson handed over the party bowl and Shay bypassed the straw and took a big gulp.

God, it was good. Maybe she'd just sit there all day on her patio, in the summer sun, sucking a few of these down. Three tops and she would be well on her way to forgetting why she was upset. But then tomorrow she'd still be sad *and* hungover.

"I don't know," Shay said, setting the party bowl down. "He was wrong about some things, but mostly he was spot-on in his assessment. We are just so different. He is determined to walk the line, and I walk it until I find where it fades."

"As long as you end up in the same place, that's all that really matters," Harper said and Shay nodded, unable to speak.

Clovis looked at them as if they were dimwitted. "We are talking about a man, right? Because as far as I know, it's about tabs and slots, dear, not lines." At the other women's confused expressions, Clovis continued, "As in putting tab *A* in slot *B*?"

"Grandma," Harper said, covering her ears.

Clovis made a serious face and leaned in. "Unless the tab and slot don't line up. Is that the problem? If so, they've got pills these days. In fact, I think I have a few left from my trip to Mexico."

Clovis started digging through her purse and Shay stopped her.

"Tab and slot are just fine." As far as Shay was concerned they lined up perfectly in that department. In fact, they lined up in every way that was important, except for one. "He doesn't love me."

Clovis waited, as if expecting Shay to go on. When she didn't, the older woman shook her head. "Honey, he's a man who felt cornered and was showing his teeth, nothing more. He wouldn't know love if Cupid himself was standing in front of him flashing his arrow. You've got to get creative."

Harper lifted a brow. "Like placing false claims to have him arrested?"

Clovis smiled. "You laugh but I didn't sleep alone last night."

"You and Giles?" Shay asked, happy for Clovis.

"Every night this week," she admitted, trussing up her sagging top. Harper was back to covering her ears. "And it took me years to get him to come around. But I didn't put my life on hold, waiting for him to get a clue. I went about my life, did what made me happy, and finally he came to his senses." She looked at Shay's St. Paws polo shirt and frowned. "Maybe show a little more if you want him to come around sooner."

"You're right," Shay said, ignoring the last part and standing. "Today is about St. Paws and my animals." Although she would rather have Jonah there to celebrate a day he had helped make possible, she needed to go out there and find some families.

Clovis stood too and knocked her cane over. It landed with a clank. A second later, Shay heard claws pounding on the cobblestone and Jabba came tearing out the door and onto the patio. He picked up Clovis's cane in his mouth, made three laps around the yard, and then dropped it at the woman's feet, tail wagging, eyes excited.

"Well, look at that." Clovis gave a caring ruffle of the ears, then picked up her cane, and Shay wondered if Jabba had already found his family. "Now, if no one shows, I got Giles and his fellas on standby, ready to model my man-hammocks for a good cause."

When Shay walked in she knew they would be spared the geriatric Chippendales, because the shop was packed full of people and pets. They were eating and smiling and admiring her work. It was a wall-to-wall party, with a line zigzagging all the way through the space and out the front door.

Gratitude filled Shay's chest and she whispered, "Thank you."

"Oh, this wasn't us," Clovis said, then looked at the man-hammock convention by the register. "Well, they're here for me, but the rest of them are here because of him."

Clovis pointed to a table at the front and Shay felt all of the air whoosh out of her lungs. Because sitting near the entrance, under a Cuties with Booties banner, was the one person who could take this day from amazing to perfect.

Jonah wasn't just sitting under any sign. Nope, this Cuties with Booties sign had a huge picture of everyone's favorite deputy, showing off that no-Kevlar-needed chest and posing in nothing but regulation pants, shooting glasses, and a pair of range-grade headphones. A silhouette target with a shot straight through the heart was the backdrop, and to his right, in matching glasses and muffs, sitting on his combat boots was Socks. The tagline read, ADOPT THIS CUTIE AND I'LL SHOW YOU MY BOOTY.

As though sensing her presence, Jonah looked up and immediately zeroed in on Shay. His gaze was so intense and direct, she felt her breath catch and her stomach go into a free fall until all she could do was stare back.

A hush settled over the room as Jonah stood and made his way around the table and through the parting crowd, his strides sure and purposeful, not slowing until he was in front of her.

No distance, no guard up, no games—he looked too tired for games.

"Why are you here?"

"Because I want Socks to go to a good home and to a family that loves her for all that she is."

Shay looked at Socks sitting on the table in her little doggie bed, happy as a clam with her earmuffs, and Shay told herself not to cry. Jonah was being Jonah, a good guy supporting a good cause. "I do too."

"So do we," someone said from behind, who sounded a lot like Ida. "Because then we get to see his booty."

Jonah shot a warning at Ida, who waved apologetically for him to continue, then he looked back to Shay. "I also came because, like you, I protect what I love."

Shay shook her head, unable to get past the fear that instead of a door opening, this was yet another one closing. "You said I didn't know what love was."

"I was wrong." He cupped her face. "About so many things. I was so busy trying to find all the reasons why this could never work that I overlooked the most important piece of evidence. I love you." He stepped close, their bodies brushing, Shay's heart melting at the three words she'd waited a lifetime to hear. "You are strong and passionate and so damn loveable." He ran a finger over her cheek. "You are the color in my black-and-white world, and I love every shade that you are."

"Even the ones that steal kittens and drive you crazy?"

"Especially those," he said, and Shay's heart stopped in her chest as he reached into his pocket and pulled out a key. It was a custom one with little kittens on it and hung from a house-shaped key chain. "You are the best part of my world, the best part of my day, and even though I don't deserve you, I don't want to wake up tomorrow morning without you."

"How about the morning after that?" she asked, because she wasn't looking for a temporary stopover. She wanted the real deal. And she wanted it with him.

"I heard that you specialize in forever families," he said quietly. "And Kitty Fantastic and I were hoping you'd let us be a part of yours."

"Kitty Fantastic?" she asked, because last she'd heard Mr. Gillis was petitioning to get him back—along with the gift card. She'd also learned that Goldilocks was his neighbor and had been stealing his "food supply," as he'd called them, for months. Turns out the kittens weren't her first rescues, they were just the first ones she couldn't place herself.

"I filled out my application to adopt him this morning, right after I arrested Mr. Gillis for possession of an illegal python."

"You arrested him?" she asked, shocked that he'd even taken her accusations that the kittens had been mistreated seriously. Then she realized that Jonah had always taken her seriously. And he'd never gone back on his word.

Not once.

Shay looked into his eyes and laid it on the line. "I don't do returns, Jonah. And Kitty Fantastic, although adorable, can be difficult and temperamental and a whole lot of trouble. And he won't change. Ever."

"I like adorable, and I love trouble." Jonah held up the key. "Take it, Shay. Take it and come home. With me."

Shay closed her hand around the key and Jonah's smile started in his eyes, and by the time he captured her lips she could feel the happiness radiating off of him, feel the want and the love.

Being there in his arms, she felt everything, all at once, then felt it fall into place. A place, she realized, that had been made specifically for her. After all of her tries and near misses, Shay had found her forever family.

"This is for keeps," she said against him.

"Trouble, with you it has always been for keeps." He lifted her fingers to his mouth and kissed them, then placed her hand on his heart, the beat sure and steady. "I need you, for keeps."

And that sounded like the best kind of forever Shay could imagine.

acknowledgments

Thanks to my editors, Maria Gomez and Lindsay Guzzardo, and the rest of the Author Team at Montlake, for all of the amazing work and support throughout this series, and for making my dreams a reality. And to my agent, Jill Marsal, for everything you do, for me, my career, and my family—your dedication and unwavering belief changed our lives.

As always, a special thanks to my husband and daughter for their support and love. And to Awesome Bob, Suki, and all of the furry friends whom I have been blessed enough to have in my life, your unconditional love inspired this book and gave me hope when I needed it most.

Read on for a sneak peek of Marina Adair's
next heartwarming romance from her
Heroes of St. Helena series

need you for mine

Available October 2015 on Amazon

need you
for mine

Heroes of St. Helena series

MARINA ADAIR

chapter
one

"You need to get laid," Emerson Blake explained to the line of uniformed soldiers funneling off the party bus and into the St. Helena VFW dance hall.

She'd always had a thing for a man in uniform. It was something about the way they perpetually looked ready—for anything—that had her happy spots singing.

But there was no singing to be had, not today anyway, because these men and these uniforms smelled like mothballs. And the lei in question? That had more to do with the hundreds of flowered necklaces in her hand than belting out a hearty *Oh My* anthem. Not to mention, her body hadn't so much as hummed in months and she had no idea why.

Okay, so she had a pretty good idea why, but that would be fodder for thought for another rainy day. *This* rainy day was to be spent catering to the few hundred seniors who had come out in support of the Veterans of Foreign Wars monthly Wartime Mixer.

With an open bar, live band, and Copacabana theme, the turnout was bigger than Emerson had anticipated, or prepped for. Heroes from every one of the past five wars were present, which meant that every single silver-haired lady over sixty was there, ready to be seen and heard. Including winter herself, who sent Emerson a you-can-suck-it reminder from the universe in the form of an icy blast of wind that blew into the dance hall—and up Emerson's grass skirt.

"Have you been laid?" she asked the first man to exit the bus.

"Not since I was stationed at Pearl Harbor," retired Gunnery Sargeant Carl Dabney said, waggling a bushy brow. "So don't try to give me one of them no-salt-allowed yellow leis. I want a pink one."

"If I give you a pink one you'll go home in an ambulance," Emerson said, handing him a yellow one. The old man refused to take it.

"If I can't have any salt, what kind of message is that sending to the ladies standing at the salsa bar?"

"That you have high blood pressure?"

"That I'm a pansy, *hashtag real men wear pink!*" Carl was in his early nineties, carried a cane and a gun at all times, and was a regular customer at Emerson's food cart in town. He'd also, according to Emerson's little medical printout, compliments of Valley Vintage Senior Community, survived three wars, two triple bypasses, and a stroke—which made him far from a pansy. It also meant he was stubborn enough to beat death.

Too bad for him, death didn't have anything on Emerson.

"Yellow means low sodium," she explained, and Carl snorted as though he could take on sodium and the entire periodic table without even dropping his cane. "I can always give you a white one."

He looked the white lei over carefully. "What does that one get me?"

"Low sodium, low fat, and if I see you with alcohol anywhere near your person, silver star or not, I get to kick you out. No refund."

He wasn't sold. And wasn't that just great. With three years of the finest culinary training and five generations of family recipes in her arsenal, Emerson should have been well on her way to cementing herself as a serious contender in the world of Greek cuisine. Yet there she was, still in her small hometown of St. Helena, California, the entire fate of her career—and her reputation—hinging on her ability to corral disgruntled seniors while wearing a pair of coconut shells.

Because when your mother's ALS goes nuclear five months before graduation and you forgo finishing culinary school to take care of her, shells are bound to happen. Not that she regretted one second of it, but after her mother's death, the rebound had been brutal—on everyone. Unable to ignore what her family needed, Emerson had given up her dream of finishing school to help with the aftermath, be there for her sister, Sadie, who had only been four at the time, and her father, who had lost his best friend.

Emerson became the family glue and she was okay with that—most days. But today she needed things to go her way.

Not that catering the VFW's monthly mixer was the most glamorous job Emerson would have asked for. In fact, she hadn't asked for it at all, but they'd been desperate for a caterer who wouldn't mind getting into costume, and Emerson wanted to take her business to the next level.

Two years ago, after realizing the only positions open in wine country for a chef lacking the right pedigree was a line cook, Emerson had taken the money her mother had left her and bought a food cart. It gave her the chance to cook the kind of cuisine she was passionate about and gave her the illusion she was in control of her own life.

Which she so wasn't.

Illusions could be dangerous, and Emerson knew that better than most. But even though she'd accepted that life doesn't always play fair and dreams die, every day for everyone, she was determined to keep this one alive. Determined to make her mother proud—make their dream of a Greek restaurant a reality and in turn make her mark in the culinary world.

So the Pita Peddler was a cart and not quite the sit-down affair they had dreamed of. So what? It was a start. A small one, but a start nonetheless.

Food doesn't have to be pretentious to be delectable, it just has to have heart. That had been her mom's motto. One that Emerson tried to embrace. She had delectable down, but she wasn't sure she had enough faith left in love to nail the last part. But she was trying.

So no one was more surprised when her "little pita cart," as her culinary school friends had teased, turned out to make serious dough—and fast. Dough that had risen and doubled in size, and now this year Emerson had bigger plans. Plans that needed the extra two grand this VFW event would bring her. If catering the occasional kid's birthday or wearing humiliating costumes meant upgrading her food cart to a twenty-seven-foot custom-designed gourmet food truck with Sub-Zero fridge and freezer, dual fryers, four burners, a Tornado speed-cook oven, and a twelve-thousand-watt diesel generator all wrapped in Pita Peddler Streatery vinyl—then she'd shell up.

Emerson handed out a few more leis, ignoring the goose bumps covering every inch of her bare skin—which was nearly all of her inches. Behind her, the wind picked up, scattering a thin sheet of water over the marble floor of the entry to the dance hall, her leis whipping her in the face. Outside, the freezing-cold rain continued to pound the sidewalk, bending the branches of the maples that lined Main Street and rushing down the already full gutters.

No wonder it was so packed inside. With the potted palm trees, pineapple party mugs, and bottomless mai tai bar, it was like a tropical paradise in the middle of an arctic typhoon.

Double-checking to make sure all essential body parts were securely tucked in, Emerson took a deep, humbling breath and held up the yellow lei. "At least with this you can do some body shots off Mrs. Rose."

Carl peered through the door at Mrs. Rose, current head of the Hunting Club, who was already inside and standing by the bar. Dressed in a blue-and-white-striped sailor's dress and red flats, she looked like a one-woman USO. She was also wearing a yellow lei. "You think she's packing tonight?"

"I heard in the ladies' room that she swapped out her holster for a garter belt and she's looking to score." Emerson wiggled the yellow flowers again. "Last chance."

He looked at the lei and frowned. "Real men wear—"

"Pink, yeah, yeah," Emerson cut in, then looked at the large group of seniors still waiting to be checked in and sighed. It was only a matter of time before a riot broke out, and if Carl kept yammering on, it would only get worse. She'd seen it happen too many times with her sister's Lady Bug troop—one bad bug could lead to an angry swarm.

Time to get tough. "You can either take Mrs. Rose on a twirl around the dance floor or have me escort you out. Your choice."

Carl studied the yellow lei thoroughly, then sized Emerson up, most likely to see if he could take her. She flexed her guns and narrowed her eyes. "Remember when your grandson Colt came home with a busted face senior year? That was me. And I was only a seventh grader."

She might be small but she was scrappy.

With a resigned sigh, *smart man*, he gave the lei one last skeptical glare. "If I promise no salt, do I to have to wear that?"

"Rules are rules." Emerson leaned in close—real close. Close enough that Carl could see the seriousness in her eyes, and if that didn't work, she hoped he'd be too distracted by her coconut shells to argue.

And wasn't that a man for you, one well-calculated breath and his eyes glazed over, his mouth snapped shut, and he stopped yammering. "You got to get laid before you can do a body shot, Carl."

"Not much point in body shots if I can't salt her up first," Carl grumbled, but he took the lei anyway, dropping his twenty on the table before hobbling off.

One down, fifty to go, she thought, taking in the still-growing crowd.

"With rules like that, I'm glad I came." A cocky but oh-so-sexy chuckle came from beside her and she froze, then closed her eyes. It didn't help. She could still feel the weight of an intense, masculine, and very amused gaze, as her whole body instantly heated and—

Oh boy, hummed.

Because it wasn't just any low, husky chuckle. It was the same panty-melting chuckle from her past that had spurred her every teen fantasy. In her more recent past, say, oh, five months ago, it had whispered wicked promises in her ear.

Promises that took an entire night to fulfill and five months to forget. Not that she'd forgotten. Far from it. But she'd tried.

Never one to run from her past, or anything for that matter, Emerson opened her eyes and—*sweet baby Jesus*, the wry amusement and combustible heat in those dark blue pools made her knees go weak. And *that* pissed Emerson off—more than the wet grass skirt that was bleeding green dye down her legs.

Emerson didn't do weak, not even for a guy who looked like Captain America, GI Joe, and an underwear model all wrapped up in a big, bad-assed army-of-one package.

Oh, Dax Baudouin wasn't just insanely handsome. Handsome she could handle. He was also dark, inside and out, and dangerous in that mysterious way that tempted her even when she knew better. His body was massive—everywhere—and today it was soaked. All the way through.

Like he hadn't bothered to get naked before showering.

His white button-up was wet around the collar and down his chest, the material translucent, clinging to his hard-cut upper body and hinting at the impressive collection of tattoos that were hidden beneath.

Great, now she was thinking about him naked. In her shower. His smirk said he knew it. Just what she needed, a little game of *I've seen you naked* to make her already humiliating day that much more humiliating.

Clearly, karma was bitch slapping her for her one transgression.

Then again, Dax Baudouin was one hell of a transgression to have, but she had known that the second she'd agreed to go back to his hotel room. He was her first and only one-night stand, a no-panties-allowed kind of affair that blew her mind. It blew some other parts too, but she didn't want to think about that here. Not with her goal of her Greek restaurant just in arm's reach.

"Dax," she said, forcing what she hoped was a professional and unaffected smile. He smiled back. It started as an amused twinkle in his eyes then spread to his face and—

She was a goner.

That was all it took, a single flash of those perfect teeth and her body started humming. There was no other word for what happened to her whenever he so much as shot a dimple her way. It was as if he jump-started her entire body—brought it to life.

His gaze took a long trip down her body and back up, the corners of that smile turning up farther, and Emerson could practically hear the gears turning in his head, trying to come up with the perfect smart-ass remark about her attire.

"Now back to those rules," he said.

"Yeah, no."

He laughed softly. "No? To getting laid or the drink?"

"No to both the lei and the drink." To be as clear as possible, she added, "And no, you can't mow my grass, put a lime in my coconut, or any other unoriginal comment you were going to say."

"I'm very original." He leaned forward, resting his hands on the table, which did amazing things to his biceps. "Creative, even."

Didn't she know it. "Shouldn't you be off in some war-torn country defending mankind from the supervillains of the world?"

"Someone else is handling that today," he said as though it would be just another day at the office. Emerson snorted.

As a Force Recon marine, Dax was a weapon of mass destruction in a sea of already lethal weapons, handpicked and trained by Uncle Sam to fight the battles that very few soldiers were equipped to fight. He'd been to some terrible places, seen the worst parts of human nature, Emerson was sure, yet he kept going back, his need to serve stronger than his fear of death. On the rare occasion when he wasn't on supersecret missions or hiding out in caves, he lived in San Diego, a good nine hours south of St. Helena, which was why she'd agreed to the one-night stand to begin with.

And okay, she'd just watched her best friend, Shay, marry Dax's older brother Jonah in an incredibly romantic ceremony overlooking the Golden Gate Bridge, and all the talk of forever and partnership and a kissy-boo future had gotten to her. Not that she wanted a kissy-boo future, but sometimes she thought about what that would be like. To not have to fight every battle alone.

Then she'd seen Dax at the bar looking bigger than life in his dress blues—and as out of place in all of that happiness as she was, and before she knew what was happening they were . . . bonding. Over Jack and Johnny Walker. In a momentary lapse in judgment, she found herself in his room, her bridesmaid dress around her waist like a Hula-Hoop, staring down her one secret fantasy, who offered her something she desperately needed.

Escape.

One night to forget about everything, be selfish, and lose herself without the fear of *losing* herself, because she wasn't looking for forever. Good thing, because Dax was not a forever kind of guy.

"If I give you a lei, will you go away?" she asked.

"Is that your way of saying you don't want to talk about the wedding?"

"First rule about one-night stands," she said as though she was a foremost expert on the subject, "what happens between the wedding party, stays between the wedding party. No post expectations, no post conversations, and no ties."

"Actually, first rule of one-night stands, Emi, is that they last all night. You cut out before dawn." He lowered his voice. "And to be clear, you liked my tie."

She had. A whole lot. Almost as much as she'd liked him. Which was why she'd cut out. Somehow, if she was the one to walk, it felt like she was still in control of her emotions—in control of her life.

"I had things to do."

"At three in the morning?"

"What did you expect?" She laughed. "To cuddle and hold hands while swapping embarrassing childhood secrets and life goals? And it isn't like you called me the next day anyway."

He grinned. Big and wide and he slipped something out of his pocket. A phone.

He gave a few confident swipes of the finger and a second later, hers rang. She leveled him with her most lethal glare. When it kept ringing she crossed her arms, so not going to play this game.

Dax stood there, patient and unfazed, as though he was confident she'd answer as it rang and rang until it went to voice mail. Emerson could hear the muffled message she'd recorded and threw her hands in the air. "Oh, for God's sake, hang up the—"

He held up a silencing finger. *Beep.*

Emerson had a finger of her own to hold up, but since she was working, she refrained.

"Hey, Emi," he said into the phone, charm and swagger dialed to full. "Wanted to let you know that I had an amazing time the other night—"

"Five months and nine days ago."

He flashed her a *do you mind, I'm busy here* look. "I'm in town for a bit and I'd love to see you. Say grab a drink, maybe after you get off work? I know the perfect place, coconut shells welcomed."

Then he ended the call, slid it in his back pocket, and smiled. "You were saying?"

"You're infuriating."

He shrugged as though he'd been called worse, then slipped a twenty into the cash box and took a lei, a pink one, and held it out for her. She rolled her eyes.

"Now, slip this flower necklace around my neck so I can go get us a drink."

"There is no us."

"If you say so."

"I say so." But she didn't sound all that convinced. Maybe it was because as she said it she swayed closer. "And I'm not going on a date with you."

Dax slid the lei over his head and winked. "Who said anything about a date?"

about the author

PHOTO © TOSH TANAKA

Marina Adair is a #1 national bestselling author of romance novels and holds a master of fine arts in creative writing. Along with the St. Helena Vineyard series, she is also the author of *Sugar's Twice as Sweet*, part of the Sugar, Georgia series. She lives with her husband, daughter, and two neurotic cats in Northern California. She loves to hear from readers and likes to keep in touch, so be sure to sign up for her newsletter at www.marinaadair.com/newsletter.